Psychological War
Ryan Mundy

Cover Design: izabeladesigns
Editing: Susan Keillor
Proofreading: Susan Keillor

Paperback ISBN: 979-8-9877506-1-2

Content Warning:

Below is a list of triggers in the following book. Please be aware that your mental health matters. The book mentions the following:

Rape and other forms of sexual violence mentioned
Violence
Physical assault
Mental health flashbacks
Mention of rape, including other non-consensual sexual scene
Bodily waste, such as vomit and urine
Nudity
Blood
Kidnapping
Murder
Family loss
Childhood trauma
Graphic sexual scenes

Please take care of yourself and be safe.

Music Playlist

Evil - AViVA
Psycho - AViVA
Hella Good - Izzy Reign
Murder Party - NOT THE MAIN CHARACTERS
Sink My Fangs - Alejandro Lema
Aimed to Kill - Jade LeMac
Achilles Heel - J. Maya
Easy for You - Gracey
Demons - Vi
Up in Flames - Ruelle
Psychological War - RØRY

To anyone who didn't believe I'd make it.

Fuck you.

Salem

Everything was ripped away from me when I was a child. I watched as they took my family away. They tried to get rid of me as well. I survived. I watched and learned. Learned until it was time. Time for them to meet their worst nightmare. They think I died that night. She did. Only someone else was born. Ghost.

Zane

I'm just the enforcer for the Bratva. I don't care about much. Not until I find her. Except something is different about her. She's not scared of anything. She walks into danger, and she fights like her life has no meaning. I can't understand why she hides the secrets she does. All I know is I want to know more. I want to know who she is.

Prologue

Zane

December

My nose was definitely broken.

For fuck's sake

My head was definitely going to explode any minute from whatever hit me.

And I was definitely going to kill Dimitri. He was the reason I was on this stupid mission to begin with. I was his enforcer, not everyone else's. But here I was, barely standing, pressing my hand to my nose.

And the thing was, I couldn't even tell who it was. I kept my distance, following this person, who had to be female from how small they were.

"Fuck," I roared when something bashed into my kneecap. My body lunged forward, landing on my hands and knees. I couldn't tell if I was angry with the fact I was getting my shit rocked this easily or that I hadn't even tried to fight back yet.

Pushing up to sit on my knees, I didn't have time to do anything before the crack of my skull. Everything was fading until the blackness took over.

Salem

I rested my baseball bat against my leg, kneeling down to the unconscious body. Pushing him over with my bat onto his back, I couldn't help the smile that spread across my face from that broken nose. I don't know what he was thinking, trying to follow me, but he was stupid. Very stupid for thinking he could just follow me.

I didn't wait for him to say anything or do anything before I hit him with my bat.

This fucker was huge. More than double my size.

Patting him down, I pulled out his wallet, and took out his license, reading; Zane Theodore Rivera, twenty-nine years old, June fourteenth, 260 pounds, six feet, six inches.

My eyes widened; this fucker *was* huge. Looking back down, I took in the blood coating his entire mouth and chin, a gash above his eyebrow bleeding down the side of his face. He had dark, sharp angler eyebrows, and a single teardrop tattoo under his left eye, along with a nose hoop on the left nostril. His hair was dirty blond, slicked back. The urge to run my fingers through it caught me off guard. But I couldn't.

Shaking that thought off, I reached into my pocket and pulled out a card with a ghost on it. Tucking it into his hand, I stood up and walked away. Forcing myself to not turn back around and wait for him to wake up, I continued walking, blending into the night.

Chapter 1

Salem

February

Another blow to my stomach had me almost doubling over with the amount of bile that rose in my throat. But I refused to let them see me break, nor did I allow myself to break. They didn't deserve it, and I wouldn't let it happen.

They couldn't break me.

I also couldn't exactly double over due to the fact my legs were tied along with my arms. It would be rather difficult to bend over tied up like this.

"Where is Mario?" one of them yelled in my face. Not sure which one it was due to the amount of blood dripping into my eyes.

I barely had time to recover from the last punch before there was another one, causing me to feel a sharp pain in my kidney. The air left my lungs. I tried taking in a breath, but everything hurt. I couldn't take in a full breath.

"Where the fuck is Mario?" another one yelled from further back. I really wanted to scream at them that they were all stupid and if they looked hard enough, they'd figure it out.

He was dead.

He was dead and waiting inside the shipping container for Luca to find. Just biding time until he found him.

The problem was the slight flaw in my plan. Matteo's men weren't supposed to find me just yet. They were supposed to find Mario in the Cosa Nostra shipping crate. But they caught up to me faster than I would have liked. Which brings us to now, Matteo's men torturing me, wanting to know where Mario, their under boss, was.

"Where is he? You stupid fuc—" One of the guards sneered at me before getting cut off from the door slamming open. Another guard stepped into the room, wincing when he saw the condition I was in. It was almost comical. From his expression he couldn't handle the way I looked. With bruises covering my body, my face was black and purple.

"Boss wants you to take her into the room with the other," one of the men said in Spanish. They often spoke it, thinking I had no idea what they were saying. If only they knew I could understand every single word they spoke.

Blinking a few more times, I could see it was Hugo. Oh, he was my favorite. He loved taking his time punishing me. He was going to die a beautiful death when I got out of here. Which shouldn't be too much longer, maybe a few days at most.

Hugo let out a heavy growl, motioning for one of the men to untie my legs and hands from the chair. Once I was free, Hugo grabbed hold of my collar, dragging me out the door and down the hall. Once the door was open, he shoved me inside before slamming the door closed.

"Oh my god." I barely had time to pick myself up before a very quiet voice whispered beside me. Turning over, I nearly knocked into a red head who was reaching out for me. Snatching my arm away from her like she was on fire, I backed away. "I'm sorry. I didn't mean to scare you." Rolling my eyes, I shook my head before crawling to the far wall, resting my head against the cool cement wall. My ribs sent a sharp stinging sensation up my sides. I could feel it in my fingertips. That would be if I had actual feeling in my fingertips.

The smallest sound of her stepping forward caused me to lift my head, and her eyes widened. Either from my glare or because I was covered in blood and sweat, and most likely other bodily fluids I didn't want to think about. It wasn't like they would allow me to shower. I almost chuckled at the thought of it. I had been here for three days already, and with the amount of blood covering my body, I knew I looked rough.

"Are you okay?" she whispered, eyes glued to my face.

I snorted.

"I'm sorry. You're not okay, obviously." Again she kept talking, when I really just wanted it to be quiet. I needed to be quiet so I could prepare myself for what would come next. I just needed to hold on for two more days.

"I'm Mila, what's your name?"

I continued just staring at her. She didn't need to know my name. I was a dead girl walking. No one needed to know my name.

"You don't talk much, do you?" Mila asked. "I didn't speak much before either. I'm finding myself wanting to stop talking again."

Mila began to pace back and forth across from me. She should save her energy. I had no idea why she was here, but whatever the reason was she should definitely sit down and rest.

14

"They're going to find us soon." I had no idea who she was talking about, or if she truly believed someone was going to find her. But this was Matteo's compound. No one was getting inside. And no one was getting out. Not unless I killed them.

All of them.

Two days.

Two days and I would end all of them.

"I know you probably want quiet, but I need to talk. If I retreat back to my head I'll probably stay there." She stopped pacing, focusing her attention back onto me. "I'm sorry," she whispered.

Mila dropped her gaze down to the floor, as though she was used to being submissive. I hated that she felt like she had to submit like that to me. There was no reason she had to fear me. Sure, I was a killer. I've murdered plenty of people. But those people deserved it.

Those people hurt those who couldn't defend themselves. I was doing the world a favor. I was helping the world by getting rid of those people.

Swallowing the lump in my throat, I should just ignore her, close my eyes and wait for the next set of guards that came in to take me away. Instead, I found myself saying, "You can keep talking."

Mila's head snapped up, her eyes filling with tears. "Are you sure?"

Nodding my head slower than I should, Mila finally sat down against the wall across from me.

"Do you want my shirt to stop the bleeding on your forehead?" I shook my head no. I didn't need her taking her shirt off just to have the men come in here and see her. I was hurting and as much as I loved a good fight and taking care of the trash problem, I don't think my body could take a fight right now.

"You're right, I shouldn't take off my clothes. You'd think I'd know that since I've been through this before." Looking up at her, Mila tried holding her tears in as she spoke. "Yeah, I was kidnapped

15

before, actually three times." A small smile tugged at her lips. "The first time was Matteo. He actually bought me from my piece of shit birth giver. I was held by his associates for a few weeks before my husband found me."

So for the next what I'm only assuming could be hours, I listened to Mila talk about how she ended up here. She never spoke her husband's name. But apparently, while Mila was being transported to Matteo's, her husband saw her and saved her. She said she didn't think that when he took her that it was an actual kidnapping. I wanted to roll my eyes; pretty sure I did. Kidnapping was kidnapping. Didn't matter how nice or sweet they were.

Mila even talked about her goals of opening her own art gallery. I couldn't lie to myself that I enjoyed listening to her talk about her artwork. She had been drawing since she was ten, and her dream had always been to open one.

At some point, I must have fallen asleep because the next thing I knew, the door was slamming open. Hugo and another guard I hadn't seen before stood in the doorway. Mila was still against the furthest wall lying on the ground.

"Jose, grab her." Hugo pointed at me. Getting to my feet, Jose's hand gripped my elbow, dragging me across the dirt floor. Mila sat up, eyes pained as she saw me being taken away. I shook my head at her. I didn't need her trying to defend me. It would just end worse for her. I didn't need anyone to defend me.

I was taken down the hall to another room, being shoved into a chair. I didn't fight them as they chained my arms down along with my legs to the side.

"Where is Mario?" Hugo once again yelled at me. I wondered how many times he planned to yell at me about Mario before he realized I wouldn't talk. No matter what they did, I wouldn't.

"Oh, this is going to be fun," Jose muttered to no one. I knew it was going to be bad, taking a deep breath. The last one I knew I was going to get for a while. I turned my focus onto the wall in front of me. I wouldn't let them break me.

Chapter 2

Salem

Dada always woke up early to feed the animals. He also went to bed late, making sure everyone else was asleep, and that we were all safe. I tried to stay awake with him a lot, but I never made it past ten. It was probably because I always woke up with Dada at four. He always tried to get me to go back to sleep, but I refused. I helped feed most of the animals, and then I passed out, usually in the hay, before Dada carried me into the house. I liked working with Dada. When I woke up on the couch, it was always the smell of breakfast cooking.

"I like the name Toby," Mama whispered while pouring more pancake mix into the frying pan. I wasn't a fan of pancakes, but my older sister Emily loved them, and so did my older brother.

18

"Me too, Mama." I giggled. I don't know where I got Toby from, but it was a good name, and I knew it would be perfect for a baby brother. He would be perfect.

"Dada wants me to have a conversation with you. I think you already know this, but you know your father." Mama flipped the pancakes before turning to me. "You're not going to be the baby anymore, but I want you to understand that you'll always be our baby girl," Mama said. But I already knew this. Mama and Dada loved all their children. Each of us was different, but they loved us. Emily was a brat, but she was the best brat and she never let anyone mess with me. Lee was the same—he never let anyone bully me. He was the best big brother. He taught me how to drive a four-wheeler, and how to drive a stick. Mama and Dada didn't know that. It was a secret between us.

"I know this, Mama, you love us all." I smiled. I just couldn't wait for Toby to be here. I would protect him. No one would bully him, and no one would hurt him.

I jolted awake.

It felt like all was a lie. Toby was hurt. He was hurt really badly, and I couldn't do anything to protect him or any of them. I wanted to hate myself for not being able to save them. But I was only nine. What nine-year-old could fight back?

I was angry. I was more than angry.

But soon, soon it would be okay. I would make sure it was.

Looking around, Mila laid in a ball in the corner. She was there when they dragged my body back a few hours ago. She hadn't woken up, and no one bothered her. I didn't know what they wanted with her. Besides the fact she mentioned Matteo had bought her before her husband saved her.

I watched her sleeping for a while, knowing I looked like a creep. I still didn't bother to look away. I felt the urge of protectiveness over her, like I knew she wouldn't fight back if someone came in here for her. I felt as though if I didn't keep an eye on her, she was going to disappear.

Trying to shift my body to lean on the side that was completely covered in bruises and cuts, I hissed. As soon as Mila shot up, her eyes were wild, flickering around everywhere. Finally settling on me, she winced once she got a good enough look.

"Oh…m-my…" She gasped, jumping to her feet. Taking a few steps forward, she began battling over whether to come closer. Giving her the closest thing to a nod that I could manage, ever so slowly, she inched towards me, finally bending down and sitting next to me. "What's your name?"

I should have told her a lie, maybe not even given her a name. But I heard myself saying, "Salem."

"That's a beautiful name."

"Thank you." My voice was rough and raspier than it'd been before.

"What do they want?"

"Information." I mean, what else would the Cartel want? Information and whores.

"You're stronger than me. I don't know if I would be able to handle what they seem to be doing to you. Actually, that's a lie. I wouldn't be able to."

"You're stronger than you think." Closing my eyes, I tried my best to focus on breathing slowly. I'm pretty sure a few of my ribs were broken. If not broken, definitely bruised.

"I'm not strong like you."

"Everyone is strong in their own way, Mila." My eyes began to grow heavy. "I need to rest my eyes for a moment," I barely mumbled before my body fell sideways, and I fell asleep.

I woke up to Mila running her fingers through my hair. She was humming softly, and though I couldn't hear the exact song she was singing, it reminded me of Mama. Even with my pounding headache, I listened to her hum song after song.

"The first thing I'm doing when we get out of here is showering and then eating anything I can get my hands on." She continued brushing my black hair with her fingers. "I think I could honestly eat a whole cow at this point."

I wanted to roll my eyes, but any physical movement honestly hurt.

"Where are you from?" she asked.

I almost lied, but she already knew my name. And at this point I was too tired to care.

"Mississippi," I whispered.

"I would love to visit it there. Maybe one day I can. I'm originally from Springfield, Massachusetts." She sighed. "I live in Moscow now with my husband. He's pretty scary, but he's nice to me. Sometimes in the beginning I wondered why he was nice to me, but he told me it was love at first sight. Matteo bought me, but Dimitri saved me fr—"

BOOM.

Mila jumped up, which caused me to land on my side. Grunting in pain, I looked around before what sounded like another explosion. *Fuck.*

"I know I don't know you, but you can come with us," Mila blurted out before the sound of a gun rang out.

Jumping to my feet I looked at Mila. She was a few inches taller than me, but just as skinny. Her face was covered in dirt, but I could still see freckles covering her entire face, arms, and legs. Her hair was a complete mess, but in a way, she was still beautiful.

"I can't come with you," I said, shaking my head. I could try and get her to the point where she would be able to get out, but I couldn't go with her.

"Salem, please!" she begged, grabbing hold of my hands. "I can't leave knowing what they'll do to you."

Shaking my head again, I said, "Mila, I can get you out, but I'm not. I can't leave."

Hurt, sadness, and worry passed over her face. But I didn't need all of that. I didn't know why she would be hurt. We'd known each other for maybe two days. She didn't need to worry about me.

"Mila, I appreciate your offering, and I would love nothing more than to just walk out of this place with you. But I have…" I trailed off. I couldn't tell her.

"Okay, I understand," she muttered under her breath, dropping my hands. She backed away slowly, putting some distance between us.

"Okay, they'll come in here soon and I'll need you to stick close to me. Listen to everything I tell you, do you und—" I was cut off from the side door banging open, Jose stepping in.

"Let's go!" he snapped. Smirking at him, I stepped in front of her, blocking the view of her. "Stupid bitch, you want another fucking beat down!" Jose stepped forward to try and backhand me. It was fucking time.

Grabbing hold of his wrist, I twisted, breaking the bone. He screamed in pain. I grabbed hold of his knife that was sticking from his back pocket. Twisting him around, I yanked the knife back before drilling it into his throat. He didn't have time to react or think before I shoved his body down. Turning around to Mila I caught her eyes that widened down at the now dead Jose back to me. As quickly as she looked scared, she nodded her head and stepped forward.

"Stay close," I whispered. Mila didn't speak as I looked into the hallway. I could still hear the sound of guns shooting out from above us. I knew we were in the basement, so now it was just time to find Donato and then get out of here.

She kept close the whole time we walked between the hallways, leading to a set of stairs. I had no idea where any of the guards were, but they all seemed preoccupied with whatever was happening upstairs.

Keeping close to the wall, I continued on my way. Mila kept up by holding onto the back of my dirt covered shirt. As soon as she touched my back, I almost slammed my fist into her face. I hated anyone touching me, especially my back. My inside burned with the need to snatch her hand away, but I knew this was the only way to get her out of here safe.

Once we reached the top of the stairs, I slowly opened the door. Looking out, I could see parts of the wall on the floor, and everything looked destroyed. There was barely any light. Most of the walls were now falling apart. A few dead bodies laid around, gunshot wounds covering their body.

"HEY, GET BACK!" someone screamed from our left. Glancing over, Hugo and a few guards had their guns trained at the side door. Hugo was stuck between aiming his own gun at the door and us.

Grabbing the handle of the knife, I threw it, my shoulder aching in pain. The knife flew through the air, lodging in Hugo's throat. Before his body hit the ground, I rushed forward yanking the AR-15. The other guards were blind to what was even happening behind them. I checked the magazine before taking aim. Four guards dropped dead, leaving Mila and me alone.

"Wow, you really know how to work that," Mila whispered from behind me. Rolling my eyes, I ignored her as I shifted through the dead bodies on the ground. Opening the side door, I walked through with Mila still at my back. This room was barely lit like the rest of this place. Pointing to the corner I nodded my head towards it. Mila rushed forward before kneeling down and tucking herself back.

Scanning the room, I took in the large, empty area. All the walls were a pale gray color, and a dirt floor, with a broken ceiling light. Just as I was about to tell Mila to stay there, the door we'd just walked through banged open.

"YOU!" one of them screamed in Spanish. Yes, it was me, me who was going to kill him and make sure he knew it was me who finally got him. "Put the gun down now, fucking whore."

Shaking my head, I smirked before shooting both knees. He screamed out, and his gun dropped to the ground. The other three took aim, but I was faster. Shooting the other three dead, the one on the ground began screaming, "AHH, YOU FUCKING WHORE!" His words were mixed between English and Spanish.

Looking closer, I realized it was Nero, the bastard that liked to come in and burn my legs along with my arms.

"You asked who I was. I'll tell you, but first answer something for me." Walking closer, I kneeled down, keeping the AR-15 in his direction.

He nodded his head.

Fucking pussy.

"Where is Donato?" His name tasted sour.

His eyes bugged out before shaking his head. "Where is he?" I forced the words out.

"He-he's held in the side room," Nero mumbled.

"Thank you." I smiled.

"Who are you?" he rushed out before I held the gun to his forehead.

"Ghost," I whispered, blowing his brains out.

Mila stood from the corner, making her way towards me. Her eyes trained on Nero's dead body, but I didn't have time to just stand here and stare at him. I had places to be. Donato was a dead man.

"He used to like coming into my room," she whispered, her eyes glistening. "You're kind of scary," Mila choked. Shrugging my shoulders, I turned back towards the door. I could hear faint gun shots before the voices. I couldn't recognize them, but Mila smiled. "It's them."

"No one can know about me." I turned my full attention to her. "No one."

I don't know what fully passed over her expression. She almost looked scared for a moment. But finally, what seemed like minutes later, Mila nodded shakily.

"Go, they'll be here any minute. Go do what you have to do, *Ghost*," she said, smirking at my name.

I didn't waste any time. I slowly backed away, slipping into the small, hidden door. I watched the side door burst open. A large man rushed inside, wild eyes searching everywhere before landing on Mila. Her knees nearly buckled as he reached her, scooping her into his arms. Mila sobbed, and I smiled.

At least she got her happy ending.

She was safe.

Now it was Donato time.

And his time was up.

Chapter 3

Zane

Four years later

"Uncle Zaney." Tobias's little feet carry him faster than should be possible for a four-year-old. I barely have time to reach down as he throws himself into my arms. Resting him on my hip, I head out of the foyer to the kitchen. Tobias is my best friend Dimitri's son. Four years ago, the three of us, Dimitri, Killian and I, were on a mission to find who was stealing shipments of drugs. As we got convinced that it was Matteo from the Cartel, we made our stakeout. After hours of waiting for the Cartel to show up, we almost left until a van appeared. There a girl was being dragged from the vehicle, and from that moment Dimitri became obsessed with her.

It didn't take long for the two of them to fall in love with each other. The only problem was Matteo was also obsessed with her. Only Matteo wanted her as a sex slave, where Dimitri wanted to make her his queen. Unfortunately, while we were staying in Boston, Matteo got hold of Mila. While those were the worst two days Dimitri had been through, nothing took us by surprise when we finally arrived, only to see multiple men dead.

The worst was when we found Mila standing over Nero and three other men. We searched high and low for Matteo, since Dimitri refused to leave him alive. Not after he thought he could just take her. After an hour of searching, we found parts of him. Yes, parts of him.

He had multiple bullet holes. His body was tied to a chair and his groin was, let's just say, everything was missing. And next to him was Donato. All of us were confused as to why Donato was there. He was one of Luca's Cosa Nostra Mob men. Donato was completely mutilated. I almost felt sorry for the fucker, if it were possible for me to feel. His throat was cut, and both eyes were cut out of their socket. His cock was laying by his feet, along with his guts hanging in his lap.

I shivered just thinking about it.

And no matter the amount of times any of us asked Mila who could have done that, she refused to tell us. Just saying she had no idea and that she simply walked out of the room she was being held in. But it didn't make any sense. Matteo knew we were attacking. It's why his men were fighting us when we first arrived. Yet the moment we got inside the large building in the compound, all the men were basically murdered.

"Uncle Zaney?" Tobias's little voice broke me from my thoughts. "Can you get me a snack?" he asked, placing his small hands on either side of my face. No hint of fear laid in his vibrant green eyes. I liked the fact that he wasn't afraid of me. Most were. Mila was scared of me when she first arrived. She could never be in the same room as me without fearing I was going to snap and kill her.

I could.

But Dimitri would most likely murder me for touching her. It wasn't until after we rescued her that Mila finally began to trust me.

Thankfully, my size never deterred Tobias. I was larger than most men at six foot six, weighing 270 pounds. It also just meant I was perfect to be Dimitri's enforcer. Dimitri's the Pakhan, the Bratva leader. He was ruthless. Just not as ruthless as I am.

"What kind of snack?" I asked him to sit down on the countertop. Something I learned about myself once Tobias arrived was that I'm a big push over. But only to him. Tobias could ask me for anything, and I would get it for him. Which he knew because last year he asked for a BB gun. And me being the best uncle I got him three. Mila did not like that one bit.

"I think…" He tapped his chin as though he was in deep thought of what he wanted. "COOKIES!" he shouted.

"If you want cookies, I think it's best if you don't yell," I smirked. Turning around, I headed for the cookie jar Mila tried to keep hidden away.

"You know you're smart." Tobias giggled.

Grabbing two cookies, I held one out to Tobias and shoved the other one in my mouth.

"You need milk, little dude?" I asked, grabbing the gallon from the fridge, pouring myself a small glass.

"Yeah," Tobias said around a mouthful of cookie.

"I know you're not talking with your mouth full," Killian said, walking into the kitchen and snatching the rest of the cookie from Tobias hand. Tobias glared at Killian before swallowing.

"You're being a bully," he growled. When Tobias got like this, he reminded me so much of Dimitri. He's the perfect mix between Mila and Dimitri.

"It's okay little dude, I'll get you another one." Already doing so, I handed him another cookie and a small cup of milk. "Are you coming in here for a reason or just to steal a four-year-old's cookie?" I glared over at Killian. Killian was the third friend in the group. While I'm the enforcer, I also handle most of the men. Killian handled all security. He was in charge of watching all the accounts and books. He was also a genius, scary smart. Killian was the best hacker/computer nerd out there. For someone who was as smart as himself, he was also the dumbest. A year after Dimitri and I met, we were sitting at a club back in Boston, where Killian decided it was a good idea to march up to the table and demand a job from Dimitri. I was surprised when he hadn't killed Killian on the spot for it. But he proved himself to be smart and the best hacker. Therefore, he did get a job and slowly became one of our closest friends.

"Both." Killian grinned over at Tobias inching to steal his cookie again.

"You try to steal my snack again, I'll sic Uncle Zaney on you," Tobias threatened, shoving more of his snack into his mouth. "And he'll kick your ass."

I couldn't help laughter escaping my lips at Tobias's swearing and using me to beat Killian's ass.

"Tobias Volkov!" Killian gasped, acting as though he was hurt. "Zane could *not* beat my ass."

Tobias fell into a fit of giggles. Ever since he was born everything around here changed. At first, I hated it. I hated the change. But around the time he was three months old Dimitri was out with Killian. Mila had asked me to watch him while she took a quick shower after he got sick all over her. I was scared shitless. I may be a ruthless killer, someone who could blow someone else's brains out. But watching a three-month-old, who waited until his mother was showering to shit his own brains out... Those ten minutes Mila was out of commission, Tobias managed to shit so much it got all over his clothes. A blowout they call it. Which of course, somehow, he thought he was completely hilarious. I was running around with a shitty baby trying to find where the diapers and wipes were. But once he was laughing after I got the situation under control, I found myself smiling and laughing with him.

Ever since then I was okay with the change around the house.

"We're taking a trip," Dimitri announced as he walked into the kitchen. "Mila wants to go visit home again. And Luca has been asking about setting up a meeting."

"What is the meeting about?" Killian asked.

"I'm not really sure, but I think it has something to do with Leonardo, Finn, and Donato's deaths."

"Donato was killed along with Matteo four years ago." Four years ago when Matteo took Mila, we found Donato as well. There was a rumor going around that there was a man called Ghost who was taking out the Cosa Nostra. After Finn, Leonardo and Donato were brutally murdered, and Luca took his remaining close men underground. I don't know why he decided now was the time to come back to the land of the living.

"Yes, and from what he's saying he believes Ghost is going to come back once he makes his appearance again." I sat back against the kitchen sink as Dimitri walked over to his son, picking him up. It was odd at first watching Dimitri, the man who hated any physical contact like myself, show so much affection towards his wife and son.

"Hate to keep asking questions, but what does that have to do with us?" Killian always had questions about every little detail.

Dimitri shrugged as he carried him towards a set of stairs. "I don't know, which is why I need you to hack into his accounts to see what he's been doing. See what you can find out, anything at all." Turning his focus towards me, he said, "When we arrive I'll need you to follow the lower rank of his men and see what they're doing."

Grunting, I nodded my head in agreement. I was better at watching and following people than most other things.

"When are we leaving?" Killian asked.

"Mommy wants to leave today." Tobias cheered in his father's arms. Tobias was the only four-year-old I knew who loved traveling as much as he did. Though he's also the only four-year-old I knew.

"And where is Mommy?" I asked quietly.

"Packing." He giggles. Of course he also knew that we were taking this trip. He also knew before any of us did. The first year Mila walked around eggshells around us, even after the number of times all three of us told her she was safe. It wasn't until Dimitri accidentally dropped one of her pieces of artwork in the house that she let loose. I cringed remembering the little fireball she became.

Now Mila did whatever she wanted and, though Dimitri had very few hard no's for her, whenever Mila wanted to go back to the states we went. It wasn't hard to do because Dimitri conducted most of his drug operation from the states.

Dimitri smirked over at us, the knowing look that it would be soon. Thankfully, I always had a bag packed. Dimitri headed out of the kitchen with Tobias.

"I have a bad feeling about Luca," Killian muttered around another cookie.

"You always have a bad feeling." I rolled my eyes leaving him behind in the kitchen. I had a bad feeling too. I didn't voice it though. I didn't trust Luca, no matter how much he had helped us in the past with finding Matteo.

Everything felt off about this trip. And I didn't like that feeling.

Chapter 4

Salem

My heart pounded faster and my mouth dried to cotton as I felt someone's eyes on me. But that couldn't be possible; not when I lived alone on a farm miles away from any civilization. But I could feel eyes on me, and the hair on my arms prickled. The scar across my throat tugged at my skin, aching, causing a sharp pain in my heart.

I stopped washing the cast iron pan, turning off the water, and I stood there listening. I couldn't hear anything, but I could *feel* the eyes. Glancing around, nothing looked out of place. The sunlight was shining through into the dining room.

Drying my hands I reached under the kitchen island and grabbed the Glock I kept under there. Scanning the kitchen area, I checked the mag. Once I made sure it was full, I tiptoed to the doorway. My hands firmly on my gun, I searched the lower level leading to the living room.

As soon as I saw her sitting in the recliner, I lowered the gun, clicking the safety back on. Taking a deep breath I dropped the gun on the entryway table.

"You know sneaking into someone's house could really get you hurt if not killed." Walking over to the couch I fell down. "And sneaking into my house would just get you killed."

Aziza ignored me as she tapped away at her computer. There's something about Aziza when she's focused, especially when it comes to anything on her computer. She'd been my best friend since we were five. When we were in kindergarten, we were at some punk's birthday party. He started making fun of her, Aziza was too nice and just walked away. I, on the other hand, was not as nice and pushed him into the pool. Did I know he couldn't swim? Yes. Did I care? No.

I was grounded for a month. And every day Aziza showed up asking if I was ungrounded only to be sent away. The last day I was supposed to be grounded Dada finally let me out to play. And ever since then we'd been stuck to the hip.

"You wouldn't hurt me. You might threaten me, but you wouldn't actually hurt me," she smirked, not even bothering to look up from her lap. She's also great at multitasking. She may be a natural blonde, but she was highly smart. Smarter than anyone ever gave her credit for, and she was a wizard at hacking into basically anything.

"You keep pushing your luck," I snarked back. As much shit talk as I might do, she's right. I might be a killer and take a lot of people. But I could never hurt her. I would never hurt her.

So as much as I would like to demand her to stop typing away on her computer and to answer the many questions sprouting around in my brain, instead, I sat back against the couch and closed my eyes.

Whatever she was thinking about must be important especially if she was still ignoring me.

Aziza and I could not be more opposite if we tried. She was a natural blonde, with dark blue eyes and full lips. She stood only an inch taller than me at five foot six, and even though she hated it she was curvy. Medium size hipes, and not overly large chest. Whereas I was five foot five with small hips and small chested. Looking at me you wouldn't have guessed I could murder men double my size.

"You have your murder face on." Aziza broke me from my thoughts.

Glancing over her laptop was closed as she stared at me, smirking. Of course she was smirking at me. Besides our looks being completely different, she was sassy, a smart ass. I was too serious, always focusing on the task at hand.

"What murder face?" I raised my brows at her, uncertain of what face she was talking about. I knew I had that resting bitch face down. But a murder face? I certainly did not have that.

"Yes, oh yes you do, my friend." Poking a finger at me, she said, "That face right there. You have a mean murder face going on."

"Yeah, what do you call the face you have going on?" I asked poking at her. Sitting up I crossed my legs waiting for her to explain her reasoning.

"Wow, you're in a sour mood."

"And yet here you are, ignoring my sour mood." Done with this part of the useless conversation, I stood up and headed back to the dirty dishes in my sink.

"You're always in a sour mood." She laughs following me into the kitchen.

"Is there a point to this conversation?" Turning the water on I continued with washing my breakfast dishes. Aziza walked over and began drying the clean ones.

"There is, but first how are you?"

Rolling my eyes, I glared over at her. How am I? I hated it when she asked me this, which she did very often. Almost every day, but most of the time she called me, blowing my phone up until I finally answered and then asked why I was angry and why I was ignoring her. It wasn't that I was mad or trying to ignore her per se. I mean, yes, I ignored her because I didn't need her asking me every day how I was.

It was sweet, but overwhelming.

"I'm fine," I finally answered as I handed her the last dish. Drying my hands I leaned against the counter and crossed my arms. Aziza took her sweet time drying the last one before taking the plate over to the cabinet and placing it inside.

"You didn't ask how I am, which is completely rude by the way. But I'm good, great, actually. I got a call this morning, New York is looking for a new role, the lead role." Aziza was a dancer, an amazing dancer at that. Ever since she was nine, she danced religiously, either ballet or hip-hop. The way she could move her body made my joints hurt. "It's for *Swan Lake*. I guess the composer wants a blonde, apparently." Aziza smiled over at me.

"That's great!" Which was true, I'm happy she's getting this chance. Besides hacking into companies, dance was the other thing she's amazing at. I could watch her for hours. "I'm actually really happy for you." I finally smiled at her.

"Thank you," she said, her southern accent coming out thick. Aziza and I had very thick accents. We grew up in Mississippi, her family's farmhouse right across from my family.

"And now we've both talked about how we're doing, I would really like to know what the point of this conversation is."

"First, you need to promise me something."

Grinding my molars, I glared at her. Swallowing the lump I forced the words out, "Promise."

"I got entangled a few nights ago. I didn't know how accurate it was until I did a lot of digging last night. Which for your infor—"

"Spill it," I interrupted her.

"I found them," she finally spoke.

My body tensed. Everything around me faded away as I replayed her words over and over again.

I found them. I found them.

Aziza found them. Four years they were underground, with no way for Aziza to find them. I waited four years, thinking I would never get the chance again. I never voiced or allowed myself to think that they would just get away with it. But somewhere inside I had the sickening feeling it would be true. That they got away.

But she found them.

"Salem…" Aziza's cold hand grabbed my shoulder. Jumping to the side, I hadn't realized she was trying to get my attention until I felt the coldness of her skin on my own. Her eyes widened at my sudden movements. I felt like a complete asshole now. She was just trying to comfort me, and I was acting like she was a nobody to me.

"Shit, I'm sorry," I whispered my voice rough from the emotions swirling around. I wish I could feel happy that she found the monsters, but I was angry. I was so angry that my hands ached from the tight grip I held them in.

"You don't need to apologize, Salem." But I did.

"What information have you found?" I spat out, finding it rather difficult to think about anything besides murdering them. To watch all of their eyes as they took that last breath.

"I haven't found any sightings of most of them, but Giulio and Leonzo both have been using their accounts from Maine back to Boston. I checked security cameras around the area and found them entering their old penthouse."

Nodding my head along with her, it took me a moment to realize they were close. They were no longer underground. Which meant I could finally end this, even though it was just two of them right now. I could finally get one step closer to ending them.

"We could be there in a few hours if we leave now," Aziza said, turning on her heel heading to the foyer where the stairs leading to the second level were.

Letting out a sigh I followed her. As soon as my foot hit the top of stairs, my brain finally caught up to the fact she said we.

"Wait, wait, wait, Aziza!" I called. Stepping into my room I saw that she was already shoving clothes into my suitcase. "Aziza."

She paid me no mind as she shoved more socks than I should probably have inside. I didn't know why she thought she was coming with me, but she definitely is not.

"Aziza!" I snapped. She dropped the clothes in her hand and turned slowly facing me. "There's no one here, I'm going alone," I said, crossing my arms over my chest, refusing to budge on this.

Rolling her eyes she went back to packing my clothes like I hadn't just said something. "Honey, I'm going with you. It'll be easier, plus I'll end up going to New York anyway."

"Azi—"

"No," she said, cutting me off.

"Don't get an attitude with me," I growl. "Aziza, I'm going to Boston to murder the men who hurt my family! I'm going to kill them all, you understand that right. How am I supposed to go after them and look after you." None of it came out a question. She may act like she's not bothered by me murdering people in cold blood. But no one in the right mind could be okay with it.

I could accept I wasn't right in the head anymore. Not after what they did to them, not after what I witnessed. But Aziza, she was innocent in all this. Sure she tracked them down, hacked into their accounts. She stayed back, she was safe here. No one could touch her if she stayed right here.

"Salem Wren Gray." My full name, thick with her accent. I cringed. She only used my full name when she was done playing around. She was being too serious. Hands on her hips. "You listen to me and listen to every word," she said, pointing a finger at me. "I know *exactly* what you do. Don't you forget I hide what you do! I make sure you're not caught on security cameras. Sure we don't do field trips while you do your thing. But I know what you do, Salem. Now I'm coming with you, either driving with you right now, or I'll get into my own damn car, and I'll meet you there."

"Aziza, I rea—"

"NO!" she yells. Flinching from her outburst, she rarely got like this. Only very few things would set Aziza off. Dance, animal rights, and me.

"Listen to me, please." She nodded her head. "I can't protect you and find them."

"Honey, I can take care of myself. You've trained with me. Though you could definitely kick my ass, even with a broken arm." She laughed, probably remembering the fact that I had indeed trained with her. Though my arm wasn't broken, it was my elbow, and it was sprained.

I knew Aziza could handle herself, to a certain degree. She knew how to handle a gun, and she knew how to throw a knife to a point. But she didn't train everyday like I did. She knew how to get out of most situations. But I still couldn't protect her.

But Aziza was also stubborn, so I knew if she didn't travel with me now, she'd find her own way and show up on my doorstep there.

"You stay inside the house. You keep your head down, you listen to me, and I swear to everything in life, Aziza, you do not and I fucking repeat you DO NOT put yourself in any harm's way."

Putting her hands up, she said, "Oh, come on. You know, I'd never do any of that anyway."

"Yeah, which means if they come after me and I tell you to fucking run, guess what, *honey?*" I rolled my eyes.

"Yeah, yeah, yeah, come on. Let's get your shit packed, so we can hit the road."

"Aziza, I'm serious here. If they find us, find me. You run, you don't come back for me, you run to the safehouse." This was something I wouldn't back down from. I didn't care if I was about to die. All of them were about to kill me. She needed to run, run hard and fast.

"I understand," she said, giving me her pinky finger. "Aeternum."

Letting out a breath I didn't realize I was holding, I hooked my pinky with her. "Aeternum."

I just had to hope that, besides taking down the last of these monsters, nothing else would happen.

Chapter 5

Salem

It was a miracle when we arrived at my house at eight. Aziza only had to stop a total of three times. But with my driving I was able to get us back on track. As soon as we got to the house, we took turns showering. When I got out, Aziza gave me the news that both Giulio and Leonzo were at some nightclub downtown. It was a little soon for me to move, but after hearing they were back after four years of nothing, I was ready to get back into the swing of things.

By ten I was dancing in between two guys, the beat of the song pounding in my head. The floors were beginning to move from all the bodies slamming against each other around the song, and was spilling over many drinks from them holding it above their heads trying to get through the crowd. I smelled like the bottom of the floor with how much that was spilling on me.

Everyone else was distracted, drinking, looking for an easy hook up, like the two men who were grinding on me. I could feel their erection digging into me, but I was more focused on the top floor. No one was a concern of mine except for the two men who sat upstairs and were in deep conversation with a few other men.

The moment I laid my eyes on them I refused to let them out of my sight, but just looking at them pissed me off. I could feel my skin getting hot even in this skintight outfit. My hands itched to clench into a fist, and my body wanted to jump the wall and kill them both right there. But the chances of me getting out of this overly crowded club alive, with the amount of security that was here and on that floor, were very slim.

Doable, but slim.

Plus, I was a little out of practice, even if I did train every day. But work on my throwing knife skills and shooting range—I could admit I was a little rusty.

So as much as every fiber in my being ached to murder those two up there I couldn't. Not yet.

Six names.

Six monsters.

Six more deaths.

Then I could be set free.

Looking up at the high ceiling, I allowed myself just a moment to get lost in the bass of the music. The blue strobe lights danced around everyone. I could almost hear Emmy laughing at me. *"Never pegged you for a party animal."* She would laugh, she would think it was hilarious that I was here. For as long as I could remember I wanted to be like Dada, taking care of the farm.

I felt like none of them could rest. They couldn't be at peace with those monsters still walking the streets. They couldn't. And I couldn't be at peace. I couldn't rest.

My brows furrowed, shaking my head. I locked my eyes onto Giulio's face as he threw his head back letting out a booming laugh.

End them. Kill them, the little voice in my head told me. Reminding me that they deserved everything I planned to give them.

"Hi ba-baby," someone slurred in my ear. I barely caught myself cringing at their hot breath against my neck. "We should get out of here," he whispered as his tongue caressed my earlobe.

Shooting a glare over my shoulder, I nudged him back with my elbow. He grunted as his hands shot to his ribs.

"Fucking bitch," he growled.

"Come on, we should get out of here, baby girl." The other tried reaching for my arm.

Shaking my head no, I stepped back. Done with this interaction, I focused on their faces. Remembering them. The blond had a mole on his upper lip and a small bump on the bridge of his nose. The other had dark brown hair, almost black, and his eyes were dead. He almost held no emotions.

Both men stood next to each other, glaring at me.

"Come on." The blond elbowed his friend, backing away. Both of them disappeared from the line of sight. Taking a deep breath I turned around, instantly realizing both chairs that Giulio and Leonzo had been sitting in were now empty. Scanning the upper level I barely caught them as they opened the back door and left.

Making my way to the exit I ignored all the stares of the men eye fucking me. It was a relief to be getting out of here. Being social was tiring. All I wanted right now was a hot shower and some Chinese. Taking out my phone I sent Aziza a text asking if she was in the mood for food.

As soon as the back-alley door shut behind me I was shoved. My head connected with the concrete wall, and my forehead bust opened. The blood began to trail down the side of my face. Looking over I narrowed my eyes at the two figures who stepped forward. Blinking a few times, I realized it was the two men who were dancing and trying to get me to leave with them.

Fucking idiots.

Taking a step from the wall, Blondie smirked at me while the one other one looked like this was the last place he wanted to be.

"She's pretty ain't she?" Blondie took a step forward. I didn't move. "Brave girl, but I told you I think you should leave with us."

He's even more stupid then. Did he really think I would leave with him? And now he's attacking me, thinking I would now leave with him. They were both stupid, even if the brunette thought he could just stand back and not do a thing.

These pants were so tight I couldn't hide a gun, or even a freaking knife. So my fist was going to have to be it.

"Martin, grab her," Blondie barked. The brunette who was named Martin glanced at Blondie before taking a step towards me. My lip curled in disgust. If he thought I would let his nasty fingers touch me he was mistaken.

"Come on, make this easy." Martin reached for me. Rearing back I punched him in the face, the feel of nose crunching, my knuckles busted on impact. *Fuck I was rusty.*

"UGH, you stupid bitch!" Martin screamed. His voice turned angry, and he glared at me through his now broken nose. "You stupid fucking girl!" Oh so here was the true nature of Mister Martin. He liked to hide behind the curtain, to act like he was the real one in charge. He was. They thought I was stupid, that I had no idea the game they were playing.

Martin again went to grab at me. This time I ducked and kicked him in the shin. I didn't want to kill them really but making sure they were hurt was making my skin itch. Fuck these guys.

They both charged forward trying to grab at me. Grinning at them I grabbed hold of Martin's head before shoving him forward into the wall, his body slumped to the ground. Blondie snarled at me grabbing hold of both wrists.

"You're going to regret that, fucking cunt!"

Raising my eyebrow I raised my foot kicking him where it most hurt. They had no idea what they were doing. The moment my boot connected with his balls his grip on my wrist fell. He let out a loud scream, echoing in the alleyway. Soon someone was going to come out here and I didn't feel like being caught. Grabbing his head, I was about to ram my knee into his face before he started screaming, "W-wait, please. Please don't. I'm sorry."

Cocking my head to the side I thought for a moment about letting him stay awake, but I didn't need him following me or worse getting himself killed for trying to come at me again. I could see the moment he thought I was going to let him go. In that moment I moved faster than he could think, ramming his face into my knee.

Pushing his unconscious body to the side I let out a sigh. This was not how I thought the night was going to go. Pulling my phone out I checked my text from Aziza. She was ordering it to be delivered. Which was much better. I was bone tired, and just wanted my bed.

Taking a deep breath I turned on my heel ready to leave the alleyway, only to see an overly large man standing a few feet in front of me. His hood covered his face so I couldn't see it.

My bed was just going to have to wait it seemed like.

Chapter 6

Zane

I hated this fucking city.

I haven't been back in four years and even though I knew we were coming back to this city, I really wished it wasn't true. I left America thinking I'd never come back. I mean, Dimitri found me when I was eighteen, after I had killed three men. I thought Dimitri was going to make number four. Instead, he made me an offer to be his enforcer. I didn't think too much about it, just said, "Sure."

Then I was off, traveling back to Russia with him. The rest was history. I mean, a year later Killian came along. Therefore, I never thought we'd come back here as much as we have.

And I hated this city.

This city made my skin itch.

Four years ago, Dimitri asked me to do a stupid task. A stupid task that ended with me knocked out in an alleyway with a broken nose and my kneecaps bruised. My ego was shot, and I refused to tell anyone who I ended up with said injuries.

I mean it was a female, I knew that. But she caught me off guard.

"Where's Luca?" Dimitri inquired. Locking eyes on Giulio and Leonzo they both showed disrespect. It made my murderly ways crawl up, making me want to drill my fist into their faces.

We arrived in Boston two days ago, trying to adjust to the time change. Luca set up a meeting for tonight only for us to show up and with no Luca. Instead two underbosses that were in charge of Luca's clubs. Which didn't make any sense because the whole point of this meeting was Luca announcing he was done being a little bitch. When he went underground years ago no one knew where he went. Suddenly he's back, so you would think he would shop up and show up with his security men.

Not the club bosses.

"He couldn't make it." Giulio shrugged like it was no big deal. But it was, it meant Luca didn't respect Dimitri.

"Hmm."

"Luca just wanted us to meet you here to welcome you. He sent his apologies for not being able to make it." Leonzo followed suit and shrugged, laughing it off as no big deal.

None of us followed suit. None of us wanted to be here. Killian most likely wanted to shove his face into his computer. I wanted to just lie in my bed and Dimitri wanted to be with his family.

"Well, welcome is appreciated." Dimitri kept his expression cold. He was not happy; it was a thing I could pick up on. Just like Killian was thinking about anything but this meeting. He hated doing any of this, only doing it if he absolutely needed to. "I think we're just going to finish this drink and head out."

"How's the wife and that child you have?" Giulio asked.

Dimitri barely let on that they made a mistake of mentioning his family. They both laughed, which only caused Dimitri to tense up even more. Killian glanced at me, making it look more like he was just blinking. No one would've put together that he was warning me to be prepared.

"I didn't come here to discuss my family." Dimitri smiled. The smile was all for play. I don't know why either of them thought it would be a good idea to bring up a man's family.

"All is well." Giulio stood up buttoning his suit jacket up. "It was nice to see you again, *Dimitri.*"

We watched as both men walked away, leaving out the door to my left. No one spoke for a few minutes, but I could tell Dimitri was close to losing his patience.

"I have eyes on them, D." Killian nudged his shoulder trying to show him his phone. I'm sure Mila had no idea that Dimitri had the house bugged, cameras in every room, microphone everywhere. He was surely paranoid. But that would happen when your wife was kidnapped by sex traffickers, and then sold, just to be kidnapped again, and then taken from the person who bought her.

Mila literally had the worst luck of anyone I ever knew.

"Killian, keep eyes on them until I get there. Zane, I'm assuming you let them know."

I nodded my head. I had six men posted around the house, and another three inside. It wasn't a lot, but Dimitri preferred not to have too many guards. Less men around Mila, who made her highly uncomfortable. She only trusted the three of us.

"I'm going to head there now. I don't care what you guys do. Tomorrow, I'll need you both at seven."

Leaving without another word, Dimitri headed downstairs. Our three men who were hiding followed behind him.

"I'm getting food, you game?" Killian asked, pocketing his phone, standing from the couch.

"Sure, I'll head out in a few."

Killian nodded his head, leaving the same way Dimitri had. I don't know why I wanted to stay for a little bit, but for some reason I was not ready to leave. Even though I hated this type of scene; I hated being social. I almost didn't feel human.

Walking over to the railing I looked down at the crowd of adults dancing against each other. I never found the appeal of wanting to be that close to another person. It was disgusting. I sometimes wondered what it was like to have someone you wanted to touch, wanted to spend time with. I wondered if Dimitri ever had those thoughts about Mila, or if he truly just looked at her and wanted her.

From the moment he saw her, he wanted her, wanted to take care of her. I had no idea if it was love, or what it was exactly. Mila, it took a little bit for her to warm up, but that was understandable with her background. She went through hell but looking at her now you'd never know that.

Even dealing with me, I put her through hell. I hated her for just being there. But once I finally tried to give her a chance, I somewhat accepted her. More like I just dealt with her.

Turning around I headed for the door and took the stairs down to another door that led outside. Stepping outside, the alleyway was barely lit, and I was expecting not to see anyone. But as soon as I looked left, I noticed two average-sized figures staring down at a much smaller one.

At first, it appeared like they were all drunk until the one closest to me, standing on the right, went to grab the smaller one. They punched the guy in the face causing him to yell in pain, most likely breaking his nose from the sound of his gurgling howl. Stepping forward, I watched as they both went to charge at the smaller one. The smaller figure grabbed hold of the first one, ramming their head into the wall, and they fell to the ground like a sack of potatoes. The other one cursed rushing forward with no regard; she just knocked his buddy out without an ounce of care. Just as he reached her she kicked her leg out.

I winced as her platform shoes connected with his junk. Gripping my balls with my hands, I cringed just imagining what he was feeling.

The moment his hands dropped from her shoulders, she grabbed hold of his head, ramming her knee into his face. And he dropped to the ground.

Fuck I was getting hard just watching her beat these two shits. It wasn't the first time watching someone inflict pain caused my cock to react.

I stepped close enough that I could get a good look at who she was. I took in her tight black leather pants, fitting tightly around her ass. It was nice and round. I never was much of an ass man, but she had a great one. Her boots were chunky, and did not look easy to walk in. Glancing up at her shirt, her back was bare. Even in the dimly lit alleyway I could see faint white scars.

I found myself wanting to run my hand over her back, to feel if they were rough or soft.

I was staring so hard that I didn't notice the moment she turned around. Sucking in a breath, I thought, god damn.

She was breathtaking.

Gorgeous.

Her hair was midnight black, parted down the middle, pin straight that hung over her shoulders. Fuck her eyes.

I couldn't look away from those bright blue eyes, cobalt blue. Piercing. Her eyes were pure distraction.

She had faint white scars running down that beautiful right eye. Scanning over her, a large white and red scar stood out against her throat. Like someone tried slicing her throat, but it wasn't deep enough to actually kill her.

Standing this close I could finally see how tiny she was. Her heels helped a little. But she was still extremely tiny, the top of her head barely reaching my chest. She was slim, with small hips, and a small waist and chest. I had more than a hundred pounds on her, more than double her size.

Her head cocked to the side as she stared right back at me. No fear as she studied my own face. Not many could look me right in the eye, but her. This tiny girl held zero emotions.

"You're a tiny thing, aren't you?" I found myself saying.

I watched her move slightly, taking a fighting stance. Her head was still cocked to the side. In a blink of an eye, she swung her fist connecting with the side of my face. Damn, I could feel the bruise already forming on my cheek. She threw one hell of a punch.

Snapping my head back up at her, I was able to block her next swing. Grabbing onto her wrist, she brought her knee up aiming for my dick. Swinging her around her back went against my chest. I got a good amount of her hair in my face, and I could smell vanilla and mint. She was intoxicating.

Distracting.

"You're good, but I think I'm better," I mumbled into her ear. I never really taunted my prey in the open, it wasn't my style. I liked taunting them in my controlled environment.

Which was my mistake. She rammed her head back, my grip loosening around her. That allowed her to rip herself from me, I didn't have time to think about the fact that my nose was either broken again, or severely hurt. Her body slammed me onto the ground, her legs on either side of my head. Her warm pussy rested against my throat.

I shouldn't be hard, but fuck this woman was making me want things I shouldn't want from someone who, from the looks of it, wanted to kill me. She leaned down, coming closer to my face. I don't know why I didn't move. I just laid there and let her study me. We both couldn't look away from each other.

"Who are you?" I muttered.

She continued looking at me, not speaking. Not even when the two men behind us began groaning, slowly waking up.

I looked up at her scar across her throat and wondered if maybe she couldn't speak. "Can you speak?" I blurted out. I couldn't explain the tugging at my chest wondering if in fact she couldn't talk. If that mark on her throat stopped me from being able to hear her voice.

She nodded her head, her brows furrowed. Her grip was slowly loosening around my neck, and I still didn't move. Is this what Dimitri felt when he looked at Mila? This definitely wasn't love, it couldn't be. I didn't love her. Plus, I mean I just met her. But she was nothing like anyone I had ever meant. It was… weird.

I don't know how long had passed, both of us staring at each other. Studying. Neither of us were moving, only the sound of our breathing, the two men groaning.

"Did they try to hurt you?" I finally asked. I don't know why I wanted to know. But that tugging at my heart continued. My brain told me not to care, but that beating organ in my chest didn't get the memo.

Her head cocked to the other side like an animal watching me. Ever so slowly she nodded her head. Leaning down, her breath hot against my neck, my body went rigid. Needing to press her further against me. It took everything in me to not do exactly that.

"They attacked me." Her voice was rough and raspy. If I hadn't known better, I would have guessed she smoked a lot. But I saw that scar on her throat. Her voice was rough from that mark.

And I found myself burning with anger. Angry that someone could do that to this tiny woman. My breath came in ragged as I tried focusing on this girl with cobalt eyes.

51

But within a blink of an eye she was pushing off me, running down the alleyway. Leaving me alone on the ground thinking what the fuck just happened.

Until I heard the two voices that tried to hurt her. I was moving before my brain could catch up. Kicking both of them in the face they fell unconscious again.

Time to figure out how to get them back to the house.

Chapter 7

Salem

I was angry.

No, that wasn't even close to what I was feeling.

I truly didn't understand what I was feeling. Why had I let them live? Why did I let Zane live again?

Yes.

I remembered him. I remembered him from four years ago when I broke his nose and left him knocked out in the alleyway. His hair was a little longer then, but it was still the same shade of blond. Enough gel that it stayed back, but not so much that it looked bad. His height was overwhelming now that he was no longer lying on the ground. He towered over me. His muscles strained against his long sleeves, and his thighs were overly large. He could easily squash someone's head. I hadn't been able to see his eyes the last time, but now his hazel eyes were almost like gold. The amber color was intoxicating.

The uncomfortable warmth spread through my body when I took him down. The fact he hadn't moved, that he could easily overpower me with the flick of his wrist.

I found myself getting turned on while my legs laid on either side of his head. I don't know if he knew he rested his hands on my hips, but neither of us moved.

Besides the fact that I walked away, not a worry that he would indeed take care of those two scumbags for me. The pure flash of anger when I told him they attacked me almost made me ask why. But I couldn't. I couldn't care. Not when I had a job to do.

Zane Theodore Rivera. Who is now thirty-three years old. He was no longer twenty-nine years old; he truly had aged well.

I didn't realize I ran all the way back to my house until I stopped in front of the front door. This house wasn't necessarily mine; it was Megan Carson's. Megan Carson was someone I used while I was in Boston. I didn't need the Italian mafia recognizing my name. It was a simple single-floor house, nothing special. Grayish-white siding, a brown front door, a simple driveway that held Aziza's SUV, along with my black Ford Explorer. Inside it had three bedrooms, mine, a guest room, and an office. I never used the other rooms except to keep up with appearances.

Shaking my head, I unlocked the door and rushed inside. Locking it behind me, I leaned my head against the door. Taking a deep breath I followed my old therapist's breathing technique. *In and out.*

"Uh, you good?" Aziza asked, breaking me from my thoughts, causing me to jump. I completely forgot she was even here.

Not bothering to open my eyes I nodded.

"Liar."

Taking another few minutes to myself, letting her just stare at me, I finally opened my eyes slowly. Just to meet Aziza staring very intensely at me with a mouthful of Chinese.

"I'm going to change," I muttered before rushing into my room. Quickly changing into a pair of sweatpants and sweatshirt, I washed my face from the make-up, and threw my hair into a ponytail. Grabbing a pair of socks I made my way into the living room where Aziza held out a wine glass.

"You'd think after sixteen years of knowing me you'd know I hate alcohol." Rolling my eyes, I still took the glass from her.

"Then you'd know yours is a wonderful glass of grape juice." She snickered, taking a large bite of an egg roll.

"So any knowledge from the club?" she asked, pointing to a container on the coffee table. Grabbing it, I plumped down on my worn couch, digging into my beef and broccoli. Groaning as soon as the mix hit my tongue, I couldn't stop my eyes from closing. *God why is this so much better than down south?*

Finally, chewing and swallowing, I shrugged my shoulders shoving another mouthful of food in.

"Come on, you gotta tell me, I want to know," Aziza said, grabbing her glass of wine.

"I saw them, nothing useful." I sighed. Giving her what she wanted was better than fighting with her. I swear Aziza was more stubborn than me. When she got her mind set on something, she would not let it go. Through the years you'd think I would learn to just answer her questions.

"Salem," she warned.

Looking up from my food, she was giving me that look. The look that told me she was not backing down from this. She would bug me over and over again until I got angry. But I couldn't be angry with her.

"Fine." Setting down my now cold Chinese food I slouched down pulling a blanket over me. "I really didn't find anything useful on them.... buuuut there were two men that tried attacking me in the alleyway." I barely got time to finish my sentence before she sat up and started fussing over me.

"Excuse me?" she hissed. "You thought you could just ignore the fact you were attacked? Salem Wren Gray, what is wrong with you?"

I let out a laugh at her using my full name. *Again.* Damn this was the second time in less than twenty-four hours.

"Yeah, I was attacked. But that's not the part I think you should be using my name for." I almost shied away from telling her about Zane. I hadn't told her about it four years ago, because four years ago I was more unhinged than I am now. I was so angry that everyone who came across me in the wrong manner, I killed them.

She stared at me, waiting for me to continue. I really hated dragging her into this; however, she was involved. As much as I wished she wasn't. She was the one who found the men I needed to end. So as much as I knew I should've kept my mouth shut and just let it be, I couldn't.

"Four years ago, before I got kidnapped by the cartel, I remember I ran into a man." I couldn't look at her as I spoke. Instead, I focused on swirling a string from the blanket around my finger. "I let him live." I muttered the last part.

Like I said, I was unhinged. I killed anyone who basically looked at me wrong. So someone following me, someone twice my size would have caused me to feel threatened and I would have killed him on the spot.

"You... let him... *live?*" I did not like the way she said that. Why was she saying it that way?

"Oh, come on, Aziza, you know how I was back then."

"Yeah, crazy, unhinged, a freaking psycho. Yeah, I know, you were freaking crazy outright."

I huffed out a breath. She wasn't wrong, but I did not like the sound of it.

"So what happened?" she asked.

"Uh, nothing," I lied.

"I call bullshit," she said, laughing at me. "Actually how about some snake shit? Yeah, I call it complete and utter snake shit." Rolling her eyes, she dropped her empty container on the side table crossing her arms.

"You're difficult."

"You love me."

"That's debatable." I rolled my eyes, my heart fluttering at the emotions. I didn't do well with them, but Aziza did. "Anyway, no information in the club. Two guys tried attacking me when I was leaving when I texted you. I knocked them out and when I turned around, he was standing there just watching me. He never saw me. I mean, never saw me back then. This time, yeah, he saw me." Shrugging my shoulders, I said, "He let me walk away." It was a full lie. I mean, I punched him, tackled him, sat on his neck. Then I ran away. But basically, he let me *walk* away.

"Do you know his name? I can find out anything about him."

"No," I said a little too fast.

"Salem…"

"I-I don't know his name." I kept my voice tight and calm. I was lying to her; I was lying to my best friend to cover up for some man I punched.

"I know you're lying to me," she said, cocking her head to the side. "But all is forgiven because I'm leaving tomorrow morning for that audition."

I opened my mouth, then closed it, like a fish flopping out of water. I wasn't sure what to say to her. I mean, I'm glad she was going to follow her dream, but the protectiveness inside was raging a damn war.

"That's great!" I found myself blurting out. "What time do you leave?"

"I'll probably head out around five. I have to be there at nine." Looking over at the clock, I saw that it was 1:12 a.m. I swallowed the lump in my throat.

"You should probably get some sleep while you can, I guess."

"Yeah, are you going to be okay?"

I lied for a living, so you'd think this would be easy. But lying to Aziza was like swallowing nails. I hated it, but this was her dream. She lived for dancing. She lived for it. I couldn't hold her back, especially when I was the one saying I didn't want her around the danger I was bringing in.

"Of course. I'm getting tired myself so I'm going to head to bed." I smiled, not wasting time as I hurried to my bedroom. Closing the door behind me I crawled under the covers.

I was asleep before I had time to think about the fact that I was always going to be alone.

———————

My arms and legs were numb. I couldn't feel anything, but everything hurt.

But I felt nothing. My body was cold. I was so cold, I was shaking. But something warm covered my body. Almost like it was a blanket. I tried to move my hand to cover myself up with the blanket more,

58

but nothing worked. None of it. My arms were burning. Why was I burning?

My mouth felt like sandpaper. It was like I was licking the dirt, but Mama always got mad when I did that. She got mad when I got dirty and brought it into the house. I hope I wasn't dirty. Mama would be mad.

"They're all gone!" someone screamed. Who was screaming?

I tried to yell but nothing was working. Who was gone? Mama and Dada wouldn't leave me. Lee and Emmy were probably gone. They were always busy.

"Emmy?" That voice was screaming again. They were getting close. I could tell them I was here.

My eyes tried opening, but I was so weak. I was small, but right now I felt like I was so heavy; everything was too much. Nothing even made sense in my head. I was losing too much of something. Something was draining me.

"Oh my god, they're all dead!" someone else screamed.

They were all dead? Who was all dead?

I wasn't dead, couldn't they see that?

Someone touched my arm. Something was touching me.

A high-pitched scream drowned everything around me. "Salem, oh my god, no no. Please, you can't be dead."

I wasn't dead. I tried opening my eyes again, but all I could see was red. It was blinding my sight, and I couldn't freak out. Someone was dead. I knew what that meant. But who was dead?

"Salem," they said again. "Oh my god, someone help!"

I did need help. My body was getting even more tired. How was that even possible?

"How is she even alive?"

I gasped for air. My body was shaking uncontrollably, and my neck felt like it was on fire again. Everything felt like it was cold, but the blood from my body was warming me again. The scars on my body no longer felt like scars—it felt like I was being ripped open again. I could feel the blade digging into my skin.

I wanted to scream but my throat was slashed. I couldn't scream; I couldn't move.

It's just a nightmare.

I needed to remind myself. I was not that weak girl anymore; they could not hurt me. I wouldn't let them. I couldn't. They took my world away from me, but I couldn't allow that anymore.

Forcing my eyes open, I looked around, needing to find something to focus on. Zeroing in on the brown teddy bear on my dresser, I focused on that. I had to focus on that. That was the only thing I had left of them.

That teddy bear was grounding me. It was saving me, even from myself.

After a few minutes my breathing was under control, and I wasn't shaking as much. I knew it was just a nightmare, even when I first woke up but that didn't stop my body from acting as though I was that nine-year-old girl again dying.

Dying alone, while my whole family laid on the floor in the other room, already gone, waiting to be found.

Untangling myself from my covers I made my way into the bathroom across the hall. Stripping out of my sweat covered clothes I stepped into the shower stall. Ignoring the cold water I pressed my forehead against the tile, letting the cold water wash away the fear of the little girl I was, the sadness of losing my family, and the anger that *they* are still alive.

Pushing them into the back of my mind, the only thing left that my brain decided to think about was Zane.

As much as I didn't want to think about him, I couldn't help myself. He was bad all around. He was all edges, and something about him had me zeroing in on him. We didn't speak; I had no idea who he was. He didn't seem bothered that I was just staring at him. He was looking at me like he wanted to devour me. And man did I want him to.

I hated that I wanted his touch. I hated that somewhere deep down I wanted him. I was completely disgusted with myself. I was a murderer.

I shouldn't imagine how strong he was, how tall, and well built. He worked out, you could definitely tell. He took my punch like it was a grain of salt, while most men would fall to the ground.

I remembered him standing there, his dark blue jeans, his black boots, and the black T-shirt straining against his muscles. I almost wanted to tell him he needed a bigger size. I couldn't make out much of his tattoos in the dark, but I was keen on seeing detail. The right hand had half a sun around the wrist, with smaller ones, and a fire. Both arms had a ram's head. But they looked evil, with a triangle above them.

This man was dripping with sex, and just thinking about him had my legs tensing with the need to touch myself. I wanted to slip my hand between my legs, but I refused. I refused to give him power over the reactions of my body.

Ignoring everything that wanted to push into my brain, I showered quickly. I wouldn't think about Zane, and I wouldn't think about them. Not just yet.

Chapter 8

Zane

"Whoa, what happened to you?" Killian asked as soon as I stepped into the kitchen. "Holy shit," he muttered under his breath. Yeah, I knew I looked rough; the whole side of my face was bruised. That girl could pack a damn punch. For a tiny thing she sure as fuck was strong. Didn't make much sense since she was nothing but skin and bone. But apparently there was muscle as well.

My head pounded from when she tackled me to the ground. But that was the least of my worries. I was more worried about why I hadn't reacted. When was the last time I let someone get the drop on me? Four years ago, that's when. When someone hit my knee with that bat and broke my fucking nose.

"Ran into the wall," I mumbled. Walking around the island I headed to the fridge and pulled out a water bottle. What I really wanted was something stronger, but I still had work to do.

"You truly expect me to believe that?" Killian laughed, giving me a pointed look. Which only caused me to glare back at him. Killian was like a lie detector. I mean, I was good. I could tell when someone was lying. But I also knew how to lie, how to not have any tells. But Killian was a lie detector, and he was calling me out.

I grunted, finishing off my water bottle.

"I heard the basement hatch open and some loud noises. What's going on?" he said, closing his computer. Shrugging my shoulders I grabbed another bottle of water. "Zane, stop lying."

"Just a couple of men."

"A couple of men," he stated.

"Yeah, a couple of men." I didn't understand why he was asking me this. It was normal for me to do this. For me to go out on my own, it was all normal. So him questioning me was odd.

"Is there a reason you took them?"

I couldn't tell him about the mystery girl. I couldn't explain why I didn't want him to know, or anyone for that matter. I didn't know why, but something about her spoke to me. Spoke to me in a way that was deep, and it was weird. I didn't know what was wrong with me.

"They attacked some random girl. I'm just in a mood." I shrugged, trying my best to hide the lie. I mean, she was a random girl, but she was a mystery I wanted to solve, and not have the tech do it.

"Alright, well, I'll leave you to it," he mumbled getting up from the kitchen island and leaving me alone once again.

———

Making my way downstairs, I could hear muffled groans mixed with another set of yells. I smiled as I continued down listening to the panic of the men. Thankfully, the whole basement was completely soundproof. No one would be able to hear what I did down there.

The moment my boot hit the concrete the stench of piss hit my nose. I couldn't believe they were already pissing themselves, and I hadn't even started the real fun.

Opening the door at the bottom of the steps, I carefully closed it behind me. One of the men was tied to a chair in the middle of the concrete room, while the other I had chained up to the ceiling. His arms had to be hurting from the way he was hanging. There was one light on the ceiling, and it wasn't very bright.

They attacked me.

Her words repeated in my head over and over again. I could only imagine why they attacked her. But I would find out everything, and I would find out why. I had to find out everything.

I just had to decide who to start with. Martin was the one who grabbed at her, brunette hair, broad shoulders, but not very large.

Walking over to the chair, Blondie began to thrash around. As though the binds around his wrist and ankles would give out. They wouldn't.

Patting him on the head I ignored the cries escaping from his mouth. I walked around him to Martin by the wall. His head was down, eyes closed, but he wasn't asleep. You could tell from his breathing. If he thought I would let him enjoy his "sleep" he was mistaken.

Martin would be first.

"What did you want with the girl?" I asked, removing the cloth from his mouth.

Martin lifted his head up slightly, his eyes boring into me. For a moment he looked like he was going to play dumb and act like the innocent he played to be. But his upper lip tucked up a little bit.

"Tell the bitch to come out here herself if she wants to ask stupid questions," he snarled. I wish I could tell her to come out here and deal with these men herself. I wanted to see what she would do. I mean, I highly doubt she knew what I was going to do. She probably just wanted me to call the cops and report the attack. But that would not do.

Cocking my head to the side I continued to stare at him. I wondered how long it would take him to break. People always think they will last a good amount of time being tortured, but, in reality, they don't.

"I really won't ask again, so I suggest you just tell me."

He let out a laugh. "Get out here, stupid bitch!" he screamed. Well, I guess we'll see how long he lasts. Grabbing hold of my favorite knife I stepped towards Martin, his eyes widening. Yeah, he was going to be an easy one to break.

I sat back against the far wall watching blood drip down Martin's body. His left ear was laying by his foot. He had multiple cuts across his chest and arms and his blood pooled below him.

The door opened at the top of the stairs. I kept my gaze on Martin. I didn't have to look over to know who it was. Dimitri.

He was the only one who came down here besides me. Killian didn't like to get involved with anything I did. Sure he could shoot a gun, and he knew how to fight. But he didn't like to be involved with torturing men for information. He stayed with his computer. Whereas I stayed away from anything to do with the internet and focused on torturing men.

"What did they do?" Dimitri asked, handing me a mug of what I assumed was coffee.

"They pissed me off." I left it at that. I didn't need him to know a girl was involved. He would make Killian find information about her, and I didn't want that. Dimitri was paranoid. He tried to hide it. But ever since Mila was kidnapped for the second time, he had Killian do background checks on people multiple times. He only truly trusted the two of us and his wife. Everyone outside of the group was a threat in his eyes.

Which wasn't necessarily wrong.

So not telling him about the girl who'd taken up all of my goddamn head space probably warranted damage later on. I just couldn't find myself to care.

"Are they dead?"

"Blondie is, the other I'm not sure." I shrugged, taking a sip of the coffee, immediately burning my mouth, still getting the hint of sugar. "This is disgusting," I added.

"My wife made that," Dimitri deadpanned. "She probably just forgot you like your coffee dark roast and as black as your damn soul."

Mila didn't simply forget; she was fucking with me. It's something she did often, and somehow the other two never caught on. Like the one time she put peanut butter in my smoothie. I turned my back for a minute to open the protein powder, and somehow my dumb ass didn't realize the glob of butter. The moment I took that first sip I nearly spit it out everywhere. I put olives in her coffee. She nearly choked on one. But that was beside the point.

Mila and I acted like brother and sister, after we got over our initial dislike for each other. Mila never truly disliked me; she was just afraid of me due to the fact of my size.

Dimitri was the shortest of us, at six foot four. Still tall, but he wasn't as broad and as muscular as me. Killian stood in between us but was lanky. I understood why Mila was nervous around me. I was a big dude. Most of the time I had to bend down to get through doorways. People always looked at me like I was an actual giant.

66

She didn't look at you like that.

I scowled at myself. I didn't need this girl barging her way into my brain, especially when I stood in front of the Pakhan.

A groan sounded next to us. Glancing over I was surprised when I saw Martin beginning to stir. I didn't think he was still alive. Of course, the fucker had to prove me wrong.

"Looks like the fun isn't over just yet." Dimitri side-eyed Martin.

"Nah, I got what I needed from him."

"Needed?"

Shit. I should've made a better choice of words. Swallowing the lump in my throat I calmed my reaction. "Yeah, I'm calm now. They let me get the murder tendencies out." It wasn't far fetched. I usually needed a good fight or to kill someone within a few days. And it had been about a month.

"That's great because tomorrow Mila wants to take Tobias to some art exhibit around here. Which means I need you to start working on Luca's men."

Smiling, I sipped my coffee, cringing inside when I tasted the sugar. Following them I could do. It beat sitting around here waiting for whatever Luca wanted.

"I'm giving him one more chance to meet with us soon. If not we'll be headed back home."

"Fine by me." But something inside felt off. Normally I'd be fucking glad we'd be headed home, but something was different. I felt off, weird and tingling inside.

Dimitri nodded, sparing one more glance at the bodies before turning around and going back upstairs.

Swallowing the rest of my coffee, I ignored the feeling of gagging. I grabbed my Beretta 90-Two from the table and shot Martin between the eyes. I didn't have to kill either of them. In reality, I could have let them go. But the moment Martin told me they planned on taking advantage of her because she simply looked like an easy target, he signed their death warrants.

Making my way up the stairs, I rounded the corner, rushing through the house so I could get to my room before Mila or Tobias even saw me. Just as I rounded the entryway, I hadn't realized Mila was standing there until I knocked her off her feet. Wrapping an arm around her waist, I steadied her before backing away quickly. If Dimitri caught me with my arms around Mila, he'd kill me. Even if it was as simple as trying to make sure I didn't knock her off her feet.

"Oh shoot," she muttered. "Oh he—" her voice cut off, simply looking down at my forearms, which were covered in blood. Mila knew what I did, and she knew I had a key for getting messy. I liked it, getting more personal than just shooting them and getting their death out of the way. But it helped me get my rage out, to make it personal.

"I know, I'm sorry. I'm going to clean up," I mumbled. "Thanks for the coffee," I said, rolling my eyes.

"Oh you're welcome," Mila smirked. "I'm glad you *enjoyed* it." I wouldn't say I enjoyed it. I hated coffee. But I would get her back, somehow, some way.

Glaring down at her, I winced. She had spots of blood on her arm and clothes.

"Your shirt," I motioned towards the blood.

Mila looked down before I could visibly see her swallow. "Yeah I-I'm going to go change." She tapped my shoulder before rushing off.

Headed to my room, I slammed the door closed and began kicking my shoes off. Reaching down, I tugged my shirt off and dropped my pants.

Immediately my thoughts went to the mystery girl. My dick was now hard, begging to be touched by the thought of her. To the outfit she wore, the thin material stretched across her breasts, hooking around her neck, leaving her back and stomach completely open. The leather pants she wore left nothing to the imagination. Even her boots added to the appeal. I wanted to bend her over the alleyway, rip her pants down, and sink my cock into her wetness.

I shouldn't even be thinking of her like that; she was no one to me. Just a random chick outside the club. Trying my best to ignore my raging hard-on, I stepped into the cold shower, and tried to calm my breathing, and the itching need to stroke my cock.

"Harder, please I need it harder." I could imagine her screaming, asking me to fuck her harder. To grab her hair and punish her for unknown reasons.

Fuck it.

It'd been forever since I fucked a girl, let alone actually jacked off to the idea of one. Wrapping my hand around the base, I began slowly stroking. I hissed at the contact. It was too long. Closing my eyes I began fucking my hand harder.

I wanted to wrap my hand around her throat while I fucked her from behind. Her moans would be cut off because of my hand, her hands pinned to the wall to stop herself from falling forward. Her wet cunt would fit my cock so well, she would beg me to fuck her faster and harder. But she couldn't get a word out because I would choke her, on the verge of passing out.

Jerking my dick faster, I could feel the buildup of release begging to rip out of me.

I would deny her own release, making her wait until my own. I was a bastard.

"Fuck, fuck, fuck," I chanted, my body jerking forward, my warm cum shooting out onto the shower wall.

I kept my eyes closed and dropped my hand. I waited until my breathing calmed down before I quickly rinsed the evidence of what I'd done. Shampooing and washing my body in record time, I dried off, pulling on my black jeans, dark gray sweatshirt, and black biker boots. Grabbing my wallet and keys I closed the door behind me as I made my way into the kitchen.

I wanted to ignore what I just did, and I wanted the girl out of my mind.

Chapter 9

Zane

One week later

"Yeah, yeah, yeah," I muttered into the phone. "Yes, Killian, I fucking remember," I growled as I prowled down the sidewalk leading to the Chinese restaurant Killian begged me to stop at.

"Listen attitude, I've been busy. I don't have time to go out and get my favorite Chi—"

"Is there a point to this conversation!" I snapped. I wasn't mad at him, not truly.

The mystery girl was missing. I had no idea where she was, and it was beginning to bother me. And I couldn't ask Killian because I didn't have a name. If I involved Killian, then Dimitri would get involved as well. Then they would both learn I lied to them. Which in the end would not end up good for me.

"You're already out, just get me food and I'll find you..." He trailed off. "Oh, fuck, I gotta go." He hung up before I could say anything. Pocketing my phone, I continued down the sidewalk.

Everything in the past two weeks has been bothering me. No matter what I did, besides going to Killian, I could not find this girl, and I didn't know why I was so focused on trying to find her. After getting rid of those two people I surely would have thought I'd see her again. I couldn't explain why. But I went to that club almost every day. I walked around the area. I tried everything I could, but still she didn't appear.

"I don't know why you're freaking out," a raspy soft voice sounded nearby. I stopped dead in my tracks, that voice was so familiar. "No, I haven't, now will you stop freaking out!"

It was her. I could pick her voice out anywhere. My eyes gazed around, trying to find where she was. They didn't stop until I peeked around the corner, finding the girl standing directly in front of the Chinese restaurant I was supposed to go to.

She stood there in a pair of dark gray sweatpants and a black sweatshirt that swallowed her. A pair of tennis shoes that made her even shorter than she was the last time. Her hair was piled on top of her head in a messy bun. She had this addicting look. There was nothing special about her, but fuck if I wasn't inching towards her.

"How's the dance going?" she asked into her phone. "Oh, okay. Yeah, I'll call you tomorrow." Hanging up she shoved her phone into her pocket, tipping her head up towards the night sky. I could barely hear what she was mumbling, bits and pieces, until it was clear. "I'm too tired to eat."

Moving out of the way just as she turned, she started walking towards where I was hiding against the wall. Holding my breath I watched as she crossed the street. I know I should let her go. I know

I shouldn't follow her, but I ignored my own advice and followed her.

I followed her more than ten blocks away from the city to a small house sitting on the corner. Simple light gray siding, black door, with a black SUV sitting on the side driveway. The grass was a little overgrown, along with the bushes sitting in front of the front windows, not giving a lot of space to be able to peek inside.

I followed as she unlocked the side door and quickly shut it behind her. Ignoring the nagging feeling that was telling me to just turn around and come back at a later time, I didn't. Instead I found myself stepping around the SUV, following around to the back of the house. There were no lights on the inside that I could see. Everything was pitch black.

This was becoming useless, but at least I found out where she lived. Smiling at the thought of being able to come back and watch my kitten, I backed away leaving her house behind.

Chapter 10

Salem

The last few days I could feel eyes on me. No matter where I went, I could feel someone watching me. I just couldn't figure who it could be. I had cameras around the house, but whoever it was stayed far enough away that I couldn't see anything. I accepted to find myself nervous, fearful that I was being watched.

But I wasn't.

Instead I was intrigued. It felt almost like a game I should have told Aziza about it, told her to look into who this could be. Knowing Aziza she would be able to find them. I could, but she would be able to find anything out about my stalker.

I wondered if it could be Zane. I hadn't seen him since Martin and Blondie tried attacking me. And for some reason it bothered me. I wanted to see him, I wanted to find out where he lived. What he was doing, what he was even eating. It wasn't like me. I had a job to do; I had men to take care of.

I couldn't believe I let my mind wander anywhere else. My eyes were no longer focused on them. Glaring up I refocused my full attention on the top floor. Giulio and Leonzo were both standing on the second floor of the club talking with each other. I couldn't tell what they were saying since I was blending into the back, but they were both having fun. Giulio threw his head back, letting out a deep laugh that had me gritting my teeth. My back molars were going to break from the amount of pressure I was biting down on. The second floor was empty besides two guards that stood with guns in their holsters.

Easy pickings.

I kept my back against the wall, I kept my face lowered to the ground, making sure the hood covered enough of my face.

I watched as they talked and laughed. Not knowing tonight was going to be the last night. They were going to die. I was done waiting.

I was done with it all. All of them were going to die. Starting with these two.

Giulio finished his drink first then followed Leonzo to the exit. Both guards followed close behind them. I had about ninety seconds until they were in the cars, and I would lose them. Once the exit door was closed, I rushed down the stairs to the exit. I ignored the pulls and the gazes of men eye fucking me.

Jogging to get to the door faster I made it just as the side alley door swung open. Neither of them looked over to where I came out, *fucking stupid.*

The wind wrapped around me as I inched closer. Both guards stood behind the men. The left one was much bigger. He might have been a problem, but I felt the anger ripping through me.

The adrenaline coursed through me. Hand on my blade I made quick work as I threw it into the back of the big guy's neck. None of them had time, the big guy choked on his blood falling forward. The other guard turned around just as I threw my other blade into his throat. His eyes went wide.

Giulio turned. "What the fu—" I already had my Glock 43 and aimed, shooting him in the kneecap. Leonzo had enough time to take his own gun out and took aim.

"Who the fuck are you!" he yelled. His voice echoed off the alleyway. We both stood taking aim at each other. Giulio was moaning in pain on the ground. "Who are you!" he screamed.

Most would be scared if they were in my situation. Most feared men like Giulio and Leonzo. They were so used to telling people to jump, waiting for them to ask how high. What they didn't realize was that I was not just some random person on the street. I wasn't scared of them. They would soon learn they needed to be scared of me. They would learn they messed with the wrong family, and I was here to remind them of that.

"I'm going to give you to the count of three to tell me, who th—" I didn't let him finish. My left hand held my last blade. Not taking my eyes off Leonzo, I threw the knife, impaling him in the shoulder. It was amazing what you could do being ambidextrous.

He fell to the ground, the gun falling onto concrete. Both men were screaming like a bunch of pussies. They acted like they'd never been shot or stabbed before.

Maybe they hadn't been.

But I have.

I know what it feels like.

Both of them stared at me. Slowly I took steps towards them, my black chunky heeled boots sloshing around in the puddles.

"Hold her down," Giulio snarled at his brother. His breath felt like fire sneaking around my throat. I could smell the whiskey on his breath.

I tried twisting around in the chair, but nothing I did worked.

"Hurry the fuck up," Giulio barked at Leonzo. A scream pierced through the living room. I wanted to look over where I knew they were.

But all I saw was Giulio and Leonzo laughing as he began tying my hands with rope.

I hated the memories of them.

I used to cry when I would remember, when I had memories of that night. But now all I felt was anger. I was angry. I wanted them to feel the pain of what I felt. They needed to know what they had done.

I wouldn't feel bad about it.

Not anymore.

I refused to let them have that power over me again.

No one would have that over me again.

Shaking my head as I stepped in front of them. I cocked my head to the side, both of them staring up at me.

Leonzo tried opening his mouth to talk, and I lost it. Bringing my foot up, I kicked him in the face, his nose obviously broken as I could hear the crunch of bones. A pained wheezing broke from his mouth.

"You fucking cunt," Giulio screamed trying to move. Bringing the gun up I aimed it at him, making him freeze on the spot.

"I'm going to give you two options," I said quietly. "First option, I can kill your brother here slowly. Very very painfully, making him regret his life. Or…. you can shoot your brother and put him out of his misery." Shrugging I kept my gun aimed at Giulio.

They both stared at me like I was dumb.

"I'm not killing my own brother you stupid fucking c—" I cut him off kicking Leonzo again, this time ramming my heel down into his leg. The crack of his shin caused me to shiver in pleasure.

"Giulio, just fucking do it," he hissed.

"I'm not killing you!" Giulio snapped glancing towards his brother on the ground. His mistake, never take your eye off the person with the gun. Gripping it a little tighter, I bashed him over the head. His body slumped down.

"Who are you?" Leonzo begged. Looking over at him, I could see the tears beginning to fall.

"You really don't remember?" I asked. I couldn't tell if I was bothered more by the fact he forgot who I was, or if he didn't. Because I wished I could forget it.

"N-no. I d-don't. Please, just le-let us go," he begged.

"Please let the kids go, let them go," Mama begged. "They aren't involved in this," Mama begged over and over again. I could see the blood dripping down her leg.

She was hurting badly. I could see the dried tears. I could see the pained look on her face.

"Please, I'm begging you, let them go."

Mama never spoke again after that. They made sure of it.

"They begged you, they begged everyone there." I started crouching down, so we were more eye level. "I begged you to not tie me. I begged and cried. I fucking screamed." My voice was beginning to get louder and louder. I felt good, being heard finally. Finally speaking to those who hurt me.

I watched as he finally realized. He did remember.

He knew who I was. They all thought I died. They had no idea I was the one who killed the other three before them. He finally realized he'd made a mistake.

"No no no no," he repeated over and over again. "Yo-you can't be here," he spoke to himself, whispering things under his breath. "She's dead, we made sure."

Kicking him in the stomach, I kicked and kicked over and over again. He was my own fucking punching bag. I hated him, I hated them all.

"P-pl-please," he stuttered.

"I begged; we all did. We wouldn't have told the police. We wanted to be left alone. They didn't deserve what you fucking put them through. Yet none of you cared. You laughed when I was screaming. You laughed when Luca ordered his son to slit my throat."

"I'm sorry." I barely heard him.

"You're *sorry*?" I couldn't help but spit back at him. He was sorry for what he did to me? I was losing my patience, but I knew I couldn't let that happen. It was how you got caught; it was how you lost yourself in revenge. I needed to stick to my plan.

Gritting my teeth, I took a deep breath. Looking over at Giulio I took aim and shot him between the eyes. Leonzo sobbed watching as his brother's body fell. I felt relief when I saw that bullet hole in his forehead.

"What's my name?" I asked.

"I do-don't know it," he admitted.

"Who do you think killed your old partners?" I smiled like a psychopath. I liked the terror in his eyes.

"You."

"Yes, me, again. What's my name?" I kept eye contact with him as he was piecing it all together.

"Gho-ghost. That was who killed them. They were all slaughtered."

"Yes, and now it's your turn," I mumbled.

He was going to die a painful death.

Chapter 11

Zane

In every story there is the truth and then there is a make-believe tale that everyone believes is the truth. In fairy tales they are told to children, so they grew up with this make-believe reality. Most others don't want the truth. They want someone to blame when reality comes down to kick them in the ass.

Hence why we're sitting with the Cosa Nostra. Luca called an emergency meeting last night, wanting to meet this morning bright and fucking early. I was pissed when Dimitri barged into my room telling me to get ready when I had just laid my head down ready to finally try and fucking sleep. I was ready to shove Dimitri down the hall and tell him to go fuck himself.

The moment we stepped into the building Luca acted like a bitch. He tried to act as though he wasn't scared, but you could see the tremble in his body. His voice shook when he spoke, his hand was not as steady as it should be, and his eyes wandered everywhere when he didn't think anyone was paying attention.

Before Dimitri was even able to sit his ass on the chair Luca was going on about how two of his men were killed last night. Giulio and Leonzo.

I barely remembered them, but what Killian gathered before we got there was that they were both found dead in the alleyway outside the club. They had two guards who were also dead, both found with knives in their throat. Giulio had a gunshot to his kneecap and his forehead. He died quickly.

Whereas Leonzo was a different story. He had a knife sticking from his shoulder, but the worst part was his face. His nose was broken in places that I didn't realize it could be broken. Trust me, I've had my fair share of broken noses. He was stripped bare, left completely naked like the day he was born, with multiple stab wounds to his stomach. And his cock was missing.

Where was it you might ask?

Shoved down Giulio's throat. His own brother.

I mentally shivered thinking about it, my own cock shrinking from the pure thought of being cut off.

"What are we supposed to do about it?" Dimitri asked coolly.

Luca sat twirling his whiskey glass, the ice clinking against the side. My skin itched with the need to shoot the glass. Grinding my molars, I clenched my fist at my side.

I don't know who Luca thought he was. A small fish in an extremely large pond. No one demanded Dimitri to do anything, yet Luca thought he could.

"I want to hire your services," he finally stated.

"My services?"

"Yes. It's a terrible loss, Giulio and Leonzo." He rubbed his graying mustache. "But Ghost is real. I've had my men trying to find who it is, but I've come up with nothing so far."

I couldn't stop myself from rolling my eyes at the mention of *Ghost.*

The fairy tale I was talking about earlier was this. Around four years ago there was a rumor going around about some person who went by Ghost. Whoever this person was, was believed to have taken out three of Luca's men. Now apparently five. It was also believed they took out half the Cartel.

None of us had any idea on who actually took out Matteo and his men. When we arrived four years ago to save Mila, half the cartel had been found dead in the basement where we found Mila just standing in the corner waiting for us. Dimitri tried asking her who it was, because obviously it wasn't her. But she refused to tell any of us. She said she had no idea. Which was a lie. Mila had a tell—she tugged at her earlobe after tucking a piece of hair behind her ear.

Dimitri never pushed, so out of respect I never did. It was soon after rescuing her we found out she was pregnant. Therefore, none of us pushed her or asked again.

Ghost was something that someone made up to scare other operations. I don't know who started this rumor, but that's all Ghost was. A rumor. Someone making a joke, and whoever it was or whoever *they* were always left a playing card with a simple ghost drawn on it.

I had one.

It burned a hole in my wallet, and I have no idea why I decided to keep it. Just a weird gut feeling, but I did.

"Why do you believe it was this Ghost person?" Dimitri asked.

"They left their mark, and whoever he is came after me four years ago. I don't know why they stopped, but they're here again." Luca's voice trembled slightly. I looked around the empty club where we sat, Luca in the middle of Orlando and Remo.

They were both in charge of security, which meant if this Ghost guy was after Luca's men, they would be next. Leonzo and Giulio were in charge of the clubs, which brought in legal money, and helped them. Orlando and Remo were in charge of the security, which they obviously were shit about because if this guy could get to two of Luca's "best" men, then they were all fucked. If these two got taken out, Dante would be next. Then Luca.

I couldn't give a shit if they were.

"I don't like asking twice, but since you helped me once I can possibly return the favor," Dimitri said, finishing off his Vodka.

"What are you saying?" Orlando couldn't help himself, finally speaking for the first time since we arrived. But Dimitri didn't like being asked, especially by a nobody.

He snapped his gaze over to Orlando, giving him that look that caused Orlando to curl into himself. If they thought I was their nightmare, Dimitri was worse. I loved my fair share of fights and killing. But before Mila came into his life, Dimitri was cold-blooded. He was the last fucker I ever imagined taking a wife and having a child. A wife who was innocent and sweet. And who gave birth to her clone. Tobias was just as sweet and though he had a temper like his father, he cared and loved like his mother.

"I'll find out who this Ghost person is," Dimitri stated. He was getting involved but wasn't putting himself out there. It was smart.

"So many have tried, what makes you think it would be so easy?" Luca questioned. No one apparently listened to him because Dimitri did not like being questioned.

"Don't question me," he spat out. His temper was going to start shining through. Cracking my neck side to side I glared down at Luca. His gaze noticed me for the first time.

"Any help would be appreciated, so finding this Ghost would be delightful," he rushed out.

Smart.

"Great, I'll contact you when I find anything. Until then I can recommend getting better security." Dimitri smirked at the men before getting to his feet. Killian followed closely behind him, while I waited until they were halfway to the exit.

Sending them one last glare I turned on my heel and walked out of the club.

———————

It had been five days since Dimitri sent me out to gather any information I could at the underground. I went to six underground fight clubs, ready to throw the towel in until some twenty-year-old came up whispering that he'd heard about this Ghost guy. Being bored was never a good thing for me because I got inside my head a bit too much. Which meant I didn't care that I followed this twenty-year-old to meet with a contact he had. Thankfully, nothing happened.

Not until I started asking questions, and he got a bit ballsy. He tried throwing a weak punch at my face.

Men never learned that when you're my height, and you were several inches shorter than me you should never go to the face. I could see it coming. As soon as his fist was halfway thrown, I grabbed his wrist and twisted until he screamed like a little girl. Punching him directly in the face he fell to the ground out cold.

———————

Getting this twenty-year-old into the SUV and back to the warehouse was more difficult than it should have been. After dragging him to the middle of the warehouse I finally got him chained to the chair.

I waited for Killian to show up since it was nearly three in the morning, and I needed coffee. After ten minutes, I watched as he struggled, holding two cups of coffee and trying to open the door.

Finally, after struggling, Killian righted himself before walking over.

"You couldn't have helped?" he asked, handing me a small white cup.

Taking a sip I nearly spat all over the ground. No one could ever get my coffee right. They always added creamer or sugar. Never made sense on how it was hard to fuck up a black coffee.

Literally black. Pour it directly from the pot, that fucking easy.

"No."

"What'd he do?"

I debated on telling him. I doubted he knew anything about Ghost, just like I doubted Ghost was even real.

"He was at one of the underground fight clubs, and says he knows about Ghost," I finally answered. I didn't care if we found this "Ghost" because that's all they were to me. A fucking ghost. I could give two shits if they took out Luca and his men. I could give two shits if this thing was real or not. Right now I was just playing a little role for Dimitri.

"Do you think Ghost is real?"

"No." It was the truth. Ghost was just a lie and was a stupid joke. A dumb one.

"Luca thinks it's true." Killian took a sip of his coffee. "God, Mila makes the best coffee."

Frowning over at him, he tried hiding a smirk behind his cup. Of course, Mila made the coffee, which explains why it tasted like shit. Fucking sugar.

"If you don't believe this person exists then why are you even looking into it?"

Simply because I was trying to do anything to distract myself from following the girl around. After I found where her house was a week ago, I barely stopped myself from becoming a full-blown stalker. I went by her house every day, seeing her SUV had not moved. She was either inside and I couldn't see her, or she was outside doing yard work.

She looked tired every time I was able to get a peek at her. It was still mind boggling seeing her in everyday clothes. She always wore leggings or sweatpants, and an overly large shirt. I couldn't help but think it was because of the scars covering her back and neck. I wondered if the rest of her body had scars as well.

She never wore makeup either, and her hair was always tied back into a high ponytail or a braid trailing down her back. Her eyes still took my breath away from the cobalt brightness.

Shaking myself from her, I took another sip of my coffee.

"Dimitri said he'd find who it was," I lied.

"That's interesting, I've never seen you so hyped to look in—" He was cut off as the guy began to groan. Killian winced, finally sparing the guy a look.

"Are you going to beat him up?"

I nodded my head. Of course, I was. If he didn't talk, then I was going to have to force him to. Hence why I was the enforcer, and Killian was the computer nerd.

"Well, I'm going to leave you to it." He laughed waving a hand as he backed out of the warehouse.

Turning around I looked over at the guy. I no longer cared about Ghost at all. Right now I just wanted to find the girl and see what dirty secrets she could be hiding from me.

"Glad you're finally awake," I mumbled, walking closer to him. "What's your name?" I asked. I didn't really care what his name was, but normal people thought when they asked what it was, they were going to be nice. It was a mind game.

"Thomas," he whispered.

"Wow, that was easy, Thomas. I thought I was really going to need some of my toys to get that out of you," I smirked. "Who's Ghost?"

Thomas snapped his head up at me, sending me a death glare. It could almost be comical if he really thought that scared me. No one scared me.

"I really don't have the patience to play this game with you. I have a date to get to." The date was getting to her house and finally getting to her. Who she was with, even what her fucking place looked like inside. I wanted to know every little detail, and it was beginning to piss me off with how much I wanted to know her.

I never cared about females. They were a good fuck, but once I was done, they had to leave. I never allowed them to stay over, and I never let them touch. It was always from the back. Top rule, no kissing. Absolutely no kissing.

"Who is Ghost?" I demanded standing a few feet in front of him.

Instead of answering me he tried his best to spit at me. I couldn't help the chuckle slipping out when it landed on his chin. Without a second thought I grabbed the hammer and slammed it into his kneecap.

He wasn't walking out of here anyway. Thomas threw his head back shouting in pain.

"Who is it?" I asked again.

Nothing.

His other kneecap was blown.

"Who?"

Nothing.

Cocking my head to the side, I looked over at the table where my tools were placed, laying out waiting for me. Deciding on what to pick up I smiled when I saw Beauty, my favorite. Picking up my favorite hatchet that yes, I've named Beauty, I turned around, and Thomas's eyes widened.

"Which hand do you use the most?"

I could see in that moment when he knew I was no longer playing games with him. His body was shaking already but now he was jerking against the chains and chair, hoping somehow that he would break free of them.

"P-please don't!" he begged. "I'LL TELL YOU!"

Too late, I lost my patience. I brought the hatchet down on his right hand.

Clean cut.

His hand was now laying on the floor, and he was crying in pain, thrashing around, blood coating the ground.

I smiled.

"Who's Ghost?" I kept my voice level. For a moment, I thought he wasn't going to say anything again.

"He's a story, he's not real. Not until you mess with someone they deem important. I do-don't know wh-who they truly are. They they li-live in the dark…" his words became faint. His eyes fluttered closed.

"Fuck," I muttered to myself. I shouldn't have chopped his hand off. He lost too much blood. And I hadn't gotten anything from him.

Everyone believed this Ghost was a monster, someone in the darkness that killed at random. I didn't know what to actually believe. Dimitri was the only other one who didn't believe this story, but everyone else seemed to think Ghost played a part.

It didn't make sense on why he would go after the Cartel and kill most of them, as well as go after the Italian.

Rolling my shoulder I pulled my phone out, sending a text to the cleanup crew. I headed out to my truck, ready to see my kitten. I just needed to see her.

Chapter 12

Salem

I can feel eyes on me again. The hair on my arms prickled as I sat up on the couch. The TV was playing *Bones*, subtitles on, volume off. I couldn't hear anything, I never did. But I could feel someone's eyes. They always watched me while I was home. It was never while I was out, stalking my own men. But at home I could feel them.

Standing up, I headed straight forward into the kitchen. The oven light was on. I couldn't see anything that was out of place, but the feeling of someone in my house was strong. Reaching behind the fridge I grabbed hold of one of the guns strapped there. I knew the magazine was full, but that still didn't stop me from checking. Flipping the safety off, I kept my eyes aware of any movement.

Searching each room, I cleared them, leaving my bedroom last. Taking a steady breath, keeping my gun aimed, I opened the door.

My eyes immediately felt the massive build in front of my window. Their hands reached for the window, trying to open it to sneak out.

"Who are you?" My voice was rough and raspy. They bowed their heads as if getting caught hadn't even crossed their mind. I don't know how they got past my cameras, or without tripping the wire around each window and door. But they had.

"I won't ask again. Who. Are. You," I snapped. Losing my patience.

"Hello, Kitten." That voice was familiar, too familiar. Only when they turned their head towards me, I sucked in a ragged breath. He couldn't be here. How did he find me?

I couldn't breathe. If he found me, anyone could. He must have been the one stalking me. His eyes were the ones on me while I've been home. Why did he take so long? Why was he even here? What was he planning?

I hadn't been this caught off guard in such a long time, that even as he stepped closer, I struggled with holding a gun to his chest. He didn't flinch as I readjusted my hand.

"Hi." *Why the fuck did I just say hi?* Here I am, a gun aimed at his chest, saying hi to the man who I first knocked out, second ran into over a week ago, and who just broke into my goddamn house!

"You sound nervous."

"I'm not nervous," I lied. I was nervous. No, nervous didn't even reach what I was feeling. I didn't know what I was feeling.

"You plan to keep that gun aimed at me the whole time?" Cocking his head to the side, my eyes tracked over how large he truly was. Here I stood barefoot, and my head would barely reach his chest. But he didn't scare me. No, I was completely aroused. I was turned on by his size. His murderous eyes engaged me, boring into me. My thighs pressed together, and I could feel my nipples press against my tank top. A tank top I realized showed everything. His watchful eyes dropped down to my breast. And if it was even possible, I got wetter.

"What's your name, Kitten?" he asked.

I should have told him a lie, told him to get out of my house. There were a million things I should have done. But when I opened my mouth, "Salem," came out. I flushed realizing I told him my real name, a name I kept hidden from everyone. I mean, my house wasn't even in my name.

"You're cute when you blush, sweetness." His knuckles brushed against my collarbone. If it was possible to become even redder, I did. My body broke out in goosebumps. If he were to rip my pants down right now and have his way with me, I found I would let him.

He was so close I could feel the heat from his body.

A loud ringing sounded, causing my body to jump. Blinking rapidly, I tried to get rid of the aching feeling I had. I watched as Zane's eyes changed from softness to anger. Reaching into his pocket he pulled his phone out, answering it. Never breaking eye contact.

"Da." *Yes.* Whoever was on the other line spoke low and soft. I couldn't hear anything.

"Net ya nichego ne nashel." *No I haven't found anything.* He was speaking Russian. I masked my expression. He didn't know I understood what he was saying.

"Khorosho, da. YA otpravlyus' tuda pryamo seychas." *Alright, yeah. I'll head there right now.*

I wanted to demand he tell me where he was going, but I shouldn't care. He was no one important to me.

"Do svidaniya." *Bye.* Then he was hanging up, blinking like he was shaking off a feeling he had. I understood.

We stared at each other. None of us moved. His hands clutched at his sides; my gun pressed against his chest. He held no fear. Instead, it was almost like he liked it.

Finally he smirked, breaking whatever trance we both had. "I have to go, Kitten," he mumbled. Dropping the gun to my side, I flipped the safety on. Slowly he bent down, pressing his lips against my forehead. I wanted to lean into him, beg him not to leave. It didn't make sense. But oddly I was comfortable around him.

Breaking away quicker than I would have preferred, Zane walked around me heading towards the front door. I didn't move until I heard the front door close. Suddenly I realized I had my chance.

Grabbing my keys, I rushed to my SUV, and getting inside, I followed him. Thankfully I had a blackout outfit stored inside. I could change and see where he was rushing off too.

Chapter 13

Zane

Everything you'd think could go wrong did.

The moment we arrived at the warehouse for the shipment of cocaine we got ambushed. I have no idea where any of the men came from, but we were outnumbered, and I have a nice gash above my eyebrow. When we walked into the warehouse, two men attacked me, bashing me over the head with a gun. They dragged me further into the empty large space. Killian's hands were tied behind his back when I finally got the chance to focus. Dimitri was sitting on the ground with a similar gash but this one was further on top of his head. Blood trailed down the side of his face.

I couldn't even remember the last time someone got the upper hand on me. Probably that fuck face from four years ago that left me with the Ghost card and with a broken nose.

If you wondered if I was still pissed about it, the answer was yes.

I was also angry because I don't know why I didn't think to bring more men, or to bring more than just my Glock. I thought having a few magazines on me would be good enough, but I fucked up.

I was the head of security for them, and I failed.

I sat back on my heels, both hands on the concrete. Looking around, four men had their guns aimed at Killian and Dimitri. I could tell from the look on Killian's face that he was pissed about even being here. Dimitri was pissed about having a gun shoved in his face. It wasn't his first time. But it had been a long time since someone dared to do that.

Shaking my head, I tried my best to ignore the pounding headache coursing its way down to my neck.

"Montón de jodidos idiotas que no vuelven a subir," one of them said from behind me. I was mentally kicking myself for not learning other languages. None of us knew anything besides English and Russian. Dimitri was more fluent in Russian since he was born there, while Killian and I were from America. But apparently not knowing anything else was going to be an issue.

"Ah si jodidamente estúpido." That didn't need much translation. We were stupid. I couldn't exactly be mad at them for calling us stupid. I could assume they were talking about us not bringing any back up or being more prepared for this.

Yes, we were fucking stupid.

Killian kept his gaze down on the floor while Dimitri glared at the men who were behind me. I had no idea how many, but I could only assume it was decent. The sound of the door slamming shut made me glance over to the left to see who was walking through.

I couldn't recognize him, but with short black greasy hair, he had a dark mustache that did not fit him well at all. He looked like a damn creep.

I kept his gaze as he slowly made his way over to us, a cigar hanging from his lips.

"Golpea al grande," he demanded. I didn't have time to think about what he said when I felt a solid punch land on my temple. A normal person might have been knocked out, but I'd been hit so many times it didn't make a difference.

I didn't make a sound. I didn't move.

Sitting back up I faced Dimitri, giving him a reassuring nod. It was alright. I could handle whatever they gave me.

"Otra vez."

Another blow, this time to my side.

"Otra vez."

They repeated it over and over again. I could taste the bruises forming on my back and sides.

"Suficiente." He laughed. The blows stopped, and I felt whoever was throwing them back away from me. "I think it's time to introduce myself." The greasy dude smiled, his teeth stained yellow. "I'm Carlos Herrera, the new Matteo if you will." His accent was thick and almost hard to understand.

I ignored the fucker when he said Matteo. He seemed oblivious to the fact that he was holding a gun to Dimitri Volkov. Or if he knew he was stupid.

Very stupid.

"Now I think it's time you introduce yourselves and why you're in my warehouse."

I couldn't help the chuckle slipping again. I was becoming a real shit about controlling my emotions when someone said something stupid. If this Carlos character really thought this was his warehouse, then he would get a reality check soon. Dimitri owned six warehouses just here in Boston. Two of them were for weapons, two were just empty, and one I kept as mine since I couldn't always bring people back to the house since that's where Mila and Tobias lived. I didn't need Mila kicking my ass if he somehow got through the lock and went downstairs. And the last was for his drug imports.

I knew he had a problem with someone getting hold of the drugs, but I had no idea it would be this fucker trying to be like Matteo, who was dead, and I was really tired of him still being active in our lives. He died four years ago; he just needed to stay fucking dead.

"Estúpido," Carlos snapped. "Who are y—" He was cut off from a large explosion outside.

Shouting quickly followed with rapid amounts of guns being shot off. Dimitri glanced at me, his eyebrow raised, like he was asking, "Who the fuck could that be?" We never tell people where we go. If he didn't bring backup, no one knew. So this attack had to be on Carlos and his men, which meant we had to get out of there sooner rather than later.

Carlos began shouting orders, leaving only a few men guarding us. If I played my part well, I could take at least a few of them out. Dimitri would be right behind me. Killian, I had no idea what he would do since he hated this part of our world, but I'm sure if push came to shove, he would.

Swinging my body around I grabbed hold of the guy's leg that was right behind me. Slamming his body down, I heard a commotion behind me. I was hoping it was Dimitri, but I couldn't take my eyes off the other two drawing their guns to aim them at me. Speedily I reached for the guns of the one I took down. Aiming, I shot them both before they could shoot at me. While I was busy taking out the two that were in front of me now, I hadn't paid attention to Carlos.

He kicked my hand, the gun dropping. He grabbed me around the throat. For a small man he had a tight grip. "Basta de esta mierda!" he roared, turning us around. I took in Dimitri who had killed three men, while Killian stood over one with a knife aimed at his throat.

"Lo dejó ir—" Carlos was cut off. The door slammed open.

Two men backed into the warehouse, their guns drawn, aiming for whatever was heading their way.

In a split moment two daggers went flying impaling the two men in the neck who were backing up. They fell back from the force.

It was one of those slow move films, where you can see but your actions were slowed or even stopped.

I was stopped. I'm sure I even stopped breathing.

I watched as the figure slowly walked inside as if they owned the damn place. I honestly was confused on how so many people knew about this fucking warehouse, and why so many thought they fucking owned it.

Whoever it was, was definitely female. They wore a tight ass black leather suit, long sleeved, along with black gloves. She had a thigh holster that held four more daggers, and another holster around the waist that led to the other thigh that held two guns. She looked tall, but from the look of her shoes, she had at least five-inch heels on. They reminded me of… Salem. Snapping my gaze up, she had a black mask over her mouth and nose, along with a hood that covered most of her face. But looking into their eyes, they were a bright blue.

Salem.

Salem was standing in the doorway.

It had to be her.

She was no longer wearing her sleep shorts and tank top.

Instead she was wearing leather pants, and a skintight black long sleeve shirt. Two thigh holsters, one holding a gun, another holding a set of knives. Another holster across her chest holding another gun. Her hands had a dagger in them.

I couldn't stop the groan slipping through my mouth. She looked hot, and deadly.

"¿Quién eres tú?" Carlos demanded.

Silence.

She cocked her head to the side and continued into the building. Her eyes stayed on me the entire time. A few men ran into the building, their guns staring her down, yet she didn't care.

"Stop!" Carlos screamed. Jerking, I tried moving away from his hold.

"Fuck, dude, my damn eardrum," I snarled. His grip tightened more, the knife digging into my throat. Nicking my skin I could feel the blood start to trickle down my neck.

Looking back at Salem she stopped abruptly, her nostrils flared, darting between Carlos who held me, and the dagger pressed into my throat.

If I thought differently, it was as though she cared.

Which she couldn't, could she?

"I won't ask again! WHO THE FUCK ARE YOU?" Carlos screeched.

One of the other men stepped closer to Salem. She turned her head over to him, looking down at the gun that was now less than an inch away from touching her. I had a feeling she hated being touched, and she was about to lose her shit. She looked back up at the guy's face and I could feel the anger radiating off of her.

I was beginning to become angry at myself. I didn't like the guns aimed at her. I didn't like the danger she was in now. Two guns aimed at her, and yet she looked as though they were fucking flowers.

"Solo dispárale," Carlos barked. I had no idea what he said, but I didn't like the sound of it.

I felt the pull of wanting to let Carlos do whatever the fuck he wanted to me just so I could try and save her.

I didn't *want* to save her.

Yet I did.

"Don't touch me," she said calmly. It was creepy that she had not a single care in the world. She was too calm, it was unsettling. Her raspy voice was oddly attractive, my cock threatening to harden. She hadn't even hitched in breathing. She just stared at me.

"Inmediatamente!"

I watched in slow motion as the one to the right moved, his finger moving to the trigger. I was expecting Salem's blood to be painted over the floor. To watch as her body dropped.

What I didn't expect was Salem to move at the last minute, the bullet just missing her. She swiftly grabbed him around the neck and brought his face down to her knee, twisting him around, kicking his back then shoving him down to the ground. Reaching around she grabbed the second guy by the shoulder and stabbed him repeatedly in the stomach. The moment the first one tried to get up she pointed the dagger in his direction. "Stay," she snapped.

I shouldn't have gotten hard.

But watching her give no mercy turned me on.

She was perfect.

"Who the fuck are you?" Carlos's voice slightly shook. He was scared of her, not that I could blame him. Just staring back at her, she was completely calm. After stabbing the guy she stood back like she hadn't just murdered the guy in cold blood.

Fuck.

My dick was now pressed against my god damn jeans, and I needed some relief soon.

Salem took a step closer to us.

"Lady, if you take another fucking step, I will fucking end you."
Carlos's accent was thick and heavy. I barely understood what he
was trying to say. But the moment he said he would end her I felt
the anger rise in me.

The tiniest smirk played at her lips, if you were not so observant,
you'd miss it. Stretching her foot she stepped forward.

Naughty.

It shouldn't make me want to spank her ass, but I did. I wanted to
smack her plump ass until it was black and blue. Until you could see
my handprint on it. She wouldn't sit down for weeks without feeling
me there.

I was so caught up in wanting Salem, Carlos shoved me to the
ground, barely giving me enough time to move my hands up to
catch myself. Getting to my feet quickly I glanced over as Carlos
charged at Salem. Ready to defend her myself I felt a hand grab my
shoulder.

"Don't," Dimitri ordered. I didn't have time to think about what he
said before he was grabbing hold of my arm, dragging me to the
back door, leaving Salem and Carlos.

Chapter 14

Salem

My life was out of control.

Everything was out of control.

I didn't even know how or when it became this way. But it was.

I've been in Boston for a while now. All my thoughts were surrounding Zane, and his whereabouts. I should be focused on Orlando, tracking him down. Which I have been, but my thoughts keep going back to Zane. Where was he? Who was he with?

I was becoming like a jealous girlfriend. But I didn't do relationships. I didn't do well with physical contact.

Which is why I had tracked him down to the warehouse. I planned on just following him until I saw him and the men he was with get attacked. I should have walked away, but the nagging feeling in my chest wouldn't let me.

If I had known that they would have left me, just completely disappeared while Carlos attacked me, I would have just left him to find his own way out.

The fucker left me. I could have died.

I mean highly unlikely due to the fact Carlos literally punched like a bitch, but something still could have happened. Especially when four more men showed up trying to save their poor leader.

I was fuming when I got back home. He left me alone in the warehouse after I saved his fucking ass.

I shouldn't be so angry, but I was.

I am.

I am angry.

I could take care of myself. I didn't need him or anyone else.

But something in me was fighting with my brain with the fact he just up and fucking left me.

Which is why I found myself getting my shit rocked by Orlando and his men. I followed him around for two days, trying to learn everything I could about him. I was angry at Zane and at Aziza for leaving. I had no right to be mad at any of them, maybe Zane. But Aziza left because dance was important to her; she needs it.

They all left.

They will always leave.

Another blow to my face forced me to come back to the now. I could feel the blood dripping down my face, the ache in my ribs. They were either broken or bruised badly.

"You know you're really stupid to think you could just come here and try to take me out." Orlando laughed. It was an ugly laugh; it always had been. He laughed when he ripped my sister in half. He laughed when they tore my brother apart.

They all laughed.

Just like they were now.

Laughing at me.

Locking eyes with the man coming at me again, I threw my leg up kicking him in the stomach. The moment he went down I threw my elbow into a headlock. Twisting his arm I threw him over my shoulder, and he landed on his back. Kicking his head he was out cold. The one I had kicked in the stomach got up to charge at me again. Twisting around, I kicked his chin.

"Shit," Orlando mumbled. He thought he was winning because I let two of his men get a few punches in. It was all a play.

"It's okay, Orlando, I got you," a very familiar voice appeared behind me. I didn't want to turn around and face him. That voice, god, why was he even here?

"Thank fuck," Orlando said under his breath. I don't know why he thinks Zane would save him. But he wouldn't.

"Is she giving you trouble?" he asked, walking past me and going straight to Orlando.

I couldn't stop the hurt crawling around my chest that he didn't feel the need to say anything to me. I shouldn't feel that way. The first time I knocked him out, even though he didn't know it was me. The second he saw me beating up two guys, and the third we didn't talk. Yet I saved his life.

Now he's acting like he has no idea who I am.

Once he was standing slightly in front of Orlando, he stood with his chest out, arms crossed. We both glared at each other.

"She hasn't spoken. I don't know if she fucking can't or is some deaf bitch." Orlando laughed. That annoying laugh that had me grinding my teeth. He was going to die. They both were if Zane didn't get out of my way.

I needed to remind myself no matter what, I didn't have room or time to care about anyone else. I was going to finish my list, then I was going to move on. That's all that mattered, that was all that I cared about. I refused to care about Zane and the fact he left me.

Staring at both men I could see Orlando thought Zane would save him, but when he said I was a deaf bitch, something flickered over Zane. It was there one moment and gone the next. If I didn't know better, he didn't like that Orlando called me a bitch. Which made no sense. From the looks of it, he was here to try and save Orlando from me.

"Go home," Zane called out.

Shaking my head, I held onto the small dagger in my hand. I know Orlando had no idea I had it, but something was different about Zane. I had a feeling he knew I had it.

"Just kill the fucking bitch," Orlando motioned towards me.

Zane wouldn't have the chance to kill me.

Rolling my eyes, I braced myself for whatever Zane would do next.

"Go. *Home*," he demanded. Funny because him trying to be dominant would not work. I was the monster here; I wouldn't submit to him. I never would. "For fucks sake, I really don't want to fight you. But I have orders, go home," Zane spit out at me.

Orders?

Orders to fight me, or save Orlando?

Either way I refused to back down. If he wanted a fight, then I'd give him one, but I wasn't leaving without Orlando dead.

"Seriously, just fucking kill the stupid bitch. She's obviously a mental case and needs to be taught a fucking lesson."

I was getting real sick of him calling me a bitch, and him opening his mouth in general.

"Fuck," Zane muttered. Stepping forward, he walked closer to me, reaching towards my arm. I moved out of his way. "Seriously, fucking leave. I'm not in the mood to deal with whatever is happening here," he snarled at me. His words were saying something, but his eyes were soft. Or as soft as they could be for someone who was rough.

If he hadn't shown up, I could have Orlando killed and be halfway home by now. Halfway to taking a good shower and having a good night's rest.

Zane reached for my arm again.

"Do *not* touch me," I quietly said, stepping away from him again.

"If you don't leave, I'm going to have to fight you, and I would rather not do that. You don't want to touch him, trust me, they have powerful people on their side, Salem."

I snapped my head up to look at him fully. I hated the way he said my name. I hated that I liked it so much. I wanted to hate the way he wanted to sound angry, but he wasn't. He sounded tired, but he wasn't angry about being here.

"I'm not leaving," I stated.

Just as the words left my mouth Zane kicked my legs out from under me. I fell down onto my back. He went to throw a punch into my face, trying to knock me out. Rolling he missed, barely. Doing a kip up I brought my hands up in fists. Throwing a punch into his side he grunted. I gave no chance as I punched his stomach and threw one in his face.

From the corner of my eye I saw Orlando trying to make a move to leave. I couldn't let that happen. Turning from Zane I threw the blade nailing him in the shoulder.

Just as he screamed, I was tackled to the ground. Zane's large frame covered mine completely. Forgetting everything for a moment I felt Zane everywhere. His nose brushed against mine. We both were breathing heavily. I could taste the whiskey on his breath, and I felt the urge to lock our lips together.

I was getting ready to tell him to either get the fuck off me or making him. But I felt him, I felt his hardness pressed against my stomach. He was very hard, and he was big. I couldn't stop the gasp from leaving my lips. His pupils dilated; his nostrils flared.

I wanted him.

A small sound broke my gaze from Zane. Looking over I saw Orlando making a move again, trying to find a way out.

"I have to kill him, so either step aside and let me or I will end you with him," I mumbled, just low enough he barely heard me.

I watched as he fought with himself. Was he going to actually let me kill him? Or was he going to make me take him out too? I didn't want to, but he wasn't going to stand in my way. Four more.

Four more people and it was the end. I had to.

The slightest nod from Zane gave me all I needed. Unspoken words. At the same time he threw himself off me as I moved towards Orlando.

He didn't see it coming until I was right behind him. He had no time to scream, no time to ask for help. Beg for mercy. I shoved my other knife into his gut. Falling to his knees, I tugged into him hard. Making him look at me.

"Do you remember me?" I quietly asked.

He shook his head. He had no idea, just like the others. They didn't recognize me. I mean, I couldn't blame them. I barely recognized myself most days.

"Emily and Emmy." I spoke two names I hadn't spoken in years.

His eyes widened, remembering everything. I watched as the tears began to fall from his eyes. "You-you're dead."

"Should've checked a pulse." I smiled, taking the dagger from his shoulder, ramming it into his face. He screamed, while I continued ramming the dagger into his face, into his throat. His body dropped but I couldn't stop.

I stabbed over and over again.

Blood squirted around me.

I couldn't help the overwhelming powerful feeling that coursed through my veins.

"Oh my god, she feels amazing." Orlando laughed. The tears fell from my face. I tried screaming but the rope bit into my mouth, wrapping around my head. I couldn't. I couldn't move. I could hear the shouts from Dada.

"Come on, baby, you give it so fucking good." He laughed again as my sister tried fighting. She gave it her all, but he laughed and laughed.

He was laughing while she was screaming in pain.

"He's dead," that voice broke from my memories. Letting go of the dagger it stuck out from Orlando's eye socket. There was blood everywhere. I was covered in it.

Standing above Orlando's body I glared over at Zane. I still felt the anger, the fire burning inside me. He was glaring back at me, both of us breathing heavily again. I don't know how long we stared at each other until we both grabbed at each other.

I never kissed anyone in my life, but the moment his lips slammed over mine, I stiffened but that didn't deter Zane at all. Instead, I felt his cock harden even more against my stomach. Not breaking our mouths he grabbed the back of my thighs, lifting me up. I wrapped my legs around his waist. He threw me against the wall, hard.

Letting out a grunt my back hurt from the force. My arms went around his neck searching for something, I had no idea. There was no time to think or react. I felt him undoing his belt and then his pants. I knew I should have told him, that I should have stopped this, but I couldn't stop kissing him. Our tongues fought each other, fighting for dominance. Neither of us wanted to give it up.

The next thing I knew he set me down on the ground, ripping my pants off before picking me back up and shoving me against the wall. His mouth was on mine in no time. His knuckles brushed against my folds. I couldn't control the moans that left me. Zane apparently liked everything because he was grunting and moaning all the same.

Stop this.

My brain tried reasoning with me. I really should stop this. I needed to.

Breaking away from his mouth I opened it to tell him we needed to stop, we needed to at the very least slow down. But I couldn't, not when he gave no warning before he drove his cock into my pussy.

"FUCK!" I screamed. He ripped me apart. Tears fell from my face, and Zane instantly began licking my cheek. He didn't give up, not giving my body time to acclimate to his size. He thrust into me, thrusting like a man on death row.

"Holy fuck, Salem, you're so god damn wet." He moaned.

Why were this man's moans so fucking attractive?

My hands reached around to his back. Tearing it apart, I dragged my nails into his back. He just fucked me hard, my back pressed against the wall. I would feel all this tomorrow.

"Fuck, fuck fuck!" I chanted. I couldn't catch my breath. Zane gave no indication of giving up either. He pounded into me. My orgasms took hold of my body. I couldn't move.

I couldn't breathe.

Burying my face into his neck I bit down onto his upper trap muscle, biting down hard enough to make him bleed. Zane growled, one hand holding my ass while the other reaching for my throat. Pressing against me we stared at each other.

His cock got even harder if that was possible. My nipples strained against my leather top, and I knew he could see them. Slamming his lips against mine I knew he could taste his blood from them.

"You're so fucking tight," he groaned against my lips. His thrusts became sloppy before he gave another four thrusts, slamming me into the wall before I felt the warmness of him spilling into me.

The moment he stopped moving is the same moment I realized what just happened. We stared at each other, not speaking. Slowly he lowered me to the ground. Grabbing my pants I yanked them on and when I looked back up at Zane, I could see the smirk. Like he'd just won something. He had already shoved his dick back into his pants and done them up.

In a split moment of anger I drew back punching him in his face before running off into the darkness.

What had I done?

Chapter 15

Zane

Setting her down onto the ground I tucked myself into my pants. I watched as she shoved her pants on. I had no idea what even came over me, but the moment I saw her stabbing Orlando not giving a single fuck about the blood that poured onto her, I couldn't control my actions. She took everything over. My brain couldn't process anything but wanting her.

It was like my brain shut off anything real and all I saw was her.

Salem.

I saw Salem, the beautiful masterpiece, stabbing him. I almost didn't stop her, I enjoyed her getting whatever she needed from him. I didn't know what it was, but my dick was hard for her.

Just as I was thinking of something to say to her, she reared back and punched me in the face. I didn't get a chance to curse or even blink before she ran. I didn't know what I excepted from her after fucking her hard up against the wall, but her running away was not one of them.

Wiping the blood from my nose I laughed to myself while I made a quick glance at Orlando. Poor fucker's face was basically done in. Who knew if they would even be able to tell who it was?

Shaking my head, I walked outside to my truck. I changed out of my shirt since it was the only thing that had blood on it. Once I was clean enough, I pulled away. I couldn't stop the smile spreading across my face just thinking about Salem and the way she squeezed my cock.

The moment I stepped inside the house Tobias was running towards me and jumped into my arms. It was something he did often. He knew I would always catch him.

"Uncle Zaney, you're finally home." Tobias giggled trying to tickle my neck. I gave him a little laugh, although it didn't tickle one bit. It made him happy.

"It's late, what are you doing awake?" I asked. Walking further into the house I carried him into the kitchen where Mila sat on Dimitri's lap. Killian stood at the stove making something that smelled weird. "Why is everyone awake?" I asked Tobias to sit down on the chair before taking the chair across from Dimitri and Mila.

"Luca has been blowing my phone up," Dimitri stated.

"What for?"

"He hasn't heard from Orlando in a few hours. The last thing was about someone following him."

Not reacting to this news, I cooled my facial reaction. I knew exactly where Orlando was, and why he wasn't responding. I should probably tell him but for some reason I wanted to protect Salem.

"Has Killian tracked his phone?" I asked, taking a glance over at him.

"Yeah, he was at some warehouse. I just texted Luca the location." Dimitri shrugged. "You haven't gotten any more information about this Ghost person, have you?" he inquired.

"No, it's a stupid myth, and a waste of time," I spat out. I was tired of this stupid myth. It was a waste of time for me to try and figure it out. Neither Killian nor I could find a single person who knew anything.

He nodded his head, giving Mila a kiss on her temple. "Mila wants to have a family dinner tomorrow."

"Yes, so you need to stop disappearing." She raised a brow at me, waiting for me to refuse or tell her I had something else going on.

"Why?" I barked. My voice was a little rougher than I intended. Dimitri glared at me, and I could see he was about to tell me to watch my mouth. "Sorry," I muttered, not giving him time.

Sometimes I was still a complete asshole to Mila. I didn't intend to be, but I didn't trust anyone. When she came into our lives, I tried my hardest to ignore her. But since Dimitri laid claim to her, I knew it was either accept her or live in misery for however long I stayed with them.

"Because I want to have a nice family dinner," Mila mumbled, not giving any good reason. For Dimitri it was enough, he would give her anything she wanted. Me on the other hand, I knew Mila was hiding something. She had been since we rescued her four years ago from Matteo. It shouldn't have gotten so far under my skin, but I couldn't stop the feeling. I couldn't trust Mila all the way because of this.

I didn't want a family dinner. Instead I wanted to go find Salem and bury myself in her again.

I wanted to know why she freaked out and ran away.

Not giving anyone a second glance I turned and left to go to my personal bathroom. Turning the water on as hot as I could stand it, I turned to the mirror, lifting my shirt. I looked at the deep bite mark she left on my shoulder. It was bruised to hell and back, you could see every little indentation from her teeth. My cock jumped at the memory of when she ripped the back of my shirt, and bit down on my shoulder. All I could think about was being inside her again.

Shredding the rest of my clothes I stepped towards the shower stall, and just as I was about to get inside, I caught a sight of red on my groin. Looking down I was taken back when I saw the dried blood on my cock. I couldn't stop staring. Where had this come from?

Fuck.

No no no no.

Salem. Salem was a fucking virgin, and I'd just ripped that apart like a madman up against the fucking wall.

"Shit." I slapped the counter and bowed my head, staring directly at my dick.

I never fucked a virgin before, never wanted to. But it all made sense, why she screamed. It wasn't from pleasure. No. I tore into her cunt, not giving her time to adjust.

"Fuck, fuck fuck." I was such an asshole, no wonder she ran away from me. She had just killed someone, and I fucked her like a damn whore.

Running my hands through my hair I jumped into the shower. I didn't want to think about what I was going to do when I was done, because if I gave it too much thought, I wouldn't do it.

But I had to see her. I had to make it better.

Chapter 16

Salem

I ran, ran so hard that my lungs burned. I couldn't stop.

I ran like I wanted to run away from all my problems. I wish I could run away from everything, from everyone. Especially my own damn feelings.

It was becoming too much. This was supposed to be easy. Take care of my list. No one was supposed to get involved. It was supposed to be a done deal. But the moment I laid eyes on Zane I knew something was different about him.

When I hit him with that bat I wanted to wait until he woke up, but I couldn't. I had to be somewhere else. But that didn't stop me from thinking about him. I thought about him more than I ever cared to admit. He was my little secret that I told no one about. That secret was now begging to be let out. Begging to reach for the surface so that it was getting harder to be around him. He was consuming everything about me.

I almost stopped myself from killing Orlando. I wouldn't have actually killed Zane. Putting the threat out there tasted so sour. I hated that I said it aloud. I hated that I also didn't mean it. I hated everything about him. But I didn't. I really didn't, but I wanted to.

I didn't know anything about him, but he made everything I felt fade away until all I felt was him.

He made me forget my family.

But I can't lose that. I lost my family, and I needed to get revenge for them. It was what got me through the days.

Except Zane consumed my every thought.

Pushing him from my brain, I yanked my front door open and slammed it shut. It was dark inside, and I didn't want to bother with the light. My breathing was so heavy from running miles that I didn't have a chance to realize someone else was inside.

Someone's fist connected with my jaw, and blood immediately filled my mouth. I didn't get a chance to look up or even put my arms up to block. The punches kept coming, and my face ached from the blows. Two different sets of hands grabbed both arms, holding me on my knees. My head hung down; I could barely keep my eyes open.

"I thought you'd have a bigger fight in you." A deep voice that I wanted to forget reminded me of that night.

They dragged me through the glass. My back screamed in protest. Everything in me screamed in protest. Why were they doing this? What could a nine-year-old do to them? I could cry but my tiny body ached in ways I didn't think I could. I stared blankly into the midnight skies, where everything looked peaceful. I called for peace.

Mama, Dada, my siblings, they were all gone. They left me. Now I was left here facing the monsters. Here I lay halfway off the steps leading to our house. Glass rammed into my back, my blood draining from my body. I had no fight left in me. I had nothing in me. I wanted to go back and find my family in the stars.

"Is she dead yet?" Orlando asked Remo. Remo was staring at me, while I laid there. I don't know what he was thinking, or if he even cared what they had done. But he gave nothing away. His face had no emotions.

"Not yet." His evil smile played on his face. It was a smile I could never forget, something people would have nightmares about. "Everything good to go?" he asked someone I couldn't see.

"Yeah, Luca found it in the basement."

Remo nodded.

I could hear the footsteps. I counted one, two, three… seven, and then Luca was eight.

I knew who Luca was. He was best friends with my father. Remo stayed above me. Making it nine. Nine names I would learn, nine faces I would never forget. Luca said something in Remo's ear that I could hear or make out.

But within thirty seconds of Luca walking away from me, walking away from what he had done, Remo grabbed the back of my head before slicing across my throat. I could feel the blood, I could feel my life leaving my body. My body fell down the steps.

Everything was peaceful…

"Do you know who I am?" He asked me to step closer. I could see his shiny black shoes now. I could barely see from the blood in my eyes, and the rage rushing into my veins. I hadn't planned on seeing Remo yet. I had big plans for him, but now he was here in my own space.

I let my guard down, and now I was paying for it. I wanted to blame Zane, blame my anger getting the best of me. I rushed into killing Orlando. I wanted to blame it on everyone else, but the truth was I was just spiraling out of control, and now this looked like the end.

Slowly, ever so fucking slowly, I looked up, meeting Remo's gaze. His eyes burned holes into my own.

"Who are you?" he asked. I wanted to scream at him, I wanted to scream so loud, but my brain was hurting from the pain of the punches they gave me. I felt weak, I felt weaker than I should have been.

"Okay, here's the thing, little girl. I know you killed the others. I watched you kill Orlando. You honestly did me a favor, but from the looks of it I was next." Remo began pacing back and forth in front of me. "But I won't be next, because you're going to tell me a few things. First things first, who are you?" he repeated his question.

I kept my mouth shut. I was good at that.

He nodded then I was hit with something on my back. My body launched forward, but I was quickly pulled back from the two holding onto my arms.

"Who are you?"

Nothing. He nodded again.

Bracing for the hit again, my side quickly burned from the electric stick.

Stay calm. You can do this, I reminded myself. It may have been years since I was tortured but I could. It was a mind game; the body could take a lot of pain. The thing was, though, you could trick your mind into believing you were okay.

I had to trick my mind.

I was okay.

This would not be the end. I just had to wait, and they would all see.

Or so I thought.

Chapter 17

Zane

I expected Salem to be doing a few things, showering, maybe eating, watching TV, hell even sleeping. It was four in the morning. On the way over here I drove slower than normal just because I was fighting with myself about coming to her house. I had no good reason to. I was not a good guy, never claimed I was. But she crawled into my heart and kept knocking on it. When I didn't want to think about her, I did. She had a hold of me.

I slept with plenty of women, but something was different with Salem. Something about her called to me, like my demons were controlled around her. She kept me sane.

When I parked my truck down the street, everything felt off. Something was off with this place. Then I noticed the two black

SUVs, completely blacked out. The number of times I'd been here, I had never seen them.

Running down the sidewalk to her house, the lights were off except one. Standing in front of the door, I raised my hand ready to knock when I heard a loud grunt. I had no idea what I expected when I kicked the door in. But it definitely was not two men holding Salem by her arms, while two others took turns punching and kicking her body.

Her lifeless body from the looks of it.

The other person I didn't expect to see was Remo standing against the wall watching it all unfold.

I barely knew Remo, but I knew he was just soulless. He never cared about anything.

"Well hello there, Zane." Remo smiled.

It was a smile I didn't like, something behind it. He wasn't being nice, even if he wanted to. He was hiding something.

"Remo," I growled. I couldn't help the protectiveness I was gaining from looking over at Salem moaning in pain. She looked terrible. Her nose was broken, her lip was split open, both eyes looked pretty swollen, and her side was bleeding, but I couldn't tell from what. Her body looked weak and broken down. She looked so different from the girl I saw an hour ago.

"What are you doing here?" he asked, stepping away from the wall. Remo squared his shoulders, trying to appear taller than he was. He was still shorter than me, and I almost chuckled with him trying to hide the fact that he was intimidated by me.

"I could ask you the same thing, Remo."

"Does your boss know you're here?" Remo deflected.

"Does yours?"

He tightened his jaw, and from the looks of it, Luca had no idea what Remo was doing. Dimitri never gave a shit about what Killian or I did on the side, as long as we didn't bring trouble back to him. He knew we were loyal, we were best friends, and all of that pussy bullshit.

"What'd she do?" I motioned towards Salem.

"You think just because Luca asked Dimitri for help, I'm going to spill all my secrets to you?" Remo cocked his head to the side, staring at me like I kicked his puppy. God, he was annoying the shit out of me. "She killed the men. I saw her kill Orlando..." he trailed off. Then it clicked, if he saw her killing him, that would mean he saw me, saw me letting her. Then he must have seen us, together. *Fuck*.

In a split second the two who were beating Salem rushed towards me. Yanking my knife out I sliced the throat of the first and punched the second one in the throat. He began gagging. Bringing the knife up, I stabbed his chest aiming directly for his heart. He'd die slowly.

The other two dropped Salem like a sack of potatoes. She groaned in pain, which only fired my anger even more. I didn't like that they hurt her. I didn't like that she was bleeding out and was in pain.

With a roar I grabbed hold of the blond around the throat, slamming him into the second one. Throwing the knife into the blond's neck, the second fell below the blond.

"ENOUGH!" Remo barked, causing me to look up as he held Salem. Her back was pressed against his chest, arms wrapped around her throat. Her eyes landed on mine. She looked so sad, so broken, but I had no idea why. "You need to leave, and we will never speak of this again."

"You think they won't find out about this blood bath?" I laughed. He was going to die painfully.

"If you can keep your fucking mouth shut, yes. If not, I'll just end you both right here right now. Come on, I saw her run out after you fucked her. You don't give a fuck about this whore."

I saw red.

My anger fueled me, and I charged at him. He threw Salem down as I tackled him and threw our bodies on the ground. We threw punches at each other, but I was fighting for an actual reason. I don't even remember the last time I got so angry that I threw punches, not seeing where I was even punching. I didn't care about anything. He hurt Salem.

Salem.

Bashing his head into the ground his arms went back to the side, his eyes barely open. I looked over at her. She was weakly walking back over holding a fucking cleaver. She looked amazing. Beautiful. Hot. She looked like mine. She limped over to me, standing above us.

Without her even having to speak I got up off Remo. I barely had a chance to move before she pokes him with it saying, "Ti ricordi di me?" Her voice was so low.

Remo shook his head. Pulling her hair back she showed him her neck, the scar that I saw before. His eyes widened, fearful. Tears seemed to appear in them. Fuck he was actually crying. I had no idea what Salem was to him, but I could see the fear finally seeping into his eyes.

"Dì il mio cazzo di nome," she whispered.

Shaking his head, the tears fell down his face. The smell of urine hit my nose.

"Dillo."

"S-s-Salem," his voice cracked. "Salem Gray." As her last name fell from his lips, she swung the cleaver down into his throat. His eyes widened, and blood squirted everywhere. But she kept hacking until his head had fallen from his shoulders.

Dropping the cleaver she fell to the ground. The tiniest whimper echoed around us, dropping down to her. I pulled her face in my hands. I held her face close, blood covering it, and if I hadn't somehow fallen in love with her before, I sure as shit just did. Tears fell from her face. It caused me pain to see her like this. "I won't let anything happen to you again," I vowed. Why I had said that, I have no idea. But it was the truth, I wouldn't let anything happen to her again. I had no idea what those men did to deserve to die, but after witnessing Orlando and the need in her eyes to end him, then with Remo, I saw the hurt, the anger, and everything she was trying to hide.

Without giving it a second thought I scooped Salem up, carrying her down the street to my truck. I placed her in the front seat and grabbed my phone from my pocket.

Me: I'm sending you an address. I need a cleanup crew ASAP, and I need someone to come pack a bag of clothes.

Sending that off to Taylor, I scrolled down to Killian. As much as I didn't want to talk to him or bring any of them into whatever shitshow was raining down on Salem I couldn't ignore it anymore.

"You never call me." Killian laughed while answering the phone.

"I know. Listen, I just texted Taylor for a cleanup crew. But I need you to get Dimitri and tell him we need to talk. I'm heading back to the house, and I'll be there in about thirty, but I need to take care of something when I get there." I kept it vague.

It was silent for a moment. "Alright, so meeting around what, ten?" he asked.

Glancing down at the time, I said, "Yeah."

"Does this have anything to do with you being at the same place Orlando died, and currently at the same place Remo is?" he inquired. I should have known he would know where I was and who I was with, or at least somewhat.

I grunted, not giving him an answer.

"I'll take that as a yes."

"Listen, I'll explain everything at the meeting. I've got to go," I mumbled hanging up before he could say anything else. Climbing into my truck, I peeled away.

The moment we got to the house Salem was snoring quietly in the seat beside me. I almost let her just sleep. But I knew a shower and a bed would do much better for her. Going around, I opened the passenger door and picked her up again. She didn't wake up at all. Not when I walked into the house, not when I got to my room, and not when I got into the bathroom.

Salem was so small I easily held her in one arm, her back side on my knee while I flipped the switch on. Walking over to the shower with her still in my arms, I maneuvered her body, so it was resting more against my chest and my left arm. Turning the shower on, I turned and set her on the counter while the water got hot.

"Kitten," I mumbled. Her head pressed against my chest, and I rubbed her back. "Come on, I gotta get you cleaned up."

Slowly her eyes opened, peeling her head away from me as she looked around the bathroom, clearly lost on what was happening.

"Come on, arms up," I whispered.

With the little strength she had, she did as I asked. Pulling off her shirt, I unbuttoned her pants and carefully picked her up. Unclasping her bra, I waited for the protest, but she never gave me any. Her bra fell with the rest of her clothes. Picking her up again I got rid of underwear, boots, and socks.

Salem kept her head down, as though she was ashamed of her body. It was so different from the original person she always presented herself as. Here she looked broken, scared, and unsure of herself.

Shredding myself of my own clothes, I picked her up, her legs wrapped around my waist. Carrying her into the shower, she hissed.

"Is the water okay?" I asked, cringing to myself for the fact I never cared about another fucking person in my life, yet here I was asking if the fucking water was okay.

She gave a little nod before pulling her face back from my neck. The water poured down her face, rinsing away the blood. Black make-up streaked down her face.

"I need you to stand kitten, think you can handle that?" Again she nodded.

Placing her down I grabbed my loofah, poured my body wash, and slowly began washing all the blood off her. Salem stood there, her eyes closed as I dragged the loofah across her chest. I took in the scar across her neck, a pale white line showcasing pain she took but survived. Going down her arms there were tiny cuts all over them. Going around I washed her back. Worse scars covered her entire back. Kneeling down I could feel the anger radiating off my body, pleading to be let loose. She had a long scar from the middle of her thigh to the middle of her calf on the inner part of her right leg.

Swallowing my rage I tapped her hip. Salem looked down at me, her eyes barely opened. "Lean on me," I mumbled. Her dainty hand reached for my shoulder, while the other grabbed my head. Grabbing her foot, I washed both of them before placing them back down onto the ground.

Getting up, I grabbed my shampoo and washed her hair, being careful in case they'd hit her on the head. Conditioner next, I rinsed off, grabbed a towel and wrapped it around myself. Picking her up, she snuggled into my neck again.

I carried her into my bedroom, where I dried her off. Grabbing a shirt, I tugged it over her head. "Come on, get under the covers." Tugging the blankets down she slid under them.

"Zane," her voice broke.

"It's okay," I said bringing her to my chest. "I got you."

I had no idea what that meant, but whatever it was, I was here. If that meant holding her while she felt broken or helping her shower. If that meant fighting her and letting her get her anger out. I would be whatever she needed. I had no idea what that even fucking meant, but damnit this woman had my heart. She had the cold black thing. I would rip it from my chest and let her fucking have it. I wanted to see her smile, for her to laugh.

Something about her was calling my name.

"Thank you," Salem muttered before her breathing evened out and she began softly snoring.

After Salem fell asleep, I showered quickly before making my way downstairs, where I found Mila making breakfast, Tobias watching as she did. Killian was sitting at the kitchen table with his computer open. Dimitri was sipping his steaming cup of coffee watching Mila with all the love in his eyes.

Before I had no idea why Dimitri would go to war for her, how he could have so much love for someone. It was hard for me to deal with natural human emotions. I had normal parents, they loved me, but for some reason I couldn't. I had no idea what was wrong with me, but I hated human contact. I hated humans. I was just an angry person.

Dimitri stared at his wife and son like they were the world, and to him they were.

Making my way closer to the coffee, I poured myself a cup.

"Hi, Uncle Zaney." Tobias smiled up at me. Leaning against the counter by him I nudged him with my shoulder.

"Where have you been?" he asked, shoving a piece of bacon into his mouth.

"You miss me?" I said, smirking at him.

My heart broke when he looked up at me, his eyes showing all emotions of pure sadness. "Hmm."

I hadn't realized I was gone that much, but now I saw it. The moment we arrived here I was stuck on being away as much as I could. I never left Tobias more than a few days if I needed to. I felt like complete shit realizing I hurt this child.

"Hey, how about after I talk with your dad and Uncle Killian, I take you to get some ice cream and maybe we can hit some toy store?" I wagged my eyebrows, giving him the best smile I could.

"Really?" Tobias all but screamed excitedly.

"As long as the parents say it's all good." I eyed Dimitri and Mila. Dimitri glared at me, most likely because of this meeting I called. Mila on the other hand looked like she was about to jump out of her skin from how big her damn smile was.

"Dadda." Tobias looked over at Dimitri. I waited for him to say no, and I think Mila knew this as well because just as he went to open his mouth probably to tell me to go fuck myself, Mila went and stood next to her husband placing her hand on his arm.

"I think that'll be great, Zane, plus tonight we're having that dinner, remember." Mila smiled looking between everyone. A warning that if we didn't show up, she'd rain hell down on us.

"Everyone will be there, Moy tsvetok," he muttered, kissing the side of her head, giving me a sharp look, which had me nodding my head in understanding. I was on thin ice around them. I was acting like a dick towards Mila for no reason lately. We had worked through our issues years ago. I didn't know why I am acting like this now. I mean, for fuck's sake I was the one who delivered Tobias. I didn't think Dimitri held it against me, but I also knew he was a little upset that I had seen way too much of Mila.

"Including the girl upstairs in your bed?" Killian decided to partake in this discussion. Rolling my eyes, I looked over at his smug look.

Killian had always been a smug bastard. He always had a comment somewhere shoved up from his ass, and never cared if no one wanted to hear it.

"What girl?" Mila looked over at Killian, who was now smirking at me. I was going to have to remember to beat his ass later.

"A girl?" Tobias sounded disgusted. "In your bed." *Shit.* "Mommy, why would there be a girl in the bed?" he asked, staring at his parents. Again his father was glaring at me like I was the one who opened my mouth and said there was a girl in my bed. No, that was all Killian, so why was he wanting to murder me? I had no idea.

"Hey, malen'kiy mal'chik." *Little boy.* "I have a meeting with your uncles, but after we're done, Zane is going to take you out and buy you *anything* your little heart desires."

"Anything?" He laughed, turning back towards me from the counter.

I could feel all their eyes on me, waiting for my answer. Of course, I would get Tobias anything, I always did. But the way they were saying it showed a different agenda. Swallowing the lump in my throat I smiled at him. "Yes, of course, anything you want."

"Alright, we're going to be in the office, moy tsvetok." Dimitri kissed her temple. Walking behind him we headed into the office.

Dimitri sat down, and Killian and I both took the chairs in front of the desk. I had nowhere to begin with everything I'd been doing. Thankfully, I didn't have to think too hard before Dimitri laid it all out in front of me.

"Who's the girl?" Dimitri asked, folding his hands on top of the desk. "And does it have anything to do with why Luca has been blowing my phone up?"

I couldn't lie to him. Not anymore. Especially not since she had killed Orlando, and now Remo was dead.

"Yeah, she does."

"You better talk and talk fast," Dimitri growled out. Losing his temper.

"I didn't kill any of them, just Remo's guards." I don't know why I started with that first. But I guess starting anywhere was better than not speaking at all.

"There's a but," Dimitri growled out. "Just spit everything out. We have other shit to speak about other than your bitch up there."

"Watch your mouth," I spit out before I even knew what I was doing. I never was the one who went against Dimitri, or his orders. But something inside me told me to protect Salem from him. And I'd be damned if I ignored that part of me. It was the only part of me that I felt now.

I could feel Killian stiffen next to me while Dimitri and I held each other's gaze.

"She's yours?" he asked.

"Yes." I didn't have to think about it. Yes, I was claiming the mystery girl upstairs asleep in my bed. Which reminded me the faster this meeting got over with the faster I could get upstairs and lay with her. Fuck, when did I become such a pussy?

"What's the deal with her?" Killian finally asked.

Breaking away from Dimitri's gaze I took a deep breath. "When we first got here after the meeting with Giulio and Leonzo I went to the back alley and found two shits messing with her." I decided I had to tell them everything from the beginning. "I mean, they were, but she was holding her own. She broke one of their noses, and when she saw me, she…fuck, *she took me down*," I muttered. I was a tough fucker, but her punch was hard, and I'd be crazy if she didn't make me hard. They didn't need to know all that much.

"The two fucks you were killing in the basement weeks ago?" Dimitri inquired.

"Yeah, those were the guys. I was stuck on trying to find who Ghost was, but my mind kept going back to her. I don't know how to explain it. It was like the moment my eyes laid on her, I became… obsessed. The night I was going to get Chinese," I said, motioning towards Killian. "I saw her. She was on the phone and then I followed her to her house." I laughed to myself, remembering the number of times I drove past her house just to see if she was outside, or if her car was in the driveway. She didn't even realize I was following her because she kept her head down. She wore baggy sweatpants. Even her damn sweatshirt was baggy on her. They were two sizes too big, but she looked cute. Her hair was done into a messy bun on top of her head, and her face was clear of all make-up. I could see a dusting of freckles across her nose.

"Zane," Dimitri snapped bringing me back.

"Yeah, right. Anyway, I followed Orlando, actually. I had no luck finding Ghost. Which I still don't, I really don't believe this ghost person is true." I shrugged my shoulders. "She was there. I did step in at one point. She held her own against me. She knocked me down and guys she's fucking strong. But fuck, Dimitri, when she said that she would kill me if I didn't move out of her way, something in her eyes, man." I hated thinking back to just a few hours ago. I hated remembering the sadness swirling around, the anger, every emotion swirling around her face.

"So she killed Orlando." He had no emotions about that Italian dying. "And Remo?"

"I almost did kill him. But no it was her, she chopped his head off."

I guess neither man thought a tiny girl had the power to do so because Killian gasped like a fucking girl while Dimitri's eyes bugged from his head. It was a split moment, but he still had been surprised.

"After she ran, I followed her and when I got to her house four of Remo's men were beating the shit out of her." I had no intention of telling them she was a virgin. Something primal in me snapped when I saw the blood on my cock. I had claimed her without even realizing, and she took me like a fucking champ. "Something in me snapped. I couldn't watch as they continued breaking her bones and beating her. I killed three of the guards, I don't know about the fourth." I cringed inside.

"Excuse me?" Dimitri growled.

Yeah, rule number one about killing people, leave no survivors. Especially when we were technically supposed to be helping Luca, and I had been there helping kill his men.

"Remo grabbed her, and the guy slipped out. I hadn't realized until it was too late." I fucking hated that I hadn't. I was the god damn enforcer for the fucking Bravta, and I messed up big time. Because of a girl. "I was about to kill Remo until I heard her, and she was carrying a goddamn cleaver, and she started whacking off his goddamn head," I finished. The rest of them didn't need to know that I stole her cherry, or that she spoke a different language as well. They didn't need to know about the scars covering her whole body. They didn't need to know that.

"Fuck, Zane," Dimitri barked. "If I didn't already have enough shit that I was fucking dealing with. Now this." He clenched his hands together. Probably trying to stop himself from jumping across his desk and beating me to death.

"I can't find anything about her, like at all. It's as though she's not a real person." Snapping my head over at him, I noticed his computer was set up, obviously looking into her history as we spoke. But this was the worst thing he could do in front of Dimitri. Killian was the best of the best hackers. No one could do what this man could do. If you needed to find someone he was your man. Hack into any program, anything to do with technology, he was your man. So his not being able to find Salem was a problem.

"There's literally nothing?" Dimitri said, taking his focus somewhat off me for the first time since we stepped inside the office.

I wasn't scared of Dimitri. But I also knew that he would protect Mila and Tobias no matter what, even if that meant taking out

Salem. If she was a threat to them, he would not think twice about putting her into the ground. A place I didn't want her.

"Seriously, like I cannot find a single thing about her, no matter where I look. The normal web there's nothing. Fuck, even the god damn dark web. There's nothing about her. She does not exist in this world." He sounded spooked. It should concern me more with who she was, but I couldn't find myself caring.

She could take out Luca's men, and in my eyes that was good enough. I was perfectly fine with her killing them off.

"Zane," Dimitri snapped. Looking up from the ground Dimitri was glaring at me again. This man needed to find a new look. "I'm going to set up a meeting with Luca. I will tell him we don't know what's happening. Killian is going to get rid of any type of evidence. I will tell him we are going back to Russia. Until then lay the fuck low. Keep that girl of yours in check. I don't need her going off the fucking handle and killing more people."

I nodded. I didn't know how much control I would really have over her. I had a feeling she was going to be a handful, and even then, I highly doubted she would ever let me even try to control her. I'd probably get stabbed from it.

Chapter 18

Salem

I couldn't remember the last time I woke up without having a nightmare of the men or dreaming of my parents. But the moment my eyes fluttered open I was about to close them again, ready to try and sleep more until I took in the large bed and the dark room I was currently lying in.

Sitting straight up, I hissed in pain, forgetting about my ribs that were most likely broken due to the ass beating Remo's men gave me. Clutching my chest, trying to push the pain away, I looked around the room. The bed I laid in was definitely a king, which had the most cooling covers on it that I had ever felt before. Looking around, there was a dresser directly in front of the bed, with nothing on top, a closed door to the right, and then two doors sat on the right side of the bed. One I could tell was the bathroom, and I could assume the other was a closet. Besides the bed and dresser, nothing else sat in the room.

Pushing the covers off, I swung my legs over the bed and slithered my way into the bathroom. Turning on the light, I cringed the moment I took in what I looked liked. A fucking mess. My black hair was a curly mess. I never went to bed with my hair wet for this exact reason. There were several bruises all down my arms, and my damn face looked like someone thought it was a punching bag.

Wait a minute...

Taking a step back I realized I was no longer wearing my leather outfit like I was last night. Instead, I was wearing a large red shirt that came down to my knees and swallowed me whole. Ignoring the ping of pain running through my body I pulled the shirt over my head. My eyes locked onto the deep bruises covering my entire torso and legs. This wasn't the first time I had been covered in this amount of bruises, but something felt different this time.

I had been blind-sided with the fact I lost my damn virginity. I lost it to Zane, someone who I barely knew, and someone who fucked me better than I ever thought would happen. Even thinking about Zane had me pressing my legs together. I was still sore, but that didn't stop me from wanting him again. A man I barely knew, yet I wanted to know, against my better judgment.

Rolling my shoulders back I stepped into the shower and turned it on as hot as I could stand it. Stepping in I welcomed the sting against my skin where the cuts were once clotted but now reopened. I washed my hair the best I could because the moment I tried to lift my arms higher than above my chest pain shot down my back. Finishing faster than I had before, I wrapped a towel around my head and body.

"I could've helped you," someone said from behind me. Looking over my shoulder Zane stood with his back against the bathroom door. His blond hair was a mess, like he had been pulling on it in different directions. He wore a skintight black t-shirt, showing off his muscles in his arm. The amount of tattoos this man had should not have been as attractive as it was. But, fuck, my body was reacting in ways I fully didn't understand. His gray sweatpants didn't do much to hide how thick his thighs were either. Standing there with no heels on, both of us completely barefoot, he towered over me. By a fuck ton, a full head taller than me.

"Here take these." He held out three white pills. I wasn't sure if I could trust him not to drug me. From the look on my face he must have realized that. "It's just Tylenol. Come on over here."

Slowly stepping forward I made my way over until I was standing right in front of him. Reaching forward to his hand to take the pills he closed it. "Open," he demanded. Looking up, my knees nearly buckled from the way he ordered me. Now don't get me wrong, I truly hated anyone telling me what to do. I wanted to refuse Zane, but I'd be stupid to not acknowledge the warm feeling my body got. The way my pussy was being a damn slut, ready to fucking beg this beast of a man to take me.

The moment he raised his eyebrow, waiting for me to deny him, I swallowed my pride of wanting to refuse and opened my mouth partly.

"Good girl," he murmured, sticking the three pills into my mouth. Closing my lips around his finger, I sucked. Something inside both of us must have snapped. I don't know who moved first but our lips crashed together. A new fight took over, his teeth biting down on my already split lip. I hissed while letting go of my towel. Gripping his hair, I pulled hard, and he grunted in pleasure. Zane's hand wrapped around my jaw, pushing my head back, shoving his tongue down my throat. I tried shoving against his chest, but he just held me harder against him. Taking all my might, my arms screamed in protest. I shoved him harder. He moved an inch back, his lips leaving mine. Both of us were breathing heavily. I didn't give myself a chance to think before I punched him in the jaw. His head twisted to the side ever so slowly as he brought his gaze back to me. His dangerous hazel eyes promised me too many things I was not ready to deal with.

Bringing up his hand he cupped my cheek and I leaned into it. It was the most comfort I've had from someone other than Aziza. I didn't know if I wanted to welcome or run from the warmth wrapping itself around my heart.

Grabbing me by the throat, he yanked the towel from my head. My black hair fell to a mess around my shoulders. I stood there completely naked, scars, bruises, everything bare for him to see. Yet he looked at me like I held the sun and moon for him.

I blamed the fact he must have put me in some type of trance. Maybe he truly did drug me because all I felt was him everywhere. His hand wrapped around my throat, his body pressed against mine, his tongue inside my mouth again. His other hand roamed the rest of my body, and the scars not deterring him had me wanting to tear up and spill everything to him.

I didn't have time to think too much about that because I could feel him spreading out of his sweatpants, not once breaking from my mouth until he pulled his own shirt over his head. Taking that moment I stepped back and stared at him. His chest was covered in just as many tattoos as his arm. On his chest a large skull with an owl on top with its wings reaching across onto his shoulder. I didn't have time to admire any more of his artwork on his body because my eyes traveled down. My mouth instantly went dry, and I could barely swallow.

"Oh, fuck no, you are not fucking me with that thing," I shirked. My voice broke from pure fear of what was hanging between his legs. There was no way he was getting anywhere near me with that thing.

He laughed. An actual deep laugh, one that came from his stomach. "You already had it, Kitten."

I couldn't even look up at his face. My eyes were glued to the fucking baby elephant trunk that was sticking straight out at me. There was no way he had that inside me.

Shaking my head, I took a step back. "You have got to be fucking with me. There is no way in this world, *that thing,* that thing you have attached to your damn body was inside me."

"Hold the fuck up." I knew the moment I spoke he was going to say something about it. "You have an accent."

I nodded my head.

"Tell me you want me to fuck you," he smirked. He wanted me to say that for a reason, my accent, which I worked so hard to hide. And because he knew his dick scared me.

"I'm a virgin," I blurted out, not giving a shit that my accent was no longer hidden.

Again he laughed at me. "As of last night you are not," he said cocky. He was full of himself. I should've known he would figure it out. "You know last night when you left me, I came back here, angry that you ran away from me." He slowly began walking towards me. "The moment I saw your virgin blood dried on my cock, something sparked inside me. That's why I was at your apartment." He stood in front of me. I had to crane my neck back just to look at him.

He reached down, grabbed the back of my thighs, and lifted me up. My legs wrapped around his waist, both of our noses pressed against each other.

"How sore are you?" he whispered against my lips. I wanted to lie to him and tell him I wasn't, but the way he stared into my eyes, I knew he wouldn't appreciate me lying to him.

"Just let me get used to you first," I said, hoping that would be enough of an answer for him.

Zane didn't say anything as he lifted my ass up before slowly bringing me back down. His cock kept pushing into me, fitting snuggles against my walls. Even as the air left my lungs, and I fought for more, he didn't stop until I was flushed up against him. He began breathing heavily, his eyes closed like he was losing the battle of wanting to slam into me. I never felt this full in my life, uncomfortable but also comfortable. The feeling was almost too much. My arms wrapped around his neck, my nails digging into his skin. He growled like a heart before pulling out and pushing back in. My pussy clenched around him, causing him to speed up, my body barely having time to acclimate to the invasion of his cock inside me.

Closing my eyes I threw my head back against the wall as he continued his punishment. "Fuck, Kitten, you feel so fucking good," he groaned, dragging a broken gasp from me. "You are so fucking tight, I barely fit," he growled against my lips.

Something in me snapped. I wanted him to fuck me harder, though I doubted my body could handle any of that. I ignored that rational side of me and slammed my lips against his mouth. Both of our moans mixed together, and he slammed his hips into me. Our tongues fought against each other, fighting for dominance. But we both knew he owned my body. This stranger could do anything to my body, and I wouldn't care. He was fucking me like this was his last moment on earth, slamming me against the wall. I bit down on his bottom lips, the taste of metal filling my mouth. I wanted to cringe away from the taste of his blood, but it ignited me. I felt my body tighten, my pussy strangling him. I was panting, feeling breathless. I was so close, and he knew it.

"Don't you dare, you wait," he demanded. "You won't come until I tell you."

God why was he so fucking hot? My body flooded with emotions, and my eyes welled up. I could feel the tears fall down my cheeks. His tongue licked my salty tears up, his punishment not letting up. I didn't know how long this man had been thrusting into me. Sweat coated both our bodies.

"Fuck fuck fuck," I chanted, my nails digging into his skin. I could feel the blood on my fingertips from the force. I wanted to mark him just like he was marking me, his fingertips bruising into my hips.

My eyes fluttered closed, my head leaning against the wall.

"Eyes on me." He grunted at me. My eyes flew open, and I stared down into his. "Come for me, my kitten."

That's all it took. My soul left my body, and I came. I couldn't stop the scream slipping through my lips as he thrust into me three more times until I felt warmness shoot through my body. Zane slowly stopped before resting his forehead against mine, our eyes both closed. Our breathing was too heavy to hear anything else, and I couldn't stop the smile playing on my lips.

"You have a beautiful smile, Salem." My name on his mouth sounded so sexy, and my smile grew even bigger.

"I need to shower again," I muttered. Leaning forward I rested my head in his neck, not caring about anything at the moment. "I think you just fucked the daylights out of me."

Zane gave me a small laugh. Turning around he set me down on the countertop before turning around towards the tub. Turning the water on he plugged the tub before reaching for me again. I watched Zane as he grabbed a washcloth, wetted it, and kneeled down in front of me.

My legs snapped shut as he went to reach for me, and he looked up at me. Something about this man being on his knees for me had my stomach in knots.

"I'm just cleaning you up before the bath, kitten," he mumbled.

After what seemed like forever, I finally slowly opened my legs for him. I couldn't stop feeling embarrassed with his face so close to that area of myself. I was never a sexual person, never had sex until last night. I touched myself maybe three times, but never felt fully satisfied. I never had time or cared enough to explore any sexual desire. But Zane woke something up in me.

I watched as Zane carefully cleaned me up. If I thought I was sore before this, I was definitely sore now. Everything felt sensitive, and my pussy throbbed.

Before I knew it Zane tossed the cloth onto the counter. Locking eyes with me he brought my right leg up—the leg that was littered with scars, the one that almost made me forget how to walk. His eyes traveled down to the long scar on the inner part. It started mid-calf and ended in the middle of my thigh.

"This stupid bitch won't stop fucking screaming." Remo laughed. They all laughed like my family was a joke, like our lives never mattered. I couldn't stop screaming, even if I wanted to. Dada was dead, and Lee was dead next to me. All I could smell was blood.

Then I felt the pain. My leg felt like it was being ripped from my body. My eyes were too blurry. I could barely see. My right leg was covered in so much blood, I felt dizzy, my eyes blurred. Everything was going black.

"Salem," Zane's voice sounded soft. It was so unlike him. I hadn't even noticed my eyes were closed, or that I was beginning to cry. He brought his mouth from my ankle, kissing his way up my calf, taking his time to kiss my scar. I never would have guessed Zane would be soft like this. He was all man, pure muscle, tattoos, had this dark look surrounding him. But right now he was on his knees kissing my leg.

When he reached the top of my scar, he lingered closer to my pussy before pushing to his feet, sealing his lips over mine. I was ready to shove my tongue into his mouth, but he stepped back and wrapped my legs around his waist. Turning towards the tub, he stepped inside and lowered us down.

Hissing the moment the hot water touched my pussy I dug my nails into his back until I felt the numbing take over. Once the water reached a little more than halfway he reached forward turning it off. Once he laid back down, he patted his chest and waited for me to lower my head down. I laid my stomach on his chest, like we'd done this a million times before. I couldn't stop my eyes from closing, not realizing how tired I actually was. I smiled to myself as I let sleep take me over.

A low hum woke me up, along with the freezing water. Slowly opening my eyes I realized I was still lying against Zane's hard chest. But now one hand rubbed my back while the other played with my wet hair. He hummed a song I couldn't place. It reminded me so much of my mom when she would sing to me.

"Mila is making dinner; it should be done soon," he muttered in my head. Nodding my head I looked up at him. Zane was already staring down at me.

"I should go back home," I blurted out.

Did I really want to go back? No. Should I go back? Yes. And from the dark look he was now glaring my way he did not like what I just said.

"You can't. And even if you could, I wouldn't let you out of my sight," he growled at me.

"You don't even know me." It was a weak excuse. He had already been inside me twice now. I had fallen asleep on his chest, and if that didn't scream something at both of us we were dumb.

"I know more than you think." Jumping back from his words, I opened my mouth to say something, but his hand covered my mouth, shutting me up. "But right now we need to get out of this cold ass water, get dressed, and head downstairs before Mila comes up here and tries to kick your ass," he finished giving me a quick kiss. Grabbing hold of my thigh once again, my legs wrapped around his waist. He stood without trouble, and sure I knew I was small. I mean five foot four, maybe 130 pounds. But from sitting in freezing water, this man got up with no trouble. He carried me out of the bathroom and to the door next to the bathroom. The one I assumed was the closet.

Setting me on my feet, he wrapped me in a towel I hadn't even noticed him carrying. I watched as he dried himself, pulled on a pair of dark jeans, a long sleeve Henley, and put on a pair of dark motorcycle boots. Suddenly, I felt uncomfortable standing there in nothing but a towel with hair soaking wet like a damn mop bucket.

143

He stood there looking like a dark angel, who'd fucked me into another world.

Watching him bend over I couldn't help but look deeply at his ass. He really did have a nice one.

"You done staring at my ass?" he asked, breaking me from my thoughts. Looking up at him, I hadn't even realized he was looking back at me over his shoulder. He was holding clothes in his hand, holding them out to me.

Giving him my best smile I took the clothes from him and turned for the bathroom again. I didn't know why I felt this embarrassed about changing in front of him—he had seen me completely naked and seen the scars covering my body. I hated that I felt this vulnerable. I never needed anyone anymore. I had to remind myself of that.

I already started to fall down the rabbit hole for Zane, and I couldn't fall down. I just couldn't.

Shoving my feelings down I headed into the bathroom and quickly changed into the long-sleeved Henley he gave me and a pair of leggings.

"Come on, dinners done," Zane called through the door. I needed to get away from him. Just the sound of his voice right now was doing things to me. Things I didn't want to be dealing with. I didn't want to deal with the emotions creeping through me whenever Zane was around. I was used to being alone. I needed to be alone.

"Salem, come on." He spoke softly again. It was that voice that had me melting, ready to fall into his arms. I don't even know what happened last night that caused this shift in both of us, but I didn't like it Not one bit.

Opening the door, I almost ran directly into his chest. A chest that I wanted to lay my head on. I wanted to lay on him again. To fall asleep on him. I wanted nothing more than to lean on him when everything in my life suddenly felt like it was falling apart.

Zane went to open his mouth, but I didn't want to talk. I didn't want these feelings. Shoving past I ignored him when he called my name. Storming my way downstairs, I continued on my way, not bothering to stop until I made my way to the dining room.

I don't know what I truly expected, but it was not finding four people staring at me. A man with dark brown hair and striking gray eyes was smiling at me. Another man sat at the head of the table, his black hair slicked back, green eyes glaring at me. Like he was ready to jump across the table and murder me on the spot.

Then I reached her. The woman sitting next to the one wanting to murder me.

Mila.

She sat at the table, her eyes widening at the sight of me. It couldn't be because I looked like shit. No. It was because four years ago I saved her. My body tingled as I tried to mask my surprise at her sitting here. How could this be? What luck did I have?

Mila only smiled at me before she continued cutting into a small plate of food. Then I turned my attention towards the little one. A small boy sat on the other side of the angry one. His brown hair matched Mila's, his goofy smile. From the looks of it, he couldn't have been more than four or five. My guess, she was pregnant when she was kidnapped. My heart warmed, and I was ready to burst into tears. It made me miss my family. I missed them all. The pain wanted to tear through my body, to tear me apart.

I felt Zane behind me before he even had the chance to say anything, and I found myself leaning backward into him. Wanting his comfort. I needed it.

"Sit next to me." The little voice pulled me from my thoughts. Looking over, my body went numb. Looking back at the same child, he sat on his knees, bouncing in his seat. It reminded me of myself. I always wanted Lee to sit next to me at dinner. I remember sitting next to Dada, begging Lee to sit on the other side of me. He always seemed to make a fuss, but it was all an act.

"Kitten," Zane whispered into my ear. Looking back at him, he nodded his head towards Tobias. I forgot he wanted me to sit next to him. I just wanted another moment with Lee.

"Uh, sure," I muttered. My feet were moving before I realized it. Sliding down next to him, everyone kept quiet. I was used to being quiet, but it was unsettling.

"What's your favorite color?" he asked. Looking over next to me, I tried my best to ignore the angry man shooting daggers at me.

"I don't know if I have one, but if I did, I think it would be gray." I smiled back at him.

"Hmm…" The child cocked his head to the side, as though he was thinking about my answer, determining if it was good enough or not. It made my heart flutter, and for the first time I actually felt at ease.

It seemed like forever before he finally let out a belly laugh. "Gray is a great color. I think it's my new favorite." Then just as fast he turned back towards his plate and began shoving his mouth full of food.

Turning back around I looked down at my now full plate of what looked like chicken in some type of sauce, a salad, and a few pieces of broccoli. I hadn't even realized someone made a plate.

"It's Chicken Marsala, and the salad has vinaigrette, and yeah it just has broccoli, nothing special. But yeah, um, if you don't like it, I can cook something else." Mila looked between me and her own plate. This is the same Mila that I remembered. She was shy and unsure of herself. "Or I can just order pizza, I'm sure that would be bett—"

"I'm sure it's great, thank you." I smiled. I could barely remember the last time I had a home cooked meal. Sure I knew how to cook, but normally I didn't take the time to do it.

Just to prove to Mila that she didn't need to worry about what I ate, I cut into the chicken and took a huge bite. A low moan escaped my lips before I knew it and I hadn't realized my eyes were closed until I heard someone clear their throat. Snapping my eyes open I looked right across from me. Zane was staring so hard at me I could see the vein on the side of his forehead straining. Sparing a look of anger, he had yet to pick any of his food up, and I doubted he had looked away from me either. Shifting in my seat I grew uncomfortable from the lack of quiet in this dining room. And I knew it was because of me. I was the reason they were all being so quiet.

"What's your name?" the little man asked. Looking down at him again, I shoved another piece of chicken in my mouth. Swallowing without chewing it much I tried to ignore the burning of my throat.

"Salem," I answered, not daring to look at anyone else. If he wanted to be the only one to talk to me, so be it.

"That's it?" He scratched his nose. "No middle or last name? My name is Tobias Theodore Anderson Volkov. I have Mama and Dad's last name." Tobias shrugged, grabbing his milk from the table. After taking a large drink he looked back at me. "I got Theodore from Uncle Zaney, that's his middle name. He delivered me when I came out of Mom's tummy."

"Theodore is a beautiful middle name." I grinned. It took everything in me to not laugh and turn to Zane when Tobias called him Zaney. I had to tuck that away for later. *Later.* As if I was going to be staying longer than I needed. Which I couldn't. Once dinner was done, I had to leave. I had to finish what I started.

"I think so, too. Do you have a middle name?" he asked again.

"I do, hmm tell me a good reason why I should tell you?" I whispered to him. Either way I would tell Tobias but talking here with him made me forget about my other problem and I wanted to enjoy it.

"Dada doesn't trust you, and Uncle Kill couldn't find anything about you on his 'puter." No matter how much I could be prepared for anything, the next thing that he said prepared me for nothing. "And Uncle Zaney is obsessed with you. I think he has a crush on you as well." Three things happened at that point. Kill—as Tobias called him—just smirked. It was no secret he felt something for her.

Angry man literally looked like he was about to throw the butter knife. I noticed he was now holding tightly to me. And glancing over at Zane he wore a smug look. Like he won some fucking prize.

That smug look made me want to punch his face until I felt better about the mutual feelings.

"I think that's a very good answer." I nagged his arm slightly. "Salem Wren Gray."

"What's your real name?" A low growl came from the head of the table.

Looking up at him, I took in the hold he had on the knife, along with the snarl. He was large like Zane, but not as muscular. His hair was a little light brown, and shorter. He wore a white dress shirt, and I could assume he was wearing dress pants and shoes as well.

"Salem Wren Gray," I said not to break eye contact with him. I refused to show weakness and break down.

"Interesting because Killian can't find a single fucking thing about you, *Salem.*" He said my name like a disease. Like I was a bug sitting here, and he wanted to squish me. Funny for him, I refused to die. They tried, but it didn't work.

I survived.

"Haven't you heard of a dead girl walking?" I shrugged. I knew I was getting under his skin from the small tick of his jaw. He was grinding his teeth together. He wouldn't completely lose it with his son sitting here, but he also wouldn't let me get away with provoking him. "What's your name?" I asked back finally.

"Why are you here?" He tried a different approach, not bothering with telling me his.

"I'm trying to enjoy a nice meal that your wife made, *what are you doing here?*" I shot back.

"Salem, don't provoke him," Zane warned. Glaring over at him, I hated that he was choosing his side over mine. I had no real reason, but it still bothered me. I wanted him to pick me.

"This is my house. I suggest you don't piss me off much more."

"Or what?" I blurted out.

You know when you're quiet for so long and then all of a sudden everything comes out. When you're ready to scream at anyone in your path. Yeah, that's where I was right now. He was pissing me off. I was angry about everything, and he was in my path. He thought he could talk to me like a child, like I'm his wife, and that I would bend over for him. He was wrong.

"You're playing a dangerous game," he growled.

"Dimitri, stop," Mila whispered, her hand reaching for his. Immediately his eyes softened as he looked down at his wife. "Let's just finish dinner, please."

He nodded his head. Still holding her hand, he used his other one and began eating, not daring to look away from me. No one spoke again, and I was fine with that. I kept my gaze down and waited until it was time for me to go.

Eventually, Mila took Tobias upstairs to get him ready for bed, and I was ready to make my break for it until the blaring sound of someone's phone went off. Dimitri cursed until he dragged his phone out and looked between the three of us.

"It's Luca." He scowled at me like I was the reason Luca was calling.

"Luca," Dimitri answered. I couldn't hear what he was saying on the other line, but I felt my skin burn. Everything was becoming too much. It was like Luca was right in front of me with a thin piece of glass.

"Yes, he's here," Dimitri answered what Luca asked. Switching it to speaker, I gripped the table, my knuckles turning white.

"Zane." Luca's voice sounded the same. He sounded the same as he did twelve years ago.

Chapter 19

Zane

When Salem went into the bathroom, I hadn't expected her demeanor to change, but when the door opened her emotionless eyes were back. She refused to look weak even in front of me. It shouldn't have bothered me as much, but it did. I thought I was finally breaking through the cement wall she held around herself. But it was like a step forward, three steps back, and she had another layer of cement around her. Before I could come up with anything to say to her, she stepped around me and raced downstairs.

Turning on my heel, I followed quickly. I didn't want her to step into the dining room with everyone there staring at her. Knowing Dimitri, he would think about killing her if I wasn't right there. Killian wouldn't give a shit; Tobias would probably beg her to sit next to him. Then Mila, it would be a toss-up. She wouldn't be jealous of her because Salem would most likely think of Dimitri as a bug she wanted to shoot. But she could also want to hide away. She often did that when someone new showed up.

As soon as my foot hit the bottom step, I could feel the tension before I saw Salem standing a few feet in front of me in the doorway.

Fuck.

"Sit next to me," Tobias begged.

"Kitten," I whispered into her ear when I stepped closer to her. She looked back at me as though she hadn't realized I was following her or that I was there. I wanted to sit next to her, but I also couldn't deny her sitting next to my favorite little person. Nodding my head towards Tobias, I let her know to sit by him.

"Uh, sure," she muttered, completely unsure of what to do. She slowly made her way there and slid into the seat. Sitting across from her, I sat down next to Killian.

"What's your favorite color?" Tobias asked. Salem brought her gaze from her empty plate to him, and Dimitri couldn't have been glaring any harder.

"I don't know if I have one, but if I did, I think it would be gray." She shrugged, her voice small. Her accent was completely gone, as though she was trying to hide it. Now that I heard her real voice, and not just a few words, I could tell she was trying to hide it. She was working harder at speaking.

"Hmm…" Tobias cocked his head to the side.

While she was busy talking to Tobias, I grabbed her plate and filled it with chicken, salad, and a few pieces of broccoli. I didn't know if she even ate this, but I knew she wasn't a vegetarian from her choice of Chinese.

"Gray's a great color. I think it's my new favorite." That boy always changed his mind about his favorite things. Just last week he asked me the same thing and when I said black, he laughed and said it was his new favorite. That Killian was red, and it was a weird color.

Salem turned back around and looked down at her plate. Something I couldn't quite read came across, maybe she was surprised or happy.

"It's Chicken Marsala, and the salad has vinaigrette, and yeah it just has broccoli, nothing special. But yeah, um, if you don't like it, I can cook something else," Mila stuttered looking between her own plate and Salem. "Or I can just order pizza, I'm sure that would be bett—"

"I'm sure it's great, thank you," Salem interrupted, giving her a smile. I watched as Salem grabbed her knife and fork and cut into the chicken. The moment she brought the piece of chicken to her mouth she let out a moan. My dick should not have gotten hard as fast as it did, yet now I was sitting here with my dick pressed against the zipper of my pants painfully. I felt like a fucking teenager with a hard-on ready to blow at any moment.

Salem must have realized she moaned out loud because her eyes snapped open and now, she was staring at me. I knew I looked like I was ready to attack her. She probably just didn't know it was sexual and not like I wanted to murder her.

"What's your name?" Tobias asked thankfully, breaking this tension. I was seconds away from throwing her over my shoulder and having my way with her again. I never wanted a woman more than her. Salem woke something inside me. She was able to have control over me in ways I didn't understand.

"Salem."

"That's it?" He scratched his nose. "No middle or last name? My name is Tobias Theodore Anderson Volkov. I have my mama and dad's last name." Tobias shrugged, grabbing his milk from the table. "I got Theodore from Uncle Zaney, that's his middle name. He delivered me when I came out of Mom's tummy." I couldn't look at Salem the moment he said Zaney. I had no problem with him calling me that, but now that she knew that I had to prepare myself for it coming back to bite me in the ass.

"Theodore is a beautiful middle name." That grin she gave him told me everything I needed to know. She was going to hold it against me.

"I think so too, do you have a middle name?" he asked again.

"I do. Hmm… tell me a good reason why I should tell you?" she whispered to him though she was loud enough everyone could hear.

"Dada doesn't trust you, Uncle Kill couldn't find anything about you on his 'puter, and Uncle Zaney is obsessed with you. I think he has a crush on you as well." Were men allowed to blush? Did it happen? Because if it did, I was blushing like a little girl who just found out their crush liked them back. Yet I had no idea if Salem actually felt anything towards me. I could feel my face getting redder by the moment, but the moment Salem looked at me I couldn't help but smirk at her.

"I think that's a very good answer, Salem Wren Gray." I hadn't realized I was sitting on the edge of my seat waiting for her to answer. Since we couldn't find anything about her, and she never carried around a fucking ID that I could find, I didn't realize I had no idea what her name was besides Salem. And now that I had her whole name, I never thought I could find a fucking name attractive.

Salem Wren Gray. It fits.

"What's your real name?" A low growl came from Dimitri. I had been so busy focusing on Salem and Tobias I forgot Dimitri. The guy looked like he was ready to murder her. He held a fucking butter knife, his knuckles turning white. I knew him better, that he wouldn't actually do anything unless she posed a threat with Tobias sitting right next to her. But I had no idea if Salem would do anything to push him to that point.

"Salem Wren Gray," she said not to break eye contact with him. Which no one besides the three of us sitting here had ever been able to do. It was a good thing in my book.

"Interesting because Killian can't find a single fucking thing about you, *Salem,*" he spat her name.

"Haven't you heard of a dead girl walking?" Salem shrugged. Fucking shrugged like it was no big deal she was sitting here with the most feared man in the Mafia. His jaw tightened, and if either Mila didn't diffuse him or I didn't stop Salem, they were bound to both attack each other.

"Why are you here?" He tried a different approach.

"I'm trying to enjoy a nice meal that your wife made, *what are you doing here?*" God, the balls on my fucking woman.

My woman.

It shouldn't have sounded so good, but it did. I enjoyed the feeling and the sound of her being mine. Even if it was just inside my head right now.

Looking over at Dimitri, the great thing about knowing someone for almost half your life, you learn what they tell you. And Dimitri was about to throw that knife at her, not giving a damn that his son sat next to her. Not knowing that she could easily move before it even got to her.

"Salem, don't provoke him," I warned. Salem glared at me, and something besides anger crossed her face. She looked hurt. Hurt that I was telling her to stop. But I had to. If she provoked him enough, he would attack. And I couldn't let him hurt her. I would actually hurt my best friend for her. Not kill him, but definitely hurt him.

"This is my house. I suggest you don't piss me off much more."

"Or what?"

This fucking woman. It was like she was trying to actually do harm. This was not the way this was supposed to go down. They were supposed to meet, and it was going to be awkward. But from the looks of it everything was about to end up bloody.

I couldn't control Salem. But I knew Mila could control Dimitri.

"You're playing a dangerous game," he growled. Mila looked over at me, and I gave her a nod toward Dimitri. I just hoped she understood what I meant.

"Dimitri, stop," Mila whispered, her hand reaching for his. Immediately his eyes softened as he looked down at his wife. "Let's just finish dinner, please."

Thank fuck.

Just as quickly as everything was turning to a damn fire, everyone went back to their meals. Tobias talked quietly with Mila and Dimitri while he just stared at Salem. Killian kept texting on his phone. And Salem just kept her gaze down at her plate, eating a small amount. The tension in the house could be cut with a fucking knife. It was suffocating. Shoveling food into my mouth, I finished before anyone and sat back in my chair. I was looking like a creep staring at Salem, but she was a mystery that refused to let anyone in.

After what seemed like forever Mila finally hurried Tobias upstairs for bed while the rest of us sat staring at each other awkwardly. I didn't know who was about to speak or if anyone was but the moment Dimitri's phone began to ring, I knew this was the moment everything was about to go to shit.

"It's Luca." He scowled at Salem. She looked like she was ready to claw his eyes out, but she had no idea Luca was really calling me. He knew it was me that saw Remo last. And it was her fault.

"Luca," Dimitri answered.

"Yes, he's here," Dimitri answered. Switching it to speaker, I heard my name being called by Luca. I couldn't stop myself from looking over at Salem who gripped the table so hard I'm surprised she hadn't split the fucking table in half.

It made me really wonder what they had done to her. They had to be the reason behind her scars. It was the only thing that made sense, and that had rage coursing through my body. Rage that I so desperately wanted to take out on anything near me. I wanted to break the table, and stab everyone sitting here. I don't know why the moment I heard his name everything seemed to have clicked. I knew he did something to her, and I would take a bullet in the head before I ever let him touch her again.

"Where's Remo, Zane?" A stern voice broke me from my thoughts. I had no idea who Luca was demanding of me like that. But I could see both Dimitri and Salem glaring at the phone. Dimitri most likely because he didn't like others trying to take authority over him or the two of them. Salem, I had no idea besides the fact I had a feeling she got hurt by him. But the way she was glaring at the phone said it was more than the rage she was feeling. She was feeling protective of me. It shouldn't have warmed my heart the way it did, but I felt the cold thing in my chest warming to her.

Dimitri shook his head at me, warning me not to speak.

"Why do you think we have anything to do with whatever is going on?" he asked. Thankfully, no matter if I did actually kill Remo or not. Dimitri would always have my back.

"I don't like to play games," Luca snapped, before saying something in Italian. Once again I was kicking myself for not learning anything besides Russian and wanting to kick the shit out of Dimitri for not knowing it either. How could the Pakhan not fucking know anything but Russian and English?

"Neither do I, so again I have no idea what you're talking about." Dimitri pretended to act bored, when in reality he was ready to murder me for getting them involved in this shit.

"We both know he was there when Remo was at that girl's house. But now I can't seem to get a hold of him. Zane, did you happen to forget that you left one of my men alive that was able to report everything back to me?" He switched to some Italian. I needed a god damn translator.

Looking over at Killian he was oddly quiet, so I paid him no attention. Salem was burning with anger and I was surprised she hadn't started screaming, stabbing, or done anything at this point.

"Just because he was there does not mean he knows where Remo is. And since I have you on the phone, I have to inform you that we've had no luck finding who this ghost person is." Dimitri just had to throw gasoline on this already shit show fire.

"Well that is very unfortunate." Luca once again began speaking Italian. I was getting ready to pull my phone out to get Google translate up. Everything happened too fast. One moment Salem was sitting there on the edge of her seat then the next she grabbed hold of the butter knife next to her plate and threw it at Dimitri. But instead of hitting him it was now lodged into someone none of us noticed behind him.

All hell broke loose. Four men ran in drawing their M16s taking aim at us. I don't even know when Salem had time to grab the amount of knives she had. But just as quickly as they took aim at us, Salem threw four knives, all of them embedding them in the throat. If we weren't in the middle of being attacked, I might have tossed her over my shoulder and fucked her.

"There are five more men outside, and three are heading upstairs," Salem said getting up from the table and running into the kitchen. I don't know why none of us moved, I think from the pure shock of a few things. Salem just basically saved Dimitri, and from the sounds of it she understood Italian.

"Killian, get the keys for the SUV," Dimitri ordered.

Getting to my feet, I ignored Dimitri if he even said anything to me. I found Salem in the kitchen turning the stove gas on.

"What the fuck are you doing?" I barked.

"We have two minutes to get out of this house," she said, not giving a single fuck that if anyone shot a fucking gun in here, we'd all go up. She was not thinking logically. Marching over to turn them back off, she sharply turned at me, glaring.

"If you touch those, I will tie your ass to the fucking chair and leave you." With that she grabbed a few kitchen knives, marching back out into the dining room.

Mila ran down the stairs, tears running down her face. Killian most likely was already inside the SUV ready to go. Dimitri turned the corner carrying Tobias in his arms.

"Why does it smell like gas?" he asked, heading towards the back door.

"Psycho bitch right here." I jerked my thumb towards Salem who was turning towards the basement door. "Where the fuck are you going?" I asked. You're supposed to leave the building and not go further into it when it's a minute away from blowing up.

Rushing towards the door I stopped turning towards Dimitri. "Get to the car, I'll grab her." Not leaving an option for him to say anything I fled down the stairs.

The moment my foot hit the concrete ground a solid punch to my jaw knocked me back. Blood filled my mouth, and I barely had time before another punch knocked into the side of my temple. I didn't have time to put my hands up to even try to defend myself until a bat began pounding into my body.

"Leave him alone!" Salem's raspy southern accent was thick as she screamed. I tried looking up to see who was attacking me, but the bat came down onto my head. Everything got fuzzy and my vision began having spots in it.

The last thing I heard before I blacked out was Salem screaming.

Chapter 20

Salem

"Well, that is very unfortunate." listening to Luca's voice was like swallowing glass. The anger flared through my body, my ribs ached, and my face burned with the sensation. "Una mossa di squadra." *A team go.* Luca's voice was quiet, as though he was trying to poorly hide the fact that he was ordering his men to do something. "Non lasciare superstiti." *Leave no survivors.* My eyes widened at the phone. I had a split decision to make. Get out now, and let them figure their way out. Or help and save them.

From the corner of my eye, I watched as a masked man stepped into the kitchen, his shotgun raised ready to fire. I made up my mind as I grabbed hold of the butter knife. Shooting to my feet I threw the knife towards Dimitri, barely missing him as it embedded in the man's neck.

Just as fast, four more men followed suit, M16s taking aim at everyone around. I ignored the gasp from the guys around the table. Reaching for all the knives on the table, I threw them just as fast.

"There are five more men outside, and three are heading upstairs," I muttered running from the dining table into the kitchen, dodging the dead bodies on the floor.

"Killian, get the keys for the SUV," Dimitri ordered from somewhere behind me.

Looking at the stove, I rushed over, and turning on all five knobs, I let the gas pollute the air.

"What the fuck are you doing?" Zane barked right behind me.

"We have two minutes to get out of this house." Turning over toward the island, my eyes landed on the only door I could assume was the basement. I could hear Zane doing something behind me and as soon as I turned my head, he was reaching for the stove.

"If you touch those, I will tie your ass to the fucking chair and leave you." Glaring at him, I grabbed hold of the kitchen butcher knives, marching back towards the dining room. I would *try* to save them. If he wanted to be stupid and not listen to me, that was on him.

I didn't listen as Dimitri and Zane spoke. I hurried towards the basement door, and I threw the door open. Running down the stairs, I glanced around.

"Why does it smell like gas?" he asked, heading towards the back door. At the bottom of the stairs, glancing to the right, I took in the large steel table holding a tray of medical equipment, a hatch door, and multiple black cabinets along the wall. To the left held shelves of all different kinds of knives and guns.

Rushing over, I shoved two daggers and a Glock with two clips into my pockets, checking that they were full. A smile spread across my face as I took notice of the hand grenade. Just as I reached for it, a pair of strong arms wrapped around mine, knocking me off balance. Rearing around so I was now facing the set of stairs, I couldn't believe I didn't realize Zane had followed me down.

"Leave him alone!" My voice broke, not used to yelling. My throat burned; it was as though those glass shards were stuck inside me again. They wrapped arms around my arms from behind, making me watch as four men began beating Zane. One with a bat, while the others kicked over and over again. Everything was happening too fast.

"ZANE!" I don't know why I tried screaming. My voice couldn't handle much more than a tram. Thrashing around, their arms didn't budge. My body felt weak from Remo's beatings just twenty-four hours ago. Instantly my body froze. These were Luca's men. They were ordered to hurt this family. It was like the pain in my body floated away. I was numb to the pain and all I knew was what I had to do.

Throwing my body weight down, they were forced to let go of my arms. I kicked both their knees out, causing them to fall down face first. Grabbing the kitchen knife from my back pocket, I quickly stabbed both of them in the back of the neck. The one who knocked Zane out came at me, bat raised. Throwing the knife into his stomach, he screamed in pain.

"You don't fucking touch him!" I screamed. Grabbing the knife handle, I drilled the knife over and over again, sinking into his stomach.

"DADA!" My voice broke. My throat hurt. I could barely scream anymore. I should have looked away, but I couldn't. They stabbed him over and over again. They didn't stop. Dante didn't stop. I'm

sure Dada was already dead. He had to be dead, but he continued stabbing him. There was so much blood, too much blood.

I couldn't help but gag. I wanted to throw up, but I couldn't. I had to be strong for Dada.

The crack of the knife caused me to stop stabbing. Pulling the blade out, I noticed the tip was missing. It had broken.

It was now embedded in his body.

"What the actual fuck?" someone said above me.

I cringed the moment I looked up at Dimitri standing there on the stairs. He was staring down at me standing above six dead bodies, and Zane who was knocked out. It was not a pretty sight. I could feel the blood dripping down my face. I was completely covered. I wanted the floor to swallow me whole. I didn't like the way he looked at me. Zane never looked at me like that.

Like I was a monster.

"Help me get Zane into the car. The house is going to go any minute," I said, ignoring the pang of guilt. I don't know why I felt guilty, but it was there. I didn't want to feel this way. "Now!" I snapped when he hadn't made a move.

Grabbing the rest of the supplies I saw Zane had down here I followed Dimitri as he carried Zane outside into the waiting car. I didn't waste time as I opened the passenger side and climbed into it. Killian stared at me like I'd grown another head. I didn't bother looking behind me where I knew Mila and Tobias sat. I couldn't face them right now, not when I knew what I was about to do.

"Killian, drive to the third safehouse," Dimitri demanded the moment he slid into the backseat with Mila. Killian threw the car into reverse, and taking a deep breath I pulled it from my pocket. The moment Killian backed up and threw the car into drive, I had the window open, pulled the pin, and threw the grenade as hard as I could at the house.

"DRIVE!" I yelled. Killian slammed the gas pedal, the car lurching forward.

Closing my eyes, I listened as the house exploded. I listened as Mila let out a small scream. I could imagine she was clutching Tobias to her chest, scared that I just blew their house up. It was either let them die or take care of Luca's men.

"What the fuck was that?" Dimitri snapped from the back seat. In the hour I've known Dimitri, I've grown to dislike him.

Quite a bit, too.

Ignoring him, I kept my eyes closed. That was until I felt the cold barrel of the gun pressed to the right side of my head. Dimitri was obviously trying to hide the fact he had a gun in his head from his son.

"Killian, will you please head to the warehouse on Fifth?"

"Don't listen to her. I am your boss," Dimitri spat out.

"I suggest you listen to what I say," I spoke in Russian. "Go to the warehouse and once we switch vehicles, I will explain everything." I refused to give any more than that. Dimitri would not intimidate me.

I watched the window, zoning everyone out.

I replayed the scene of them beating Zane, and the anger I felt while I watched. My body burned with hatred for Luca even more. It had been a while since I blacked out while fighting. But my body moved as my mind shut off. I could feel the warmth of blood. The blood was drying against my throat, flaking into my lap. My eyes dropped to my hands, that were coated in blood.

"Leave them alone!" Dada yelled somewhere behind us. Lee's eyes locked onto mine, like they were trying to tell me something. But I didn't understand. I don't know what he was trying to tell me. "Please, you can do whatever you want with us. Just leave the kids alone!" Mama begged. I could hear the tears in her voice. The pain she felt. I could hear it all. I know I was young. I was a child. But I could hear the dragging of something behind me.

"We're here," Killian said from beside me. Glancing up, I hadn't even realized we pulled up to the warehouse. Smirking to myself, I couldn't help but want to laugh in Dimitri's face for the simple fact that Killian listened to me instead of his boss.

Yanking the door open, I slammed it shut, making my way to Dimitri's warehouse. I ignored the shooting pain in my ribs as I flicked the lights on. This warehouse I bought five years ago, stocking it full of guns, daggers, explosives, and three different vehicles. An oversized SUV, a basic car, and a motorcycle. Grabbing the keys for the oversized SUV, I yanked the trunk open. Taking the duffle bag, I began loading up several weapons.

"Start talking," Dimitri demanded once I finished loading up as much as I could. Stopping directly in front of him, I glared back up at him. I refused to back down from men like this. I promised myself back then that I wouldn't. Dimitri was just like the others. He may not hurt the innocent like Luca, but he was still a part of that world.

"Luca."

"Yeah, what about him?"

"Are you working with him?"

"What's it matter to you?"

God this was infuriating. I should've known he was just going to be difficult.

Rolling my eyes I opened my mouth to say something until he cut me off.

"Don't fucking roll your eyes. I'm not Zane who will take it from you. I will not give a second thought to killing you right here. You can stay here, but we're le—" He never finished. Stabbing the needle into his chest, his eyes widened, his mouth stayed half opened. "What did you just stab me with?" he slurred. Instead of answering him, I waited until his eyes became glossy and finally he dropped.

The moment his body hit the ground, Killian flew from the car and stalked towards me. I wasn't in the mood to fight him, but I guess if I had to get everyone out of here, that's what I was going to have to do.

"Mind setting him in the back seat of the Tahoe?" I pointed towards it with my thumb. I didn't wait for him to answer. Going to the car, I opened the back door to Mila.

"He's fine. Just gave him something to get him to shut up," I muttered motioning for her and Tobias to get out. Mila gave me a small smile before climbing out.

"Yeah, he tends to do that when things don't go his way."

"You trust me though, right?" I had to ask. I didn't really care for Dimitri or Killian much. I wasn't sure what I felt towards Zane, but Mila and Tobias reminded me too much of myself and my family.

"Of course," she said, bending to pick Tobias up. Though for a four-year-old, he was quite tall, reaching her waist. "I just have to ask, are we going somewhere safe?" she muttered as we walked towards the warehouse door.

"Yes, this place is safe. It's just somewhere we can go to lay low, so both Zane and I can heal." What I didn't mention was the fact that Luca was playing Dimitri, and I had to figure out if I could trust Dimitri or not.

"I trust you." Mila smiled. I waited while she got into the back with Tobias, and Killian once again started stalking towards me.

"I really don't want to knock you out or fight you as well, so please just save it. Dimitri will live. I just gave him something to knock him out for the next maybe twelve hours. Maybe twenty-four hours. Can't be too sure with the dosage. I was trying to do the math, and yeah. Anyway, mind grabbing Zane and putting him in the trunk and then we can hit the road?" I shrugged.

Killian, for the first time, actually glared at me like I kicked his puppy. This was completely different from the man who smiled at me when I'd walked downstairs a few hours ago.

"I want to ask two questions before I do anything for you."

Rolling my eyes, I said, "Sure." I wasn't sure if I would actually answer him, depending on what he asked me.

"How many languages do you speak?" I almost laughed, forgetting I spoke Russian in front of them.

"Six fluent, but I can get by with eight."

"Damn, we need to catch up," he muttered to himself. But it was true. From what I gathered, they spoke two languages.

"Why can't I find anything on you?"

Wow. That was a loaded question. I could be honest with him and lay it all out for him, or I could give him the short version. Or even give him the shortest version, but I had no idea if Aziza wanted anyone to know that she was the best hacker in the world. She hid

167

the truth, so I doubted she wanted me to say anything. So I gave the shortest answer without giving her away.

"I made myself disappear from the face of the earth." Giving him one arm shrug, I turned towards the Tahoe. "I suggest grabbing him fast or I'll leave both your asses here." I wouldn't, but I was done talking or feeling.

I was just ready to get out of the city.

Chapter 21

Zane

There were a few things that felt odd the moment I felt myself gain consciousness.

The softness of the pillow pressed against my cheek, drool pooling at the corner of my mouth. The large blanket covering my body matched the most comfortable bed I'd ever laid on.

Shifting slightly, my ribs pinched in pain causing me to grit my teeth. I couldn't take in a full breath, but relaxing my body, it became easier slowly.

Lifting an eyelid, I immediately shut it when the warm sun shot directly in my face.

Fuck, that shit was bright.

Lifting my head slightly, I reopened my eyes and let them adjust to my surroundings. Which, from the looks of it, was no place I had ever been.

Where the fuck was I?

Scanning the room as much as I could, I sat in the large bed sitting against the far wall. Two side tables that were brown and worn with lamps on each. On the left one sat a glass of water with a small bottle of ibuprofen. The wall across from the front of the bed had two doors on either side, one wide open with clothes trailing out messily. The dresser laid out multiple clothes with drawers pulled halfway out. The right wall had a bay window, a bench seat with a few pillows, and the left wall had a single closed door.

Tossing the blanket to the side, my body protested from the sudden movements. But my bladder screamed at me more. Shoving through the pain I shifted to the bathroom, flicking the light on. My eyes squeezed shut at the bright overhead light. *Why does someone need such a bright light?*

Shaking my head, my eyes finally adjusted. Walking to the toilet, I relieved myself, hissing in pain as the tip of my dick burned. Small amounts of blood dripped into the toilet bowl.

What the fuck?

Scanning the bathroom, I saw a double sink, white countertops, brown cabinets, and two single mirrors above the sinks. To the right of the toilet was a large walk-in shower, with a waterfall shower spray, and a glass shower wall with two frosted windows inside the shower. There was a black honeycomb tiled floor, with a brown ceiling, and white walls. Against the wall right next to me was an oversized clawfoot tub.

Deciding to shower, I turned the water on, waiting for it to warm up. Stripping off my clothes, my eyes snapped to the bruises littering my midsection. No wonder my ribs ached; my whole stomach and ribs were black and blue. My arms were a little better, but still bruised. I took in the bruises covering my entire face. I looked like shit. The cuts and bruises looked like someone used my whole body and face as a fucking punching bag. My lip was split open pretty badly, and my nose was nearly broken.

Stepping into the shower, the warm water soothed my beaten body a little bit.
Washing my severely bruised body, I tried my best to wash my hair but ended up giving up when I could barely lift my arms up. I could get Mila to was—

Salem.

I couldn't believe I completely forgot what happened. The dinner. Dimitri wanted to murder her on the spot. Salem killed those men in the dining room. Running downstairs… I jumped.

"Leave him alone!" Her raspy voice broke when she screamed. As though it pained her to see me like that. I can't believe I forgot. I woke up in a strange room and didn't think twice about it.
Stepping out of the shower, I wrapped the towel around my hips before I realized I had no clean clothes, and I didn't even know where the fuck I was. Opening the cabinet, I found a good amount of medical supplies, gloves, and urological equipment, used for catheters. Gauze, medical tape, strips, even wound cream, along with bandages for wrapping ribs and such. Opening the other side, there were even more medical supplies, including needles and syringes. On the other side held a small basket of toothpaste, toothbrushes, and some other bath toiletries.
Thank god. Grabbing the toothpaste and brush, I cleaned my teeth more forcefully than needed. But my damn mouth was disgusting. Once I felt my mouth was clean enough, I set the brush down. Opening the middle drawers, I couldn't stop myself from snooping. I found a hairbrush, hair ties, and a few headbands. I was about to

close it when, from the corner of my eye, I noticed the pill bottle. Picking it up, it read *Salem Gray, March 30, 2001.*

Salem was young, a lot younger than I thought. I winced, thinking about the fact that I'm eleven years older than her. It's not a huge age gap, but eleven years... Fuck.

Glancing down at the clothes on the floor, I don't remember wearing sweatpants and a T-shirt. Someone must have put them on me at some point. Taking more time than I cared to admit, I finally got the pants on. I could barely lift my arm, but I managed to get the shirt on after a few tries, finally letting out a breath I was holding. I can't remember the last time I was this sore or let someone get the upper hand on me.

Finally making my way to the door, I opened it carefully, peering outside. Turning left since it was the only way to go, I followed the hallway down. The walls were off white, with a few pictures hanging of random art. Two more doors on the left-hand side, but both were closed. Rounding the corner, I took the set of stairs.

Groaning as I took them down, the bottom of the steps led me to the living room. A large black sectional couch sat in the middle with two similar recliners on either side. A flat screen TV was mounted in the middle of the wall, along with a few art pieces.

Low voices sounded to the left through a doorway. Inching closer, I could make out Mila's and Tobias's voices.

Stepping into the kitchen, I found Mila and Dimitri sitting at the blue gray island. Dimitri sipped on his coffee while Mila began cutting a piece of a pancake up.
Mila looked up as I stepped inside. "Oh, Zane, you're finally awake!" she squealed a little too loud and high pitched.

Groaning, I slowly made my way over to the kitchen table on the left side. There was no way I'd be able to get up on one of the barstools.

"Want me to get you some coffee?" she asked putting a plate of bread in front of me.

"Uh, please," I mumbled, looking down at whatever she put in front of me. It looked weird.

"It's banana bread. Salem and Tobias made it yesterday," Mila again cheerfully said, setting
a steaming cup of coffee in front of me. "Be careful, it's hot." I rolled my eyes—like I couldn't see the steam from the cup.

"I'm confused," I blurted out. What was I confused about? That would be everything.

"Where are we?" I asked, pausing to take a sip of coffee and immediately hissing. Yes, it was hot, but the goddamn sugar. "Mila," I growled out.

"Nope, no sugar promise," she said, holding her hands up in surrender. "Salem just loves anything sweet, even more than me."

"Uh, what?" My eyes flickered between them. Scanning the room, the kitchen was basic, farmhouse style. Tall ceiling, large kitchen island in the middle, dining table to the side, back door on the far wall.

"This would be Salem's house," Mila spoke with uncertainty.

"Salem's house?"

"Yes, her house," Dimitri finally muttered.

"And where is Salem, cause the last thing I remember is her and you about to rip each other's throats out," I said, cocking a very bruised eyebrow at him.

"What's the last thing you remember?" he asks, bringing his coffee to his mouth. Looking at my own cup, I took another drink, trying my best to ignore the sugary taste.

"Uh, she threw the knife at some guy behind you and then the basement where I was attacked and then I heard her screaming." I hated to admit I heard her screaming and then I was knocked out. I was the enforcer for Dimitri, and I was so easily knocked on my ass.

I don't know how long it was quiet until finally Dimitri sighed. "She killed the men that were attacking you. She was screaming about him touching you and whatnot. I carried you out and then she fucking blew my damn house up." He growled the last few words out with so much venom.

"Like, blew it up, or…?" I asked. It was stupid, and the moment he swung his glare at me instead of the table, I wished I would've kept my mouth shut.

"What do you think? She's a fucking psycho."

"She saved us!" Mila snapped. Looking over at her she had one of the most pissed off expressions I'd seen on her before.

"Yes, Moy Tevtok," Dimitri looked at his wife with love that I found myself wanting to give Salem.

"What happened after she blew the house up?" I asked, breaking the silence of them just staring at each other.

"We went to some warehouse she has, and then I don't fucking know," Dimitri snapped.

"They've had a rough friendship." Mila chuckled. "She knocked him out with some type of drug."

Widening my eyes I couldn't help but look over at him. Again, he was just glaring down at his cup like it was the thing that knocked him out.

"Yeah, he was being his normal self, and she was not having it, so she stabbed him with some drug and Killian had to put him into the backseat. And before you ask, Killian is currently sleeping somewhere upstairs. Anyway, she even threatened him, but Killian being himself, just shoved you guys into the car and she drove us here." Mila took a deep breath before she started up again. "That was four days ago. Dimitri woke up twenty-four hours after the fact. She gave you some medicine to keep you under because of the amount of damage you had to your head. She's really smart."

Nodding my head to all this information, I tried to process it all. The fact that I had been asleep for four days coupled with the fact that she drugged the leader of the Russian Mafia and she was still breathing said a lot.

"Where is s—" I never got to finish before the back door swung open and Tobias ran into Salem, following behind him. Her eyes were focused on Tobias, so she hadn't noticed me yet. She took my breath away. She looked so different from the way she did four days ago. The bruises on her face were healing nicely, but here she stood in a thin flannel, overalls that were covered in dirt, and her hair was tied into two long braids on each side.

"Uncle Zaney!" Tobias screamed.

Snapping my gaze down I prepared for him launching himself into my arms. It almost hurt my heart when he just patted me on the arm instead. "Are you feeling better?" he whispered.

"I'm feeling much better, little man." I gave him my best smile.

"Tobias, come on, let's go get cleaned up," Mila said, both of them disappearing. I couldn't force myself to look up. It felt too weird sitting here. The uneasiness of being in her space made me feel like

I was suffocating. Even with her unflinching gaze on me, I didn't like this.

"Salem." Dimitri grunted. Looking over at him, he continued staring at her like he couldn't wait to stab her when she least expected it. Salem just stood there, not saying anything, not doing anything. The tension in this room was truly becoming awkward, and I didn't do anything awkward.

"Well." Standing up Dimitri glared—no, worse than that. Whatever expression this was, he literally was barely holding back from wanting to murder Salem on the spot. "Once he's healed enough, we'll be leaving." He left no room for her to speak before he was up and stalking off. I could wonder what crawled up his ass and died, but from the looks of it, it was Salem.

Salem crawled up his ass.

Once Dimitri was gone, she finally turned her attention towards me. "You showered." That southern accent I didn't realize I enjoyed hearing so much.

"I tried to," I finally said. I watched her closely as she walked around the island and stood next to me at the dining table. With her standing this close I could smell her vanilla, but now she also smelled like the outside; sweat. I could see a light dusting of freckles across her nose and cheeks. Not as many as Mila, but I could count how many she had. Her lips oddly looked even fuller, and there was something about the way her hair laid in two braids. Her hair was frizzy, but she looked so fucking cute. She had a small smudge of dirt on her forehead that appeared like she was trying to wipe it off but just smeared it instead.

"Zane, did you hear me, or do you have more brain damage than I thought?" she smirked.

Smiling up at her, I couldn't find myself caring that I hadn't been listening to her. Instead, I was more interested in looking at her and wanting to map out the freckles on her face.

"Well, I'm going to shower. When I'm done, we can talk." She laughed. Stepping away from me, I watched as she headed towards the stairs.

Again, I had a few options. One, I could stay here and try and eat this weird looking banana bread. Honestly, who puts bananas in bread? I could sip on the sugar-laced cold coffee.
Or I could head back upstairs and shower with her even though my body hurt and ached.
I don't even know why I acted like this was a huge decision. As fast as I could, I made my way back up the stairs and down the hallway to the last room on the right.
Closing the door behind me, I made my way to the bathroom. The moment I opened the door, I was hit with steam.

I felt like a teenage boy about to see my first girl naked. I don't even know what changed, but she was different. She had this different type of energy about her that I couldn't quite understand.

Shredding my clothes once again, I opened the glass shower door. Salem was standing underneath the water, her head down. With her back to me, I could see all the different white scars, some raised and some with burn marks. Her skin was pale, a few freckles scattered across her shoulders down her arms.

"Are you going to stare all day or what?" she asked, breaking the silence. I wanted her to talk about anything just so I could hear her voice.

Stepping further into the shower with her, I couldn't help but smile. She was so tiny and fragile.

"You and Dimitri seem to be friends," I muttered, taking another step towards her.

"I think we tolerate each other." A small laugh left her mouth. I wanted to kiss and devour her. "But is that what you really want to talk about?" she said, cocking her head to the side, arching a brow.

"Are you going to tell me what happened?" I asked. Salem frowned up at me. I don't know what came across her face, or what she was thinking, but it was something unsettling. She was upset, and she didn't hide it from me. Not like she normally did.

Shaking her head, she motioned for me to step forward. Doing so, I got my hair wet and hissed when the warm water hit my split lip. Stepping back, I reopened my eyes to find Salem staring hard at me. Worry swarmed around her eyes. It warmed my heart that she was worried about me, but it also felt odd. No one truly worried about me.

"Come here." Salem stepped onto a bench in the shower. Now she was an inch or two taller than me.

Reaching over, she grabbed the shampoo bottle and poured a small amount into her hand. "Turn."

Doing as she asked, her hands began gently massaging the shampoo into my hair. The back right side of my head was tender, but she barely touched me as she washed my hair.
I don't know how long she continued to work the shampoo into my hair until her voice met my ears. "I lost control."

"When?"

I didn't think she was going to touch until finally she said, "When he knocked you out. I lost control. I didn't think I had it in me until I saw him hit you on the head and I saw your body fall." She stopped washing my hair. "Step under the water." Doing as she said, I rinsed my hair out.

Stepping back I waited until she began working conditioner into my hair.

"I didn't even check to make sure you were alive or not. I just shoved you into the trunk. I drugged your boss and then drove everyone here." I don't know if she was saying this for me, or if it was for herself.

"Where is it?" I asked.

She said nothing, still working the conditioner into my hair. I knew it didn't take that long; she was evading my question.

"Salem," I snapped.

"North Carolina, it took ten hours."

"North... Carolina?" My voice was heavy with irritation. I don't know why I was irritated we were here, but fuck.

"Salem? Did you say ten hours?"

It took too long for her to respond.

"Salem." I grunted.

"Under the water again," was all she said. Should I have said something else to her? Yes. Did I? No. I stepped under the water and once again rinsed my hair out. Salem said nothing as she washed my body, careful of every inch of me.

When I was done, Salem turned the water off and grabbed a towel. Wrapping it around her body, she grabbed another one before drying my hair and began drying my body. I don't know what I deserved to have her take care of me like this, but fuck, I needed to step my game up.

Once we were both dried off, I followed her back into her bedroom where she grabbed a large shirt and tugged it over her head. She dragged the curtains over the windows that I hadn't even realized were there. Crawling into bed she patted the spot next to her.

179

Dropping the towel I crawled in behind her and couldn't stop myself from pulling her body up against my chest. She fit and felt right with her lying against me, even if it was her back.

"I don't understand why I feel like this," she mumbled.

"I don't either, but I'm not going to fight it," I whispered into her hair. Even though I wasn't tired, I felt my eyelids closing.

"When you were lying there, I got really scared. I think it's the first time I got that scared in such a long time. I lost control when I saw you fall. It was like something took over my body. I didn't like seeing your hurt."

"When they hurt you, I felt the same way. I hated seeing them attack you. I almost felt useless," I admitted. I didn't want her to think of me as some softy, because I had no idea what that even meant. But for her I would learn. "Where are we?"

She left out a little chuckle before pushing her ass into my groin. I couldn't help the swell of my cock, pressing it further into her ass.

"You're hurt, stop grinding into me. And to answer your question, like I said North Carolina, but it's my house."

"I like being in your space," I muttered. I could blame the drowsiness, but it wasn't.
"When we arrived, Killian went and got y'all some clothes. They're in the dresser."

"I like lying here naked with you."

"Figured you would. Mila and Tobias spent a lot of time with me, helping me around the house. Tobias is my little shadow; he wants to learn to ride a horse. I think I need to do more convincing with Dimitri. He hates me."

"He doesn't hate you." *I think.*

"Oh he really does. When he woke up, I'm pretty sure he was about to kill me until I told him about Luca."

"What about him?" Her body immediately went stiff. I wanted to push and demand she tell me how she knew him, but I doubted she would tell me. Salem liked hiding her secrets. I may not know much about her, but the thing I did know for sure was that she liked hiding in the shadows. She liked her secrets.

"There are things you don't know about me, and I'm not sure I'm ready to tell you. Or if I'll ever be ready to tell you," she finally admitted. I should've known it was coming.

"Are you going to show me around the farm?" I asked. I truly couldn't believe I was talking about a farm. Growing up in the city of New York and then moving to Moscow, I never thought I would end up on a farm, yet here I was.

"Maybe when you're feeling better. Your head got hit pretty hard, and I know you broke a few ribs in there."

"Are you a doctor now?" I tried to poke fun, but instead her body stiffened again. "I'm sorry," I murmured into her hair, tugging her body closer against mine. Though I had no idea how that was even possible.

"You should get some sleep."

"I'm not tired, but I know something else that might wear me down." I moved my hips against her backside.

"Zane, you're hurt." Her weak plea trailed off as I ground against her again, swallowing the pain. It didn't matter. I would welcome any pain when it came to her.

"I just need to feel you," I tried to convince her. Rolling onto my back I brought her with me, slipping her around until she was straddling me. She looked down at me, her hair falling around her face. I almost didn't want to welcome that warm feeling in my chest. But for her, I would. I masked the pain coursing through my body. But just to have Salem on top of me was well worth it.

"Don't move." She sighed, losing the fight right in front of my eyes. Leaning up, she grabbed hold of the base of my cock. Positioning herself over me, my breath caught as she rubbed my tip along the lips of her pussy. She was dripping wet.

I couldn't stop the groan escaping my mouth as she slowly lowered herself down. Her pussy swallowed my shaft. Halfway down, she smirked before pressing her lips to my nose. I don't know why she did it, or why I felt my heart speed up at the intimate act.

Only when I thought I could finally accept air into my lungs, did she continue kissing her way to my neck. Sucking below my ear, dragging her tongue over me. I couldn't stop my hands reaching towards her hips to slam her down. It felt too good. She felt too good. She was trying to tease me.

The moment I raised my hands to her hips she shot all the way off, taking me by surprise. "I said. Do. Not. Move." Her stern voice shouldn't have turned me on this much but fuck if I didn't want to roll us over and slam myself into her. To lose myself in her.

"I won't move again." My voice was weak, pleading for her to give me what I needed.

"I'll stop if you do." Gripping my cock once more, she painfully and even slower than before lowered herself down onto me. Not stopping until her ass hit my thighs, her pussy swallowing me whole.

She felt like heaven, felt like home, and I never wanted to leave. I fought against myself to not grab her again. It took everything in me not to fight her and take what I wanted.

What I needed.

Rotating her hips, I reached up towards the headboard. I had to hold onto something because if I didn't, I would take control. Of course, Salem knew that because her little smirk told me so. I hoped she could see the desire, the need to thrust up into her.

My body screamed in protest at my reaching for the headboard. But having Salem's body on me like this, I would gladly feel this pain.

"Good boy," she moaned.

A growl rumbled through my chest, watching as she licked her bottom lip. She bounced on my dick and rotated her hips. I couldn't even comprehend that she just called me a good boy but fuck yes. I would be the best boy for her if she continued with this.

I wasn't going to last long, especially the moment she leaned back and threw her shirt off. I watched as her tits bounced every time she moved. I could feel her pussy clenching me.

"Zane, oh—oh fuck." She gasped. Losing all control, she came, causing my own release. Salem slumped forward against my chest; my arms wrapped around her back holding her against me. I didn't want to let her go.

I don't know how long we both laid there. I didn't fall asleep until I felt Salem relax and her breathing changed. I finally let myself fall asleep.

Chapter 22

Salem

I waited until I knew Zane was asleep before I peeled myself away from his chest, trying my hardest not to move around too much and wake him. It took longer and was much harder than I cared to admit. I knew he wouldn't lay and rest like his body needed. It was the only reason I kept his body under for so long. Thankfully, he finally relaxed after thinking I was asleep.

Finally untangling myself from Zane, I threw on a pair of leggings and one of my turtlenecks. Shutting the door behind me, I rested my forehead against the door.

"Sey," Tobias squealed from down the hall. Turning around, I found him running towards me with Mila hot on his tail.

"Shhh." I smiled, kneeling down so I could pick him up. "Uncle Zaney is resting," I whispered. Standing up I started walking towards Mila who was leaning up against the wall.

"Is he asleep?" she asked as we started downstairs.

"Yeah, finally. Is he always like that?"

"Unfortunately, yeah, they're all like that, honestly."

Nodding my head we stepped into the kitchen where I sat Tobias down on the island.

"Where are the other two?"

"I think Dimitri is using your punching bag outside and Killian I believe is still sleeping."

"I wanna watch a movie." Tobias looked between me and his mother. "Can we?"

"I want to watch a movie," Mila corrected.

"Mama."

"Mama, do you think the baby boy will like me?" I asked as she ran her fingers through my black curls.

"Salem, he's going to love you, he's going to love all of you," Mama reassured me. "Just like I love all of you," she said, poking my nose.

"I think he'll like me the most. I like both girl and boy things. And since he's a boy, he'll like me the most," I declared.

Except I had no idea if he would like me the most.

"Salem?" Mila was staring at me. Watching me with saddened eyes, ones I didn't want focused on me. "Are you okay?"

I didn't think, nodding my head. I hated when flashbacks reminded me of the past. I hated even more when it happened in front of others.

Mila tried smiling at me, giving me a knowing smile. "How about after lunch?" she offered Tobias. "Go wash up while I make something."

Helping Tobias down, he ran off to the bathroom. Mila turned towards the fridge and began looking around.

"Mila?"

"Hmmm."

"Do they know about me?" I asked. I didn't want anyone knowing Mila and I knew each other. It brought questions, which I would have to answer. I couldn't have that, not when I was trying to finish this.

"I haven't said anything."

Nodding my head, I turned around and looked out the kitchen window. Not even with my best friend. Aziza always joked about how I never knew what to say, and it was true. I didn't socialize well. I didn't know how to make small talk.

I just knew the moment I heard his voice on the phone. Speaking Italian. His men were ordered to attack Dimitri's house. The protectiveness washed over me. I disliked Dimitri and Killian and his fucking smile. Zane was someone I found myself relating to. But then Mila and Tobias were upstairs. Even if my brain told me to leave them, my body wouldn't let me. I had to protect them at all costs.

"Is there a reason you don't want them to know?" Mila asked, breaking me from my thoughts. Turning around I watched as she began making a sandwich for Tobias.

"Not really. I mean, I don't know. There are things about my past that no one needs to know. Not about me being there. I don't need them knowing any of it. They'll ask questions that I don't want to be asked, and things I don't want to answer."

"You know they won't look at you any different, right?"

Shrugging my shoulders I leaned against the kitchen sink. "Doesn't matter either way. I just don't need questions being asked." I also no longer wanted to talk to her about this anymore. Saved by the bell, Tobias ran back into the kitchen, jumping onto one of the bar stools.

"So after lunch we watch movies?" he asked, shoving a bite of sandwich into his mouth.

"Tobias, don't talk with your mouth full!" Mila sighed.

At the same time I asked, "What movie?"

"*Mulan.*" *Mulan.* I couldn't help but give him a little smile. He had gotten into the bin of old VHS tapes that was in the closet. He had pulled them out and told us how he hadn't seen that one.

"Sure, buddy, finish your lunch and I'll get the movie ready."

"You gots it." He giggled, turning his attention to his mom. I slipped out of the kitchen and made my way into the living room.
I didn't want to think about them, but I also couldn't stop myself. The moment I bent down to collect the movie everything came back.

"Lee, do you think things will change when Toby gets here?" I asked curled up next to him on the couch. I didn't want things to change. I liked the way everything was. I liked Lee being my older brother; he always protected me. Protected me from Emmy being mean to me and from the bullies in my dance class. He always protected me.

"Of course, things are going to change." He laughed like it was no big deal. It was a big deal for me. I just didn't tell them. I wanted a younger brother. I hated being the baby. I wanted to look after someone. I wanted to be like Lee; he kept me safe.

I must have been quiet for too long because the movie was paused, and Lee turned his full attention towards me. "Hey, don't worry your little head about it. Mom and Dad will still love you all the same, and I will still be your big brother." It was like he was reading my mind. "Plus, Mom let you name this one. You know what I wanted to name you?"

"What?" I jumped up excitedly. I had no idea Lee wanted to name me.

"Megatron." He laughed, causing me to go into a fit of my own giggles.

"But I'm a girl!

"Yes, and a very cool girl, so don't worry your little brain about it. You'll always be in this family, and you'll always be a pain in the ass."

"LEE ANDREW GRAY!" Mom yelled from the kitchen. "No cussing.'"

Lee looked down at me smirking. "Like Mom isn't a pain in the ass to us all." He lunged for me, tickling my stomach.

Little did I know that would be the last time Lee cussed in front of me, and the last time I felt safe.

"Salem?" someone behind me said. Looking over my shoulder Mila stood there with Tobias next to her. While Tobias appeared happy and ready to jump in excitement, Mila was worried. "Are you okay?"

"Yeah, sorry. I just zoned out there." I tried to sound convincing. I had no idea if I truly sounded that way. "What's up?"

"I asked if you would mind if I showered."

"Oh no, no, uh, go ahead. We're just going to watch this movie." I smiled stepping towards the large sectional couch.

"Thank you," she mumbled. "Tobias, Mommy's going to shower. Listen to whatever Salem says."

"Gots you, Mama." I tried not to flinch at that word. Instead, I watched as he lunged onto the couch next to me.

Mila nodded her head and turned on her heel, leaving both of us sitting there on the couch. Wasting no time, I turned the movie on and brought the throw blanket to cover us up.
As much as I wanted to get lost in the movie, I found myself unable to fully focus on it at all. Instead, my mind went to everything else. Zane, who I met four years ago, but he had no idea. He had no clue that I was the one who knocked him out in that alleyway when he was following me. The longer I kept it a secret the more I felt my heart ache. I didn't want to have feelings for him, because instead of staying in Boston and ending this torment, I was hiding out at home while he healed. I could handle the scars on my body from Remo and his little team he had. I wanted him to think he had easily beaten me down, until Zane showed up. The moment he appeared in my apartment doorway, the anger seeping through him gave me chills. No one had ever gotten that angry seeing me in that much pain. It ignited my heart and caused me to feel things for someone other than my family that I didn't know what to do with.

189

I didn't realize I was so wrapped up in my head when I felt the side of the couch dip down next to me. I knew who it was without having to look over, his body fitting closely next to me. I found myself curling up, wanting to be closer and feel his warmth.

"You left."

Peering up at him from my eyelashes, his face was so close to mine I could see the scar across his nose and the faint freckles that almost seemed to match my own. His eyes that bored into mine were so gorgeous that I couldn't look away.

"Salem," he warned. "Why did you leave?"

"You needed to rest." It was such a weak excuse, and he knew that, his eyebrow raising told me so.

"I've been resting for four days; I think I'm good on the whole resting shit," he barked back at me causing me to flinch. I had no idea what caused me to flinch, but the look on his face told me everything. He was honestly pissed I left him alone upstairs again. But the moment I flinched, he softened, barely. But it was there.

"Give me three more days of rest." It wasn't a question. I would knock him out again if I had to.

"One."

"No."

If it was even possible, he brought his face closer to mine, our noses touching. "One," he demanded.

"I said no." I glared back.

I could see him fighting with himself, wanting to fight me. But I would win. I had control over him even if he didn't like it.

190

"Two?"

"I can work with two." I smiled.

"Two days. I need to start training again," he muttered to himself.

Looking away from him I looked back at the movie. I watched as Mulan shot the fireworks into the mountains. I waited until Zane's focus was elsewhere until I smiled. "Two days starting tomorrow."

He whipped his head towards me, trying his best to hide the pain that shot through him.

"No discussion, no arguing, none." I didn't dare look at him. I had no idea if he had power over me to change my mind yet. And I didn't want this to be the thing that I changed my mind about.

"One condition."

"Depends." I sighed.

"What fucking movie is this?" he grunted.

I couldn't help the laugh that came from my lips. I covered my mouth with my hands, trying my best not to wake Tobias who was lying to my right. But the fact that Zane was asking me about a Disney movie had me blushing.

"*Mulan.*"

"Who is Mulan?"

"Oh, buddy, it's a good thing you have two days of full rest." I giggled.

"Why?"

"We're about to binge watch all the Disney princess movies." I kissed his chest before grabbing the remote and restarting it.

"Fuck," Zane muttered to himself. I couldn't help the butterflies swarming around threatening to break out. But for the first time I relaxed into him, finding myself in an actual calming state.

Chapter 23

Zane

After we watched *Mulan*, Salem had me sit on the couch while she and Tobias made dinner. Killian had woken at some point, barely noticing as I sat there. Besides giving me a slight nod, he hurried into the kitchen before he and Dimitri trained. I wanted to follow them outside, where apparently Salem had some sick set up, half inside a barn that led outside. But Dimitri refused and actually took her side about making me rest.

My first official day of resting, I tried staying in bed per Salem's request. But when she walked out of the bathroom wearing nothing besides a towel, I tried convincing her to ride me like she had last night. But nothing I did made her budge. Even when I told her she could ride my face, that I didn't care about my cock. I wanted her taste on my tongue. She refused.
I followed her around the house like a lovesick puppy, but she never let me go outside. I had to wait around while she finished whatever

she did outside. I knew I had to be annoying, but in a way, I actually enjoyed getting to know more about her. I knew all the basic things: her full name, favorite color, even her favorite food. Which happened to be French fries, though much to my complaint it was not actual food. I thought she was about to stab me when I told her she had the worst taste in food. Her side comment had been that she had bad taste in men. That only caused us to argue, and she ended up disappearing on me for the rest of the day.

Now it was day two, and I was clawing at myself in boredom. Which is how I found myself poking around Salem's room while she did whatever she did on the farm. I found nothing of value in her nightstands, and she had nothing under her bed. I even checked under the mattress, but I still found nothing.

Making my way into her closet, I wanted to call it a walk-in. But with the amount of clothes on the floor, I rolled my eyes as I flipped the switch. The girl had too many fucking clothes, ranging from weird looking overalls, to jeans that looked too small for her. They probably hugged her ass. My cock tented in my sweatpants at the thought of her in them. Hugging her ass. Groaning, I readjusted myself, and I knelt down. Tossing her millions of boots to the side, I noticed the small wooden box underneath them.

Pulling it out I brushed the dust off before opening the lid. On top of everything lay a single photo. Looking closely I picked Salem out right away. She was younger, much younger. Probably around eight or nine. Her black hair hung long, down to her waist, and her blue eyes somehow looked even more blue than they were now. She wore a pair of overalls with a long-sleeved shirt underneath it. But that's not what caught my eye. It was her smile. I've seen her smile before, but this smile... It was her whole face. Her eyes were bright, and her two bottom teeth were missing. But she didn't care. To her left was a man, towering over her. He had the same black hair, but not as dark. He looked around twenty maybe. Next to him was another older version of Salem, but her hair was chopped short to her shoulders and a much lighter color of black, maybe even a dark brown. Her eyes weren't blue but were brown. Besides that they looked very similar. Moving back over, on the left side of Salem was an older woman who stood about the height she was now. She had light brown hair and bright blue eyes just like Salem. Then on the end was an older man with black hair like Salem, the darkest of the bunch, brown eyes, and a smile that was just like Salem's.

This had to be her family.

It just had to be.

But where were they? Why were there no family photos around the house but this one?

Why hadn't she mentioned them? Who were they?

Setting the picture to the side, I looked through the rest of the box. Nothing really stood out: two wedding rings, a pair of earrings, a necklace with "G" on it. But besides that just other random things, like a baseball card. Until I saw an ultrasound.

In the left corner, it read November 12th, 2010. The right corner read, Emily Gray.

Wait, where's the baby?

Grabbing the picture of her family back, I looked closer at the mom. You would never have been able to tell if you hadn't known, but her stomach stuck out just a little. Her mom was pregnant. So where the fuck was the baby? Where was her family?

The sound of the back door slamming shut broke me from what I was doing. I had no idea when she would be back, and I did not feel like dealing with her if she found me snooping through her shit. Shoving everything back inside, I placed it back inside her closet and closed the door. Rushing back to the bed I lay back down just in time for Salem to open her bedroom door. She stopped as soon as she saw me awake.

"Oh, uh, hey."

"What are you doing?" I asked, sitting back up against the headboard.

"Just got done doing stuff around the farm, I have to change." Walking over to her dresser she pulled out a pair of leggings, and a sports bra. I watched as she changed and threw her clothes into the hamper. My cock twitched watching as her ass jiggled while jumping into her leggings.

"You normally shower," I commented.

"Yeah, well, Mila asked me when we left if I could show her some defensive moves." She shrugged, grabbing a pair of socks before pulling them on. I had been so focused on her that I hadn't taken in what she actually said.

"Whoa, wait, Mila wants you to show her how to fight?" I asked, standing up quickly, wincing as I did. I couldn't count the number of times Dimitri begged her to learn. After she was kidnapped the last time, he begged her for months to learn after she had Tobias. He told her he would train her, or even I could since I was the best fighter out of them. She always told him no, that she didn't want to. After a year of trying he finally gave up, and now all of a sudden, she wanted Salem to train her.

"Yeah, well I'm the best out of any of you so…" Once again, she shrugged as if it was no big fucking deal.

"I don't know about all that," I murmured, pulling on a pair of sweatpants and a shirt. If she was going to train her, I was definitely going to watch.

"You haven't seen me actually fight there, buddy." She laughed, leaving me standing in her bedroom like a fool.

By the time I made it downstairs and outside I took in the impressive set up she had. I hadn't been outside to get a good look, and now that I had a chance, the view took my breath away. I was never one that got why people loved nature and the views so much. But now standing here, I understood. The backyard wasn't just a backyard. It went on for miles. In the back you could see mountains. To the left sat a large barn with a fence around it, and small goats surrounding it. How had I not known she had fucking goats? To the right the fence went on for miles, it seemed, with horses.

One, two, three, four... seven fucking horses. How many animals did this girl have?

"Are you going to stand there gawking at the land or actually come watch the fight?" Killian asked, appearing behind me. Looking over I felt like I hadn't seen him in such a long time. I hadn't even noticed his beard was growing out more than the little stubble he usually kept.

"Where have you been?" I asked.

"The first few days I slept, honestly, traveling with both of you knocked out and listening to the three of them talk for over eight hours. That shit was rough." He laughed.

"And the other days?"

"Looking into Luca and why he would attack."

"What do you mean?"

"Luca's men were the ones who attacked us..." Killian gave me a blank expression. "Salem won't tell us anything either," he grunted as we stepped closer to the large workout mat.

Looking around, Tobias sat outside the ring with Dimitri talking away. Mila and Salem sat inside stretching and smiling at each other. I don't think I ever stretched before working out or a fight. It had me itching to step inside and start working out again. I needed to do something. But I also knew Salem would have my ass if I tried anything.

"I'll see what I can find out." I nudged his shoulder. "But I need a favor."

"Sure, what's up."

"Salem's family, have you found literally nothing about her?"

"No, nothing. Not even being here. I can't find her anywhere; it's like she doesn't exist. I don't understand, man." Killian sighed. I could tell it was beginning to really bother him not being able to find information about someone.

Turning my attention back to the girls, Mila looked nervous and still unsure if she wanted to do this. But Salem, the determination on her face was everything. You could see the strength she held just from her face. My cock twitched at the pure determination she held.

"Alright, first things first. Make a fist," Salem instructed. Mila made a weak fist, and even from this distance I could tell it was all wrong. Mila waited for Salem to laugh or even make fun of her. But not my Salem, no. *My Salem.* Instead, Salem showed Mila her own fist, showing her how to properly make one. That way she wouldn't break anything. The worst thing you could do was try and throw a punch just to end up breaking your hand.

Walking over to Dimitri I sat down next to him.

After watching Mila and Salem talk about the correct way to make a fist Dimitri finally muttered, "You're looking better."

Shrugging, I kept my gaze on the girls as Salem showed her how to throw a few punches. It made me wonder where Salem learned to fight, though I had yet to see her actually fight.

"Killian and I talked and I'm making it mandatory that we learn other languages. It's stupid we don't already know, so once we're back home all of us are going to be learning," Dimitri said, snapping me from watching them.

"I think that's smart."

"Salem told Killian she speaks six languages but can get by with eight." It took me longer to realize what he said, but the moment I realized it fully my head spun. My head snapped back over to Salem. She had Mila sitting on her, showing her how to buck someone off her. But six languages—no eight languages. How did she know so many, and why?

"I still don't trust her," Dimitri continued on.

"Why?"

"She's hiding too much. She won't talk to anyone. Killian can't find anything, and everything about this place is weird."

"Daddy." Tobias stepped between us.

"Yeah, kiddo?"

"Can Aunt Sey show me how to fight?"

"Absolutely not," Dimitri snapped.

"But why?" He pouted.

"Well first off, you're only four. You're too small to fight. Second, when it's time, Uncle Zane or I will teach you. Also, Aunt Sey?" He cocked an eyebrow at that. I also had no idea where he got that idea from. Though it did have an effect over me. I liked the idea of making Salem mine. Completely mine.

Tobias pouted but didn't bother saying anything else. Instead, he ran towards the ring and sat on the edge.

"Why do they want her to train them? You're the best fighter out of us all, and I mean I'm not far behind you. I could have taught her this whole time, but the moment we arrive here she says fuck it all?" Dimitri complained.

I never had a chance to say anything before Dimitri stood up and began walking forward. "Salem!" he barked.

She stopped showing Mila whatever move was next and stood straight up.

"Spar with me." It wasn't a question. My whole body tensed.

"Okay."

Okay? OKAY?

Everything in me screamed at her to say no. I knew she had to be a decent fighter, but Dimitri was almost as big as me. We both were 6'5" and well over two hundred pounds. Salem was a tiny person, and Dimitri would not hold back for her. He would push her buttons, and I knew if Dimitri tried to actually hurt her, I would step in. Which I truly didn't want to do.
Dimitri stripped out of his sweatshirt and shoes, leaving him in joggers and a shirt. Mila stepped out and came to sit next to me, holding onto Tobias.

"I got bets on Dimitri," Killian hollered out.

Dimitri smirked back at us, while Salem glared.

"Salem, kick his ass!" Mila laughed, causing Dimitri to cock his head to the side, raising his eyebrows at her. "Love you, babe!" she said, sending him a kiss.

"And you, Zane?" Salem threw her hand up at me.

Looking between the two I didn't know who to pick. Salem was strong, but Dimitri had size on his side. I knew who I wanted to win this sparring match.

"Dimitri," I lied. It would get under her skin, and I just hoped she would fight better.

Both of them turned towards each other and took their position. I wasn't so sure this was just a training session. This looked more like they were ready to fight each other.

"Do you think we should stop this?" Mila asked.

"I wouldn't. Dimitri has been looking for a fight and Salem can probably hold her own." Killian shrugged.

My own nerves were racking against my body, clawing at my skin. I wanted to jump inside that ring and fight against Dimitri for her. I hated that this was his way of making sure she was part of us. It was a stupid test; one I didn't want her to go through. My word about her should have been enough, but I knew Dimitri wouldn't let that happen.

I watched in slow motion as Dimitri threw the first punch in her stomach knocking Salem back. What I least expected was a smile spreading across her face. He went to kick towards her, and it looked promising until the last moment. Salem dodged it, grabbing hold of his calf and giving it a good yank. Dimitri went down. He recovered fast, throwing his elbow back into her chest. Salem fell back onto her back, giving Dimitri enough time to straddle her. Unfortunately, the look on Salem's face said everything as she bucked him off fast and hard. Getting to her feet she threw her head back and laughed.

"Are you holding back or are you just weak?" she taunted him. Usually, something like that wouldn't work, but this time it did. Dimitri charged towards her. Salem jumped and wrapped her legs around his neck before punching the back of his neck. They both fell. Dimitri landed on his front while Salem rolled and kick-flipped to her feet.

Watching her was like magic. I don't know how she moved. But everything she did was something out of a movie. Dimitri never got the chance to get his hands on her. She dodged every grab and threw him onto the ground before either kicking him or punching him.

"Come on, Dimitri, thought you were the big power Pakhan of Russia." She laughed, urging him on. "Thought you wanted to spar, not fight me. If you wanted to get your ass kicked all you had to do was ask, *Pakhan*."

Dimitri growled, rushing towards her. At the last moment, Salem swept her legs out, sweeping him to the floor.

My cock tented in my sweatpants, and I had to lean forward to hide my erection. It was hot watching her move around, fighting as if it was first nature to her.

"Alright, the next person to hold the other down for five seconds wins," Dimitri panted, getting to his feet.

"Sure." She looked as though she was barely breaking a sweat.

"Kick his ass, Salem!" Killian shouted, laughing to himself.

The words barely left his mouth before Dimitri grabbed the back of her ankles, throwing her back. It again appeared like Dimitri might actually win until she wrapped her legs around his neck again.

Choking him.

Five seconds went by, but neither of them let the other go. Not until Salem pulled him hard towards her, rolling just in time, and Dimitri's face planted onto the mat.

"FUCK!" he bellowed.

Mila shot to her feet, holding Tobias in her arms.

Dimitri rolled over onto his back. His nose was broken. Blood fell from his face onto his shirt.

"Next time you want to fucking test me, don't. I'm not some little girl you can push around. Next time you want to fight I will slit your fucking throat," was all Salem said before marching towards me. Grabbing my arm, no one said anything as she dragged me towards the horses. I had no idea what I should say, or if I even had anything to say. Everything felt like all too much suddenly.

Chapter 24

Salem

"Alright, the next person to hold the other down for five seconds wins." I cocked an eyebrow when Dimitri began panting. I was barely breaking a sweat.

"Sure."

"Kick his ass, Salem," Killian yelled.

Killian barely got those words out before Dimitri grabbed the back of my ankles, and my back smacked onto the ground. I gave him a moment, letting him think that he was going to win. Smirking, I wrapped my legs around his neck, choking him. It was well past the allotted seconds, neither of us moving. I refused to let this big buffoon get the upper hand and actually win. With all my might I pushed him back before yanking him back down, and at the last second, I rolled. His face smacked into the mat.

"FUCK!" he yelled.

I couldn't focus on any of them outside the ring. If I did, I would feel bad for breaking his nose. I shouldn't have done that. He was testing me, and I should've let him win.
Dimitri rolled over, sitting back on his heels. Blood coated his mouth and chin; his nose was definitely broken. My chest began to rise and fall. I could feel the panic threatening to rip me to pieces. I don't know what caused the fight between Dimitri and me to cause this reaction. But I couldn't breathe. I needed to get out of here, fast.

"Next time you want to fucking test me, don't," I spat out. "I'm not some little girl you can push around. Next time you want to fight I will slit your fucking throat." Would I? Probably not, but I couldn't control myself.

Finally, I looked over at Zane, who was now standing. He looked like he was ready to jump in and save me from Dimitri. I hadn't realized until this moment the feelings I had for him. Sure I cared; sure I had something there inside me. But the pure expression on his face told me everything. If I hadn't stopped Dimitri just then Zane would have. He would have pushed the pain he felt aside and stopped his best friend himself.

Shaking my head, I marched towards Zane, grabbed his arm and practically ran towards my horse. I always rode when I felt the panic rising inside me. It's what Mom taught me, even at a young age. If I had my panic attacks all I had to do was tell Dad or Mom. One of them would take me out. I was too young to ride by myself. But one of them would take me out, and they never talked until I spoke first.

I wanted that now. I needed it.

I wasted no time. I grabbed Pumpkin's mane and hiked myself up. I looked down at Zane, who was looking up at me.

"Grab his mane right here, and grab my hand," I forced out. I didn't know why I was taking him with me, but I needed him with me. He was becoming my comfort.

Zane didn't bat an eye as he reached up and pushed off, his leg swinging over. Pressing up behind me, I kicked my leg and grabbed hold of his mane before Pumpkin knew what he had to do. We did this a lot, especially during the last four years.
Pumpkin finally took off as we reached the middle of the fenced-in yard, aiming for the spot he always jumped over. I could feel Zane tense, his arms wrapped around my middle, hugging me close. I could relax into him, but I didn't allow myself to. Not yet.

"Oh, fuck," he muttered. I don't know how he could have tensed more, but he somehow did. Just in time, Pumpkin jumped. The air stuck in my lungs with the force of Zane's arms wrapped around me. The moment his hoofs touched the ground Zane let out a grunt before easing up a little bit.

I didn't think, I didn't feel. I refused to let anything take hold of me. Riding was for me. It lets me think without actually needing to think. Out here, I always felt more like myself. I felt free. Uncaring about anything that happened in the past. It was like I could see clearly and everything from my life faded away. Pumpkin knew where I always went, where everything mattered.

I don't know how long we rode; it never mattered to me. He started slowing down until he finally began a low gait along the path that my dad showed me. It was where I felt normal again.

I expected Zane to say something, but he never did. Not once the whole time we rode. I waited for what seemed like a long time, finally deciding it was time for me to speak.

"Do you ever get tired of it?" I asked.

"Of what, Kitten?" *God, I melt at that nickname.*

"The noise," I muttered. Not daring to look around at him. "Of everything."
I don't know what I expected him to say, but it definitely was not what came out of his mouth next. "With you in it, no."

"I find a lot of it hard, but the noise is the worst. Sometimes I wonder what it would be like to be normal. To have a job, worry about bills, to worry if a boy liked me or not." I don't know what I was saying exactly, but I sent a little prayer that Zane didn't speak, that he just let me talk. "I wish I could be worried about if they liked the outfit I was wearing, or even if I had food stuck in my teeth. But that seems like a completely different life now."

"I have a feeling you won't tell me why you can't have this normal life you wish for." Zane hugged me closer. His warmth gave me strength to be somewhat honest with him.

"It's not a won't, really. I can't. It doesn't just involve me, it involves others, a lot of others." My whole family. Aziza. They were the others that I couldn't tell him about. I couldn't tell him the truth because that would mean he would know truths that I couldn't bear to explain.

"Is this about your family?" he asked. Tensing, I couldn't focus on anything, the air sticking in my lungs. It was like he knew something, something I couldn't know what. Aziza wiped out my whole family. No one knew about us. "I found a picture of them when I was snooping through your closet." It was like he read my thoughts. I wanted to be angry because he went through my things, but if I was in his situation, I would have done the same. Probably sooner, but still done the same.

"I can't talk about them, Zane," I finally answered. "Can you tell me about yours?" I asked, trying to change the subject somehow.

"I had a normal childhood, honestly. I mean, both my parents were successful. My mom was a doctor, and my father was a lawyer. The best in town."

Was. That's what he was saying. They were gone.

"How did you come to work for Dimitri?" I leaned further as Pumpkin continued walking the path.

"When I was eighteen, my father wanted me to go to college, and either become like him, or become a doctor like my mother. But I didn't want either of those. I had always been different. Not in my emotions like other kids around me. It honestly was probably from my parents. They were great but didn't fully raise me. I had a few nannies, but they always quit because I was an asshole." He chuckled.

"I can't see it," I joked, smiling to myself.

"Oh, yeah, they were all crazy. Anyway, we got into a fight and when I left, I didn't speak to them for a few weeks. I cared for my parents, but it was because I had to. They gave me life, so it was expected of me to care. So one night they got into an accident, and they both died. Instantly."

"I'm sorry," I rushed out, turning my head around so I could finally look at him. Zane was staring back down at me like he had been doing the whole time, but for the first time I couldn't find the hardness that was always there. This time he had softened his expression, and I found myself wanting him closer. I wanted him to actually be mine, to help me carry this mission out that I was so hell bent on.

"You don't need to be, but thank you." Leaning forward he kissed my forehead. My heart skipped a beat, and fuck, my insides were actually beginning to burn. Sitting back he continued, "After they passed, I took off and went to New York City. I had been into wrestling through high school, fuck played football, mostly because of my size. But when I went into town, I started fucking around with fight clubs underground. It was mainly because I was good at it, but I also think it was because some part of me had blamed myself for my parents' death." Before I could even protest that he, of course, couldn't be responsible, he shushed me and continued on. "Anyway, I did that for a little, but it wasn't long before Dimitri found me. I ended up killing his enforcer. It was by mistake. I kicked him too hard in the face and his nose ended up basically puncturing his brain and he died."

All of this felt like information overload, yet I wanted to know everything about him. I wanted to ask him more about his parents. I wanted to know why Dimitri was such an asshole. I even wanted to ask about Killian and his weird attitude. Sometimes he was in a good mood, always playful, but recently he was off.

"He wanted to kill me, I think, until he realized that his enforcer was killed by someone twice as young. And someone who had no one he would be leaving behind, so he offered me a job. And before you ask, he was honest with me. Told me he was head of the Russian Mafia, and that what I would be doing was worse than anything I had done before. But I truly didn't care. I had no future. Sure I had my parents' inheritance, which was a fuck ton. But I didn't know what I was going to do with my life. I barely had emotions and I was good at punching someone's face in." He shrugged looking off into the farmland. I don't know what was going through his head that made him stop looking at me, or even stop talking. But I felt like he was inside his head and didn't want to be bothered anymore.

Turning back towards the path, I nudged Pumpkin back towards the house. It would still take a while until we got there, but I think we had spent enough time out here. I felt relaxed from the fight with Dimitri and knowing that somewhere inside he had a heart. Even if it wasn't towards me, that was okay. As long as he treated the three people well who had begun to actually matter to me, that was all that mattered.

By the time we made it back to the house it was already getting dark and everyone else appeared to be inside.

"Who taught you to fight?" Zane asked me as we got off Pumpkin. Walking him back into the fence I locked it up.

"Uh, Michael. It was a family friend who helped me in a bad situation, and he taught me everything I know." Once Pumpkin was locked up with the rest of the horses, we turned, heading back towards the house. I desperately needed to shower.

"You took Dimitri down without breaking a sweat," he whispered before we stepped into the house. Looking back, Zane stood so close I could feel his warmth on me.

"There's a lot more you don't know about me," I muttered.

"I'm beginning to realize that," he shot back.

"Salem," someone called from the hallway. Turning around I was faced with Dimitri, his arms crossed over glaring at me. His nose was back in place, but the bruising was bad. I was truly ready to knock him out and send him down to the basement.

Rolling my eyes at him, I crossed my arms right back at him. "Dimitri."

"I want to apologize for my behavior." I flinched. I don't know why, but I was not expecting that from him. He didn't look like a man that would apologize for how he'd treated someone, so I had to wonder if Mila made him do this. And if she had, why?

"I shouldn't have wanted to fight you. I have—" he growled, unsure of what he was even wanting to say. I almost stopped him, but I wanted him to grovel. "I don't trust you. But you saved Zane back in Boston, and you saved us in that warehouse. *Even if I don't want to admit it."* The last part was said so low I barely heard him. "You brought us into your home while Luca's men are hunting us an—"

"Wait, what?" Zane barked out behind me.

"You've missed a lot since you've been *resting,"* he said, rolling his eyes.

"And we're just sitting here while those Italians are hunting us!" Zane was barely holding onto his anger.

"There are other factors in this, Zane." His eyes flickered to me. Obviously, I was part of the factor, though I had no idea why. "Tomorrow we're meeting Taylor in Charlotte."

"Alright, I'll be ready in the morning." Zane nodded his head.

"Six, it's a couple hours away and Killian likes to stop a lot." Dimitri turned to leave before stopping and looking at me over his shoulder. "They'll be safe with you here." It wasn't a question.

"Always," I confirmed. Tobias and Mila would be safe no matter what.
Something, I'm not too sure what, passed between us, but his face told me he knew I was telling the truth. I would protect them with everything in me.

Chapter 25

Zane

When you look at someone who is five foot five, maybe a hundred and thirty pounds, you would never expect them to have a good amount of strength. Especially when they're sleeping. Like who can throw a good fucking punch when they're sleeping, or kick like they're life depended on it?

Salem can.

After our little horse-riding session when Salem freaked out and barely talked until we were a good distance from the house, we came back and something passed between Dimitri and her when he told me we had to travel to meet with Taylor. I had no idea what was going on since I had been "resting." After he left, Salem made us both some grilled cheese and soup, which I never thought I was an actual fan. But fuck if that wasn't the best meal I had. We barely spoke while we ate, or showered, and even before she fell asleep.

I had just fallen asleep when I got kneed in the side. At first it was cute the way she curled up into my side. Her snoring was deepening until just as I went to close my eyes again, I got socked in the jaw. For a tiny person she was fucking strong. But she had yet to wake up. Instead, the moment I sat up and turned to wake her up she full on kicked me in the stomach.

"No, no no, please stop!" She began whimpering. Salem never slept hard enough to snore let alone start sleep talking.

Reaching over I tried shaking her shoulder to wake her up. Instead, I got punched again in the jaw. I was definitely going to have a damn bruise. Just in time for my others to fade.

"Salem," I whispered into her ear. Rubbing her back, Salem began crying even harder.

"Don't leave me, please, please, no no no no, DON'T!" Her voice got louder at the end. Her breathing was rushed. I had no idea what she was dreaming about, but whatever it was she was trapped. She was trapped.

I had no idea what to do to get her to wake up, so like my natural self I reared back and smacked her cheek. It wasn't hard enough to bruise, but hard enough that her eyes shot open. Her breathing was ragged, and the pure look of disgust in her eyes had me cringing at the fact I just hit her.

"Zane," she forced out.

"Yes?"

"Did… did you just slap me?" Her voice was so low I barely heard her. I still heard the anger behind them, but there was also fear in her voice. Whatever she was dreaming about had scared her out of her mind, but I knew she wouldn't talk about it with me.

"You hit me first." I pointed to my already bruising jaw. "Plus you kicked me, and did you know you snore?" I cocked my brow.

Her mouth opened and then closed, then opened and closed again. Searching for the words, she looked cute. Her hair was a frizzy mess from going to bed with it wet, and her eyes were half closed from sleep.

"I… I don't remember what I was dreaming about. But I do not snore."

"Sure, Kitten." Smirking at her, I opened my mouth to say something else, but Salem looked over at the window. She didn't speak, she didn't move, it was like she was emotionless. I had no idea what she was thinking, or even feeling. She was hiding so much, and I had no idea about anything. It was beginning to make me feel useless. She had these walls that held so high you couldn't see the fucking top and no matter how many times I showed her she was safe with me, she refused to back down.

"Salem," I tried. But nothing. Her face was empty, blank. Nothing. It was as though she was no longer there. She was gone inside her head.
Scooting closer to her, I placed a hand on her thigh. But she didn't even react to that. Inching even closer to her face, she still didn't react.

"Take your clothes off," I demanded.

Nothing.

Her eyes were glossy, and completely gone. She wasn't there at all. I needed to figure out what happened in her past that made her zone out like this. I needed to know where her head was and why it was like that.

Sneaking my hand back to her thigh, I smacked her bare thigh.
Salem yelped and her head snapped back towards me.

"What the hell?" she growled.

"There you are." I squeezed her leg. "You went somewhere else.
You didn't react to anything. Where did you go?" I asked, dragging
her so she was now sitting in my lap on the bed.

"I don't know," she whispered.

"What can I do so you get out of your head?" Leaning forward I
kissed her nose, then kissed her forehead. Her eyes fluttered closed,
and her breathing hitched.

"What you're doing is working," she moaned.

"I want to know why you were a virgin." I continued kissing my
way around the side of her face down to her neck.

"I don't want to talk." Her hand wrapped around my arms.

"Tell me. I want to know why; I want to know." Trailing my hand
up her back I gripped her throat. She bit her lip as I pressed tighter
around her throat. The soft groan from her mouth told me she liked
this.

"I never had time for anyone. I don't have a good reason, so I hope
you're not disappointed." Her eyes narrowed when I squeezed
tighter, cutting off more air. She rocked her hips against my bulge.

Even if my ribs were begging me to protest against her rocking
against me, my cock wanted nothing more than to be inside her. A
low growl escaped my lips when she bucked hard enough that I felt
precum drip from the tip of my cock. Pulling her closer, our mouths
brushed against each other. She was so warm and soft. Flicking her
tongue out she wet her lips, causing her tongue to touch my own

215

lips. She triggered my last ounce of control, dipping down, and I crashed our lips together. It was hot, and I wanted this to last forever. I never wanted to leave the taste of her lips.

Her kiss was deep and messy. Like she was desperate for this distraction, and I was gladly offering it for her. Her finger tugged at the back of my hair, trying to get me closer. Though she couldn't get any closer, her chest pressed against my own. Her hips rocked back and forth against me.

She scraped her teeth against the bottom lip before biting down. Blood filled both our mouths. She didn't seem bothered, though. Instead, she stuck her tongue back inside my mouth, running it along my teeth.

My hands grabbed her ass, squeezing roughly. Her pussy warm against my cock, I was losing any patience I had left in me.

"Zane, please."

"Please, what?"

I could see the fight within her eyes. She didn't want to beg me. Her saying it once was far enough. But I wanted her to beg. I wanted her to tell me exactly what she wanted.

"Beg me," I taunted.

Swallowing back her pride she took a deep breath before reopening her eyes. "Please." Her fingers gripped the back of my neck trying to pull me closer to her. "Please, Zane, I'm begging you. I don't beg for anything, but I'm begging you. Touch me, take me. Control me, please!" she rattled off.

Without notice, I flipped her onto her back, nudging her thighs to fit around my waist. Hooking a finger into her panties I slipped a finger between her folds. She was already so wet and slick I wanted to sink my cock into her.

Slipping a finger into her wet channel, she was so tight and warm. I was about to blow my load just from this. She tried her best to regulate her breathing, not wanting to show how affected she was. But I wasn't having it. Pumping my finger faster, I rubbed her clit with my thumb. Her breath hitched, and her eyes closed. Her nipples hardened underneath my shirt she wore.

"I need you to come right now," I grunted. Adding a second finger, I said, "Come all over my hand right now."

"Fuck, fuck, fuck. Zane!" She came, squeezing my fingers.

Not giving her a chance to breathe, to relax, I ripped my boxer briefs off. Grabbing her hands I held them above her head. Stroking my cock I shoved my cock into her wetness.

"OH, SHIT!" she screamed. Thrusting into her, her eyes went wide as I continued fucking her, not giving a shit about the headboard banging against the wall.

"You're *mine*," I growled my eyes locked onto hers. "Say it."

"Yes, yes, shit," she panted. "I'm yours."

She spread her legs further apart, giving me a better angle, and I proceeded to pound into her. One hand wrapped around her wrists, and the other gripped her throat. Her mouth fell open, gasping for air. But I couldn't stop. I wouldn't. If she passed out, I wouldn't stop.

"Fuck, Salem," I growled out. She felt too good, too tight. Everything about her felt just right. She felt amazing. I was losing every bit of control in me. Her pussy squeezed my length, tighter and tighter.

She was so close. I could feel her pussy strangling my cock. "Zane!" she screamed, her eyes widening as she came, causing my own release. I felt my whole soul leave my body. I couldn't remember the last time I came so hard that I saw stars, and my vision blurred. My body fell halfway on top of Salem. Letting go of her hands, I expected her to push me off, but instead she wrapped them around me, pulling me closer, until my face fit perfectly into her neck. I don't know how long we laid like that, her breathing evening out, and I found myself fading into sleep.

"So what's been going on?" I asked from the driver's seat. It felt good to be back, with Killian in the back seat, nose in his laptop, and Dimitri in the front seat with his phone out, most likely texting back and forth with Mila.

"Most of Luca's men are dead. The only one left is his son. I have no idea why he's after us. The only thing I could assume is the girl," Dimitri finally answered looking up from his phone.

"Luca right now is in New York. I think he's trying to gather more men. He lost a great amount from her. If she's the one killing them all," Killian commented from the back. "All the ports are back in place, nothing missing. I think it's because she took out whoever tried to take over for Matteo."

"Have you looked into Luca at all? Maybe he could give a tell on who Salem is." I shrugged.

"I, eh, I have, but the only thing I found is a girl named Emily Willis, but she disappeared."

"Who's Emily Willis?" Dimitri asked. Looking over my shoulder, I switched lanes.

"Alright so the head of the family, Volkov, who you know never believed in arranged marriage. The cartel is not important right now, they're trying to figure out their own shit anyway. Then Caputo," Killian rattled off.

"Killian," Dimitri snapped.

"I'm getting there. Luca's dad had arranged for the Willis family's daughter to marry Luca." He continued tapping away at his computer. "Willis family here, umm. Alright, so Nathan and Mary had three children, Emily the oldest daughter, then Alexander, and then Katlyn. Nathan and Mary were both lawyers, and... wow, fuck they were rich. Nathan was the Caputo lawyer, and it looks like Mary was a lot of the other lower crime family lawyers. When Luca was twenty, it looks like Emily was set to marry him. She was three years older, but he needed a wife. After that there's nothing."

"Nothing?" Dimitri questioned.

"Yeah, they were supposed to marry April eighth, and it looks like she never showed up at the altar. Like standing him up, she disappeared. There's no sign of her anywhere else," Killian confirmed.

I had no idea how important this was. Who cared who Emily was, or this fucking family. I just wanted to know who Salem was, and why she was so secretive. I wanted to know everything about her, but now it went beyond wanting to just know the mystery of her. I wanted to know why she chose vanilla shampoo and mint body wash. I wanted to know which horse was her favorite, and her favorite movie. All of it. She was becoming something more than an obsession. I didn't even know what went beyond that. But whatever it was, I had that.

Even this two-hour road trip had my skin itching. It was more than wanting to be close to her; it was becoming a need. I needed to be around her, in her space.

"So, Zane... you and Salem seem to be... what's the word—"

"We're not talking about what's going on between the two of us," I growled back at Killian. I don't know why all of a sudden Killian wanted to gossip, but I wasn't in the mood.

"Fine, we won't talk about the two of you. We'll just talk about the crazy girl we're currently staying with."

Rolling my eyes, I continued driving not wanting to talk about Salem.

"So what is going on with you guys?" Dimitri asked, looking at me from the corner of his eye.

"Oh, fuck." Killian laughed. Dimitri rolled his eyes.

"This is going to be a long fucking drive," I muttered. Long drive indeed.

"That was a fucking pointless meeting," Killian complained for the millionth time since we'd left it five hours ago.

"If you say that again, I swear to god I'm knocking you out right here and leaving you here," I growled as we climbed the stairs to Salem's house. Though I agreed the meeting with Taylor had gone completely pointless.

"I just want to eat and see my damn wife," Dimitri muttered somewhere behind us.

Opening the front door, all of us stepped inside just to stop right away. One of the things I least expected to see was three girls, dancing to loud music. I had no idea how we hadn't even heard it from outside. But here they were. Mila held a bottle to her lips as she swung her hips to some heavy beat song. Some blonde girl was next to Mila showing her different dance moves. But she didn't hold my focus. No, that would be Salem. My eyes swung to her, and the air left my body as I stared at her. I had never seen her so carefree before. But there she stood on the coffee table, swinging her hips like the blonde was showing Mila. But the way she was doing it was completely different. Like she knew what she was doing. Her eyes were closed as she let the music flow through her. Her hair was wild, as her hands moved through her hair like it was the last thing she was meant to do.

"I don't think they realize we're here," Killian muttered.

"I think they're drunk." Dimitri sighed.

"Should we tell them we've arrived?" Killian asked.

"No," I shot out. I don't know why I didn't want them to know we were here just yet, but watching Salem dance on the table, letting loose for once was doing things to me. Things I thought I wouldn't allow to happen, but there it was. The feeling of caring for her, and it was beyond wanting her. It was becoming more.

Chapter 26

Salem

Rolling over the crinkle of paper I blinked my eyes a few times before they fully focused on the small piece of paper lying on my pillow. Lying back I brought the paper up and couldn't help the small smile spreading across my lips.

You were snoring too hard, so I didn't want to wake you.
We'll come tonight.
Zane-

"I do not snore," I muttered. It wasn't the point, but I still couldn't get rid of the happiness in my heart, or the smile that was still on my face. Zane was not what I had expected. He wanted everyone to think he was just this hard guy, someone who didn't care about others. But he did, he cared more than he wanted anyone to know.

Shoving thoughts of Zane out of my head, I made my way into the bathroom. After I finished my business, I changed into a pair of old jeans and a flannel before making my way downstairs.

"Ready to help Tobs?" I asked as I poured my coffee mug up. Tobias sat at the island eating a bowl of cereal.

"One… more… Bite." He laughed, shoving two more bites of food into his mouth. I smiled at him as he got down from the stool before walking his bowl to the sink. After he rinsed it out and set it to the side we walked out into the crisp air.

After a few minutes of us walking to the barn Tobias opened his mouth a few times before finally heaving a loud sigh.

"Ask away, little man. Remember I told you I'm an open book." I nudged him with my elbow as we stepped into the barn. Closing the door and locking it behind me, I flipped the lights on.

"I overheard Mama and Dada talking," he stated.

"Okay?"

"Dada is talking about us going back home." He didn't have to say anything else. I already knew what he wanted to say. They were leaving, and I was staying.

"It's okay, I'm sure your mom will come visit." I tried to lighten the mood.

"Uncle Zaney will want to stay with you," he said, tears threatening to fall from his eyes. I couldn't have that.

"Hey." I stopped in front of him. Crouching down so we were eye level I took his hands in mine. "I will always be here; I won't leave you."

"I don't want to go back to being nobody like I was before." He sniffled. I hated seeing him cry. This hadn't been the first time he cried, and I hated that. I wanted to wrap him up in a little burrito and promise nothing was going to hurt him. But in reality, he was going to get hurt. He was in line to take over for his dad when Dimitri was too weak or if he died. Didn't matter that he was only four years old, he was going to learn the hard life, eventually.

"You listen to me, Tobias, no matter what happens in life you know I will be right there with you. No matter what, I will help you with anything. Doesn't matter what it is. What have I promised you?"

He looked down at our hands, his breathing increased.

"Tobias," I lightly warned.

"You'd protect me," he finally choked out.

Taking his chin in my hand I brought his forehead to meet mine. "I will always protect you; I promise you. I will protect you from anyone who tries to hurt you. No matter who they are, if they are the bad guys, family, or random. I will *always* protect you. If you need help while you're in Russia, I will be on the next plane out of here. If you're here, I will be right by your side." I kissed his forehead.

"Forever…"

"And always a little bit." Our pinkie fingers intertwined, our thumbs sticking out towards each other. Both of us kissed each other's thumbs. If I couldn't save my own family, I'd save him.

"Now let's train." I laughed as we broke apart.

After I trained Tobias, we finished feeding the animals. He went off with Mila while I went upstairs and showered. After I finished and started pulling clothes on, my phone started to go off. Looking at who was calling I smiled and answered.

"Please tell me you're home." Aziza sighed, not giving me a chance to even say hello.

"I have a funny feeling you already know I am," I said, pulling a shirt over my head.

"Is that a yes or no?"

"Yes, I'm home."

"I'm bringing food and wine," was all she said before hanging up.

Dropping my phone on the dresser I closed my eyes, waiting for the headache that was going to occur.

"So you and Zane?" Mila giggled as she took another drink from her cup.

After Aziza got off the phone, I was able to clean up a bit. I told Mila that Aziza was coming over, which brought on a million questions on who she was. I couldn't tell her exactly, just the fact that she could trust Aziza. It wasn't long before she showed up carrying a box of six bottles of wine, and three boxes of pizza. Tobias ate a few slices before passing out close to seven, once I carried him to bed and got his white noise playing.

"Wait, what about them?" Aziza asked as she finished off her cup of white wine.

Shrugging my shoulders, I didn't know how to exactly explain it. I had no idea what we were, or if we were even anything at all.

"Salem, spill." Aziza tossed a napkin at me.

Looking between the two, they both stared at me like I was a movie they couldn't wait to watch. But the feeling of panic of sharing my life never came. Instead I wanted to tell them everything.

"We've hooked up a few times," I admitted.

Mila gasped.

Aziza sent me a knowing look.

"Oh my, okay you have to start from the beginning," Mila half shouted.

Sighing, I leaned back against the couch.

"The beginning?" I asked.

"Oh yes, definitely the beginning," Aziza agreed. The thing about beginnings, they had no idea how close they were to each other.

"We met four years ago." I shrugged, wincing as I said the words.

"Wait, four years ago?" Mila cocked her head to the side. "Four years ago as in when…" She looked confused, before it finally dawned on her.

"No, wait, what am I missing?" Aziza looked between us now.

I looked over at Mila, almost asking permission if I was allowed to tell even my best friend that I had known Mila beforehand.

"I should probably start at the beginning first." Mila sat back against the loveseat on the floor. "Aziza, do you know anything about a man named Matteo?" she asked.

"Not really, actually nothing besides that he's the leader of the cartel. But he's dead," Aziza answered, looking towards me. She knew I killed him, but never knew how or why.

Letting out a long and loud sigh Mila sat back hugging herself. "Yeah, well, when I was sixteen his nephew, who I had no idea were even related at all, raped me. I was a nobody at school really, the weird nerdy girl who was about to graduate school early. I turned seventeen and had been invited to a party and I don't really know why but I went. Long story short, I was raped. My life turned upside down. I barely did or went anywhere. I ended up getting a job at the local coffee shop we ran into each other at, and one night when I was walking home, I got kidnapped." Mila swallowed more of her wine before continuing on. "Gabriel had told his uncle about me, but never said what he had done. So they uh, t-thought I was a virgin when I was kidnapped. I was being groomed for Matteo to buy me. I was there for seventy-eight days. When they were bringing me for the transfer, I was um… re-kidnapped by Dimitri." She laughed at the end.

"Wait Dimitri, as in the asshole who's always growling and in a pissed off mood?" Aziza laughed.

"Yeah, I don't get involved in their business, but basically something with his ports was happening. He saw me and took me. It was rocky in the beginning, trust me, but when I finally trusted him, I asked if I could go home. I don't know why I necessarily wanted to. I mean, I don't really have parents. They passed away when I was a young child in foster care. But anyway, Matteo found out, and he kidnapped me again."

"Okay so how does this tie together between y'all?" Aziza asked, pointing between us.

"When I went to Boston, when you found them, I was being followed by someone. I thought it was one of Luca's men, but it turned out to be Zane." I cringed, remembering I broke his nose, which he still had no idea about. No one did in fact.

"Wait, what?" both girls said in unison.

"I was tracking Leonardo, and well, Zane was following me. I hit him with my bat I used to carry around and broke his nose." I shivered, remembering that night.

"Wait a damn minute. That was you!" Mila shot up to her knees. "Holy shit."

"Yeah, it was me. I never leave anyone behind. But I couldn't bring myself to kill him, so I left a note," I admitted. The note. Ghost.

What felt like a few minutes went by before Mila's eyes bugged out. "Y-you. You're what they've been looking for. You-you're Ghost." I expected her to look scared, terrified, maybe even a little nervous. But instead Mila was laughing.

"Yeah, I'm Ghost. I'm what Luca has Dimitri looking for. What Zane can't find and what has them all worried."

"That's too good," Aziza finally said laughing to herself. "Okay, anyway, what else?"

"Yeah, well after I knocked him out, I got kidnapped by Matteo and his men because Donato was having a meeting with him. It was the only way I could get close and, well, while I was there, Mila showed up."

"You hated when I would talk," Mila commented.

"Yeah, I was there on a mission not to become best buddies with someone." In the end I'm glad it worked out. But she wasn't wrong, her talking grinded my gears. "Anyway, I basically ended up killing

228

everyone there besides a few people who Dimitri took care of," I finished.

Grabbing another slice of pizza I shoved half of it into my mouth. Aziza and Mila stared at me, and suddenly I felt judged. The hair on my arms prickled with the thought that Mila wouldn't want to be around me. To not let Tobias around me anymore because I killed. A lot.

"Does Zane know it was you?" Mila asked after a few minutes of silence.

"No and honestly I don't really know if I want to tell him." I didn't want to admit I was falling for him. I could barely admit it to myself, so telling them or even the man himself sent me into a panic I didn't want to deal with.

"Why not?" Aziza asked.

"Do you want to talk about the man you're in love with but haven't seen in what, how many years?" I hissed, swinging my attention back at her. The moment her eyes narrowed down at me, but with pain behind it all, I regretted asking her. Aziza never talked about him. Never told me anything besides that he was four years older than her. When her parents would take her to visit her aunt and uncle, she'd met a boy who was her other best friend. I never met him, but Aziza never paid attention to any other men. It was always him.

"I'm sorry," I mumbled.

"No, no it's fine. I should move on, right?" Shrugging her shoulders she grabbed another bottle of wine. Not bothering with pouring any into a cup, she drank from the bottle.

"Okay, enough of this heaviness." Mila smiled, grabbing another slice of pizza. "I have some news…"

"Okay…" I trailed off.

"I'm pregnant," she whispered.

"I couldn't hear you," Aziza basically yelled.

"I'm, uh…"

"She's pregnant," I announced it to her.

"Holy… Shit…"

"Are you happy?" I asked. She didn't seem too sure about it.

"I am, I really am. We've been trying for a few years, but it wasn't looking too good for a while. But before everything happened at the house, I took a test and, well, yeah."

"You don't sound happy." Leave it to Aziza to be blunt and honest.

"I am. I just don't know how he will feel. We tried for two years, and then all this shit is happening, and it'll just add more stress on him." Mila sighed.
Before I could think about it, I blurted out, "I've been training Tobias every morning."

Mila whipped her head towards me. "Excuse me?"

"I'm sorry. When we first arrived and he was helping me with the animals, he found my second training area where I have a few cars." I couldn't look at Mila. I could feel the disappointment.

"Thank you."

What?

I don't think I could have looked at her fast enough. Or have been more confused than I was.

"Thank you," she repeated. "You saved me from Matteo again, which means you saved him. You're training him and I don't know how you can really train a four-year-old, but thank you."

"Dimitri doesn't trust me."

"Dimitri will do anything I tell him to. But I don't plan on telling him this. If Tobias needs this to feel safe, then thank you. And you have my permission if that's what you need."
Nodding my head in agreement, I knew that I would continue to show Tobias how to defend himself. Even though he was four years old, he was learning how to get out of situations. I would do anything for that little boy. Even if none of them knew.

Aziza was wasted and began to show Mila how to dance like a stripper. I tried sipping on the wine. But I hated the taste, and I needed to be aware of any possible danger.

"Oh my god, I love this song!" Mila belted out. I honestly have no idea how Tobias hadn't woken up from how loud they were being. I also had no idea what song was playing, but the moment the beat dropped I jumped onto the coffee table.

"Yes!" Aziza giggled. "Throw that ass back, bitch!" Doing as she said. I swung my hips around, letting the music flow through me. I let the song distract me long enough to forget who I was or what I was supposed to be doing. I moved my body in ways I remembered Aziza showing me. I let myself feel loose and it felt amazing.

When the song ended all of us barely stopped dancing as we began to laugh. I don't even know what made us laugh, but it felt good. It finally felt like I had a place, like someone besides Aziza who I grew up with understood me.

That was until I saw someone—not just someone, but three someone's standing in the front door entrance. I barely had time to stop moving before I locked eyes with Zane. I could feel the heat between us. It felt powerful, like I was standing on top of the world.

I didn't have time to process what was happening or let my brain catch up before Zane stalked towards me. The moment his shoulder hit my stomach I was lifted off the table. I barely even heard someone mutter, "Oh fuck." I had no idea who said that before Zane ran up the stairs, two at a time. I knew I was a small person but carrying me like this and running should've been difficult, but for him it wasn't. Before I knew it, he'd kicked my bedroom door closed and I was sliding down his front.

Both of our breathing was labored, panting before anything even began.

"You don't understand what you do to me." His voice was husky. Low and full of sexual energy that I didn't know if I could handle at all. The look on his face told me all and if I made one wrong move, he would attack me like an animal.

That still didn't stop me from backing away until I hit my bed with the back of my knees. I scanned Zane's body, his solid muscles straining against his long-sleeved Henley, his jeans tight in the right places. A rose mixed with a skull rested perfectly on his hand. I don't know why my eyes were drawn to that, but I couldn't pull my eyes away. Something was so different about it, but I'd seen that hand before. I'd seen that tattoo before.

I hadn't realized I was biting my lips until I tasted the metal. Or the fact that I was eye fucking him until my eyes finally made it back up to Zane's face. He almost appeared angry, but angry about what I had no idea. My thighs squeezed together. I could feel the wetness leaking into my panties now.

"Undress," he ordered.

I, the girl who never listened to anyone, couldn't have gotten undressed quick enough.

"Leave the heels on." Again he ordered. I was about to combust here in front of him with that tone. Earlier I had decided to put my high-heeled, ankle boots on, and now I was glad I did.
I didn't want to listen to him, yet I did. My body was not in tune with my head, because I told myself I wouldn't listen to him, that I was in charge, yet my hand tugged my tight shirt over my head. Reaching for my leggings I peeled them over the heeled boots I always wore.

"Fuck," Zane muttered, reaching into his pants to adjust himself.

Unhooking my bra I let it drop onto the floor, before tossing my panties to the side as well.

I shifted on my feet suddenly feeling uncomfortable with standing here completely naked in front of him. Every time we had sex it was dark, and it had been fast, in the moment type of stuff. But now I was standing here, naked, with scars in full view.

"Come here." That voice again. The moment I was about to take a step towards him he said, "Crawl."

Holy fuck.

My body shivered. I didn't think as I slowly slid down to my hands and knees. I felt degraded, and I was surprised by the way my body reacted to it. I didn't want to think about the scars littering my body and the way he could see them.

I ignored the ping in my gut that I looked hideous and I crawled to him. Stopping in front of him, I sat back on my knees, knowing that he most likely didn't want me to stand.

He stared down at me, as though he didn't know what he wanted to do just yet. It felt like the longest time before he reached down and cupped my cheek, stroking my jaw with his thumb while his other hand reached for his pants and began unbuttoning the top and pulling the zipper down. I wanted to look at what he was doing, but I couldn't pull my eyes away from him. We both stared at each other as he pulled himself out from his pants.

Finally, I dared to look down at him. His cock bobbed in my face. It was thick and I swallowed, realizing just how big he really was. Sure we've had plenty of sex, but for the first time I was seeing it up close, eye to eye. Literally. I squirmed realizing I had no idea what I was doing. I mean I have watched enough porn to know the basics, but beyond knowing that, I was clueless.

"Lick the head, Kitten," he encouraged me gently.

Not giving myself a chance to chicken out, I bent forward and licked the head. The taste of precum had me moaning and my eyes rolled into the back of my head.

"Suck on the tip." How he said that even gentler than I'd heard before was beyond me.

Sucking the tip, the sounds Zane made encouraged me to take him further into my mouth. The taste of more precum had me sucking him down to the back of the throat, yet he still didn't fit. He was too big.

"Fuck, Salem, your mouth feels amazing." Zane hissed, his hand curling around the back of my neck. I waited for him to take control, to do something besides holding my head. But he did nothing.

Halting, I pulled off and glared up at him.

"I didn't tell you to stop," he barked, glaring back down at me.

"Stop holding back." I grabbed his thighs. "You can be rough; I know you can," I snapped. I don't know why I was angry that he's not being rough with me. Maybe because that's all we've always done. Since the beginning it's always been rough with him, and now he was treating me… treating me like someone who mattered to him. I didn't need or want that right now.

"You don't know what you're asking for," he said, again being gentle.

"Fuck my face, Zane." I sat back on my knees.

Something passed on his face before he grabbed my hair tightly and brought his cock back to my mouth. Sucking him, he wasted no time as he bucked into my mouth with no care. He hit the back of my throat causing me to gag, but he didn't let up. No, instead it caused him to thrust harder into me. Spit dripped down my chin onto my thighs, I had no idea what I was doing.

I moved my hand down, wiping up the spit from my mouth, bringing it down between my legs. I begin rubbing circles on my clit, needing some type of release. Zane growled as I looked up at him, his eyes already focused down at my hand between my legs.

"Get yourself ready for me, Kitten," he rushed out almost in anger. "Put a finger inside your pussy now."

Somehow nodding my head with his cock buried inside my mouth, I stick my middle finger inside. *Oh, my god.* The feeling about all this was so dirty. I hadn't expected myself to be this turned on or this god damn wet. The sensation of me moaning caused Zane to hiss, his movements becoming ragged.

"I'm going to cum down your throat," he rushed out. "Do not swallow, you hear me?"

Nodding the best I could. Zane jerked before his release poured into my mouth. I pulled my hand from my legs to grab onto his thigh as he continued to cum into my mouth. I tried my best to not swallow, but his cock slipped from my mouth.

"Fuck," he grunted. His thumb wiped the corner of my mouth where I'm assuming some had leaked out. Bending down we became eye level, my mouth still opened with his cum. "Fuck, that's hot. Swallow," he smirked. Moving his cum to the back of my throat with my tongue I swallowed with my mouth half opened. I never understood liking the taste of someone, but I was screwed because I was somehow even more turned on. Opening my mouth again I stuck my tongue out, showing him my now very empty mouth.

"Good girl," he mumbled before smashing his mouth to mine. His tongue dove down my throat, and I moaned as I pressed my thighs together. I had no idea how I got so lucky with him, but fuck.

His arms tucked under my armpits. "Wrap your legs around my waist," he mumbled against my lips. Before I knew it, he was standing up, holding me up from under my arms. Wrapping my legs around him quickly, I stared down at him. He walked forward towards my bed, setting me down and he hovered over me. My legs still wrapped around him, not wanting to let him go.

"Let me fuck your pussy with my mouth." *God, his dirty words.* A pang of nervousness shot through me. I couldn't release him. I couldn't let him get that close to my legs, though I knew he had been before. Something about this time felt different. All of this felt different.

"Now," he demanded. I don't know if he knew what I was feeling and thinking or if this was all just for him. But either way I finally unhooked my legs, resting them on the side of his body.

"How was your girls' night?" he asked, sliding down my body, his face hovering over my stomach.

"It-it was good," I spat out.

"You sound a little off." He chuckled. His warm hands gripped my tits, pinching my nipples slightly. My breath hitched.

"Z-Zane, please," I begged.

"You were confident when you wanted me to fuck that mouth of yours, but all of a sudden you're shy?" he smirked. His beard tickled my stomach as he dipped down and kissed me. Right above the scar I hated so much. "I think I know why." He kissed the other scar on the side of my belly button. "Your body is full of scars…Your back, your stomach," he said, kissing along my hip bone. "The ones on your thigh, your inner leg… they're everywhere." He trailed down to my thigh. "Your throat. You wear clothes that hide your skin, even in your own home… when you're working out. You hide yourself away from everyone, even when we do this. You like the dark, you like keeping yourself away."

"Z-Z-Zane," I stuttered. The tears threatened to fall from my face. I didn't want to cry. I didn't cry. I refused to let that weakness fall. I couldn't do that in front of him.

"You won't hide from me, Salem. You will show me these scars of yours. I will kiss them better. I want to show you that you're beautiful, because you are."
Fuck I was not meant to cry, this was just supposed to be hot and heavy. But the tears began to fall. They fell as he kissed my inner thigh.

"Shh, just feel." Any words that would have left my mouth were gone the moment I felt his mouth on my pussy. His hands gripped my thighs, spreading them apart further. His tongue plunged forward into me, drawing out a long moan from me. My hands moved towards his hair as his tongue licked me from the pussy hole to my clit.

Over and over again.

He flicked his tongue over my clit at a rapid speed that had me making noises that didn't sound human. My nails started to dig into the back of his head, tugging his head closer to that part of my body.

"Za-Zane, fuck please, please, please," I begged. What I was begging for, I had no idea. Something, almost anything. I didn't care, I just couldn't have him stop.

"Fuck, you taste so fucking good." His filthy words did unspeakable things to me.

Zane slapped my thighs before he tightened his grip.

"Don't stop, don—" I was cut off when he gripped my waist, flipping us over. So I was now on top, my pussy pressed against his mouth. Bringing my knees closer to his head I lifted myself off his head.

"Salem," he said, his voice full of warning. "What are you doing?"

"What are *you* doing?" I panted, unsure of why he was even asking me this. I didn't want to suffocate the man.

"Put your pussy back on my mouth."

"Zane, I don—"

"Salem." Again, that voice was full of warning. Leaning a little closer to his mouth I still hovered over him.

"Salem, I'm not fucking around." He gripped my thighs. "Put. What. Belongs. To. Me. On. My. Fucking. Face. NOW." His voice was rough, husky, and lord with that sound I would do anything he asked me to do.

He must have still sensed my hesitation because he smacked my ass causing me to leap forward, my hands reaching for the headboard. I was no longer hovering, but now fully in his mouth.

"Oh, fuck," I moaned as he sucked my clit into his mouth. His tongue flicked over and over again. I couldn't control my movements any longer. I began rocking back and forth. I could feel his own moans underneath me. They vibrated into me, and I couldn't hold back anymore.

"Zane… fuck, I'm—I'm… fuck!" I screamed as my orgasm crashed into me. My chest heaved up and down, and I couldn't catch my breath. Especially when Zane didn't stop eating me, no matter how much I thrashed around. I felt like I was having an out-of-body moment and no matter the amount of force I put in trying to climb off his face he didn't let me.

"Mmmm," he mumbled under me. "I need another one, Salem," he said before placing me back on top of him.

My hands tightened on the headboard, my knuckles turning white. My voice a soft whisper, I said, "Please, I need your hands."

Instantly I felt Zane's finger enter me, pumping into me. His mouth closed over my clit again, giving me no warning as two fingers entered me. A high-pitched moan must have encouraged him further before he curled his fingers. Hitting a spot that had me losing control of everything inside me, I felt myself feel the urge to suddenly let my bladder go. But I needed to come, it was there on the peak.

Suddenly everything felt too much. I was seeing blackness. I lost control of my body. I threw my head back and I opened my mouth. No sounds came out. My body shook uncontrollably, and my lungs opened, letting me take a deep sharp breath.

"Fucking fuck," Zane grunted. His fingers never stopped. They continued pumping into me, drawing out this uncontrollable pleasure.

"I-I-I fuck, Zane." I don't even know what I was saying. Not when I heard him swallowing from below me. It was all too much, and my body fell forward. I could no longer hold myself up.

My eyes were closed, as I became aware of being picked up and rested against the back of his knees. Slowly opening them, it took more effort than I cared to admit to focus. Immediately, I noticed his whole face was soaking wet, along with his hair. My face flushed with embarrassment.

Zane must have realized what I was feeling because his arms tightened around my waist. "Don't you dare feel embarrassed by that." His voice left no room for argument.

Nodding slowly, I understood. But that still didn't make it go away. I had heard of girls squirting. I just never thought I would be one of them. Thinking about all the times we'd had sex, he never once made me feel less than. Even the first time, I was the one who ran away. It was always me, running away from him.

"Pick your hips up."

Doing as he said, he tugged on his cock a few times before placing it at my entrance. Placing my hands on his chest I began easing my way down onto his shaft. A groan escaped him and the overwhelming feeling that I was the one doing this to him warmed my heart.

The moment I was sitting back on his thigh Zane moved his hands to my hips. Pulling me up, he waited until I made eye contact before he thrust up into me.

"Jesus fuck," he gritted through his teeth. Ramming himself up into me left me no room to breathe, to do much of anything. "You're so fucking tight."

"Please don't stop…don't stop," I chanted over and over again. Throwing my head back, my orgasm rushed through my body.

"Salem," he hissed. "Shit, you're squeezing me so god…damn…hard…" Everything that he was doing was hitting the right spots, and I was already headed towards my fourth orgasm.

"Give me one more," he growled at me. "Fuck, give...me...one...more." His thrusts became rushed and sloppy. "Mine."

"Yes, yes, all yours!" I screamed, my fourth one skyrocketing out of me, a gush of fluid leaving my body. I once again had no idea what my body was doing, I had no control over anything. Zane barely gave me time to see things as he shoved himself into me again.

"You're going to take my cum like a good girl, aren't you?" he grunted. I couldn't even speak as he brought his hands to my clit and began rubbing it in circles. I didn't even have time to speak before Zane yanked me down, pushing his tongue into my mouth. Between him thrusting into me like a madman, the pressure he was putting on my clit with his hand, and now kissing me like he needed air, I lost myself.

"Fuck," he hissed. His movement stilled as I felt the warmth of both of our final release. My body shook, and my arms suddenly felt numb. I dropped forward, my face resting in his neck. My eyes closed, as he slowly began playing with my hair. My body relaxed, and this calmness fell over me as the sleepiness took me over.

———

The feeling of someone rubbing my back woke me from my deep sleep. I wasn't ready to fully wake up just yet. I felt like I had barely slept at all.

"Five more minutes," I mumbled sleepily into his warm chest.

"Come on, we gotta get you cleaned up." Zane still continued to rub my back, making it a little too hard to get up. "Salem, come on, Kitten." He kissed the top of my head before pulling away. I whined in protest at my personal pillow leaving me, until I looked over at the clock on my side table. Two a.m. Thank the heavens above, I could shower really quick and then get a few more hours of sleep.

Swinging my legs over the side, my muscles were all in protest. I felt like I had my ass kicked last night. Maybe a bath instead of a shower would work better to help my soreness. Slipping my hand into Zane's, I followed him into the bathroom where he must have read my mind about a bath.

"Grab those lavender salts." Zane pointed to the cabinet as he tested the water. I didn't question as I grabbed the salts before handing them to him.

Watching as he poured a good amount into the water, he held his hand out. Helping me into the water, I sat down and sighed as the warm water helped soothe my sore muscles.

"Lean up, Kitten." Zane brought my attention back to him. Leaning forward, he stepped in behind me. Wrapping an arm around my middle he pulled me against his chest.

"Will you come visit me?" I asked. I had been fighting with myself on not wanting to ask him. I didn't want to beg him to stay, but I also didn't want him to go. I was attached to him, even though I knew it was better not to be.

"What are you talking about?" He sounded annoyed that I even dared to ask something like that.

"I don't know, sorry. I shouldn't have asked. It was stupid of me." I couldn't help the worry in my voice.

"What makes you think I'm going anywhere?" He wrapped his arms tighter around my middle, his thumbs rubbing circles around on my ribs. "I don't know if I gave you the impression I was leaving, but I'm good here," he said as a matter of fact. I didn't know if I wanted to smile or fight against him saying he was staying here. I hadn't been truthful with him and now I was regretting not telling him the truth.

Instead of answering him I relaxed back and closed my eyes. Matching my breathing to his I ignored the guilt I felt for not telling him about Luca, and why it would be much better if he left. If they all just left.

Chapter 27

Salem

It had been two weeks since Zane told me he was staying here with me, even if his family went back to Russia. We hadn't talked about it, but since that night things had shifted in everyone. Killian had begun acting differently, being quiet. Aziza stopped replying to my calls. Tobias and I still trained every morning with no one knowing but Mila. He was getting faster at breaking away from me. Mila had her training, and she was getting much better. She started feeling comfortable with Dimitri training her finally. Zane got back into training, and we spent a lot of time sparring with each other.

It was odd having someone else to spar with, but it was nice. Though I still had yet to put all my training to use with him. He had asked me multiple times to not hold back, but I couldn't bring myself to actually hurt him.

I had yet to tell him about my family, or to tell him that I've known him for almost five years now. Every time I saw my bat sitting in the corner it was always there on the tip of my tongue to tell him the whole truth.

I just never got to the point where I could. It was beginning to weigh down on me that I kept my distance from everyone. Besides the three training sessions we had, I always stayed outside, usually with Pumpkin, taking him for long rides.

That's how I found myself tonight. Mila and Dimitri wanted to go out. She had planned on telling him that she was pregnant. Killian and Zane decided they were going to check out some land Killian was thinking of purchasing.

I stayed to watch Tobias, which I had no problem doing. He was lying next to me on the couch after we watched Tarzan half a dozen times. Clicking the TV off when the movie finished playing I sat back and took a moment listening to nothing but silence.
Since meeting Zane I felt like I hadn't had any silence in my life. I had always been preparing for Luca. But now here even with the small snores from Tobias, it was nice to not hear anything.
But with silence came the thoughts. How would Zane react if I told him the reasons I was killing those men? Would they understand why I had to do it?

Two more kills and I was done. It was just Dante and Luca now, and they would meet their end. I just couldn't go all this way to turn around now. As much as I wished I could, I couldn't. Nor would I.

I just hoped I was the same after, and then Zane would think I was worth it in the end. I just needed Aziza to find Dante and Luca again. That way I could finish this once and for all. Then I could get on with my life, and so could Aziza.
I wasn't the only one involved in this.

Tobias sighed, breaking me from my thoughts. I should probably get him to bed. If they came home and found him sleeping on the couch and not in his bed at midnight, they would think I let him stay up too late.

Wrapping one arm around his back and hooking the other underneath his legs I carried him up the stairs. Nudging his door open I carefully set him down on his dinosaur bed. None of them had even questioned when I got him a bunch of things for this room to feel like his. Though it had been Lee's room, it was now fully decked out in small-child decor instead of collecting dust.

Draping his blanket over him I quietly shut the door. I didn't know when any of them would be home. I had told Dimitri and Mila to stay out as long as they wanted. That in the morning I could take care of him. I had no idea what Zane and Killian were doing, but I assumed they would be home soon.

Deciding on a shower I headed to my room and into the bathroom. Turning the shower head on as hot as I could stand it, I stripped from my sweats and Zane's shirt before stepping inside. The water was a little warmer than normal, but the burn felt good.

I didn't enjoy the shower alone anymore, so I quickly washed before stepping out and wrapping myself in a towel along with my hair. After drying myself enough I made my way back into my bedroom before pulling on a pair of Zane's boxer briefs. Even if they were supposed to be form fitting, they barely stayed around my waist. Finally pulling over another white T-shirt of his I made my way back into the bathroom.

Just as I was done brushing my hair, the sound of a window breaking caused me to clench the brush. Peeking through the bathroom door I listened closely to any more noise. Before I knew what I was doing my feet pulled me towards the door. Opening it I found Tobias peeking out of his own door.

"What was that?" he asked in his sleepy voice.

"I don't know, but go back to your room," I said, stepping out into the hallway. "Lock your door and don't answer for anyone but me, understand?" I said pointing for him to go back.

Suddenly very awake Tobias nodded, "I call Dada," he said just as he turned on his heel and closed the door. I just hoped any of the guys were watching the camera system they put in my house were watching.

Waiting until I heard him lock his door I turned around and stayed in the shadows, carefully going down each step of the stairs. Listening and keeping my eyes alert to anything moving.

Getting to the bottom of the stairs I looked around the corner only to find nothing there. Taking a step I peered around the living room. Even as open as this house was, someone could hide. But I knew all the hiding places.

"They're upstairs. I saw her carry the boy up there." A man's voice spoke in Italian. Right away my mind wanted to go to that night. The night that changed everything. But I couldn't think about it, because I had Tobias to think about.

"You two, go check." *Go check.*
Fuck. Fuck. Fuck. I don't know where anyone was. I had no way of knowing how many men were here, but I wouldn't let them hurt Tobias. I would never forgive myself.

Before I could move to give them the element of surprise, two very large, heavily tattooed men turned the corner from the kitchen, stopping just as they saw me standing there. Surprise went out the window.

"Fuck," the left one cursed. Just as they stood there another one stepped up.

Three in total. I could take them.

"Take her out. Stop fucking standing there!" someone from the kitchen yelled. How he knew I was standing there was beyond me. Not a second later the one all the way to the left charged at me, his heavy footsteps echoing around the house. Grabbing hold of the vase sitting on the table I smashed it across his face and reaching around his throat I pulled myself on top of his head just as another started to charge. Kicking my leg up and around I was able to kick number two in the face, blood pouring from his now broken nose, before I wrapped my arm around number one's neck and yanked down as I landed on the floor. His large body fell with a thud onto the floor. Punching him in the throat, he began choking as I grabbed the side table and crashed the leg into his open mouth.

Dead.

Number three finally got a hint I wasn't going down easy.

"Bring it motherfucker," I snapped, cocking my eyebrow at numbers two and three. The blond charged at me. Ducking underneath him I ran to the kitchen, the third guy chasing after me.

"Dante wanted me to give you his regards," he said as he sent a punch into my gut then my face. Something in me snapped hearing Dante's name out loud. Grabbing the pizza cutter from the counter I pushed all feelings away. They were all going to die.

———————

Zane

Killian and I piled into the SUV as my phone began going off. I wasn't in the mood to talk to whoever was on the other line. Without pulling it from my pocket I silenced it as Killian pulled out of the club downtown. Just as it silenced it started ringing again.

"Fuck." Pulling it out I didn't glance at it before answering, "Fuck off."

"Zane!" I heard just before I pressed the end button. Looking down I saw it was Tobias, from the emergency burner I'd given him.

"Fuck, Tobs?" My voice quickly switched to concern. Reaching over I grabbed Killian's iPad.

"What's going on?" Killian asked. Ignoring him I made work of going to the security cameras I had installed without Salem knowing.

"SOMEONES IN THE HOUSE," he began screaming so loud my ears rang. "I-don't-I don't, HELPPP." His voice cracked between sobs.

"Killian, faster!" I snapped. "Tobias, we're almost there, a few minutes, buddy. Hold on," I screamed.

"HUR-" He cut off. The sound of two beeps seemed louder in my ear. The call had ended.

Snapping my gaze to the camera, I could hear Killian speaking, but the words didn't make sense as I switched between camera feeds. I wasn't computer savvy like he was, but since putting those cameras up, I learned how to work them. The front showed nothing, even the back, but as it switched to the stairs, I began holding my breath. Turning the volume all the way up, I couldn't focus on anything else but watching Salem being dragged down next to the staircase. A very large man covered in tattoos had hold of her hair by the fist. "Let me fucking go!" she screamed, her legs kicking as her hands gripped at his wrist.

"Killian, how long?" I barked, unable to take my eyes off the screen.

"Five minutes!" he yelled. I could tell he was listening as well. He heard her scream and could feel the tension as well as me.

The man dragged her further away from the stairs, stairs I hoped no one had climbed up. I had no idea where Tobias was, but I couldn't click away from watching her fight for her life. I should've fucking been there. I didn't care about Killian wanting to buy property here.

"Stupid bitch!" the man growled. Snapping back to the screen I watched as Salem somehow flipped her leg upward towards his head and kicked him directly in the eye. He dropped the hold he had on her hair making her fall flat on her back, which would cause anyone to get the wind knocked out of them. But Salem quickly sprung up, jumping on top of the man, her knee colliding with his face three times. She bashed his face over and over again. Another scream had her stop dead in her tracks, dropping his body, and she ran to the stairs.

Salem hurried towards the stairs, at the other high-pitched screams. FUCK. Switching the camera to the room Salem set up for his room, I watched as three large men kicked in his bedroom door.

"Killian, HURRY THE FUCK UP!" My voice cracked as I still couldn't tear myself from the screen. I felt so helpless. My heart was being torn from my chest, and I couldn't breathe.

"HELP!" Tobias screamed, tears rolling down his face. Two of the men approached him, both of them laughing as Tobias tried to hide in his closet. I would kill them all. I'm going to flay them alive and burn all their loved ones.

"Hey, fuckers!" Salem called from the doorway. She was standing there smirking at them. I had no idea where she got this confidence from, or if she was going to try and fight them off. Even if she could take me down, I was one man—she couldn't take on all three. They were huge, just as big as I was.

"Get her, I'll get the kid," the one with blond hair ordered.

"Touch a single hair on his fucking body and I will make you wish you never lived." Her voice was so calm it ran shivers down my body. I had never seen this side of her. The smile she was giving them was almost like she enjoyed the beginning of this taunt.

"You think you can fight us both little girl?" the second one asked in a mocking tone.

"Bring it, stupid fucks," Salem challenged them.

"We're around the corner," Killian said, just as I heard Salem say, "Little one, close your eyes, please." Her voice was so calm and caring.

"You need to call Dimitri." I couldn't believe I had completely forgotten about Dimitri until now.

"His phone is going straight to voicemail."

"Fuck," I cursed under my breath.

Turning back to the screen I tried to calm my beating heart from watching as Salem fought three men. She had the small dinosaur lamp, throwing it in the blond's face before grabbing hold of number two's wrist and hoisting herself up. Wrapping her legs around his thick neck, she pulled her weight back causing both of them to rock backwards before he lost his footing, and she flung forward. He fell onto his face, and she rolled onto Tobias's bed. Blondie was hot on her trail grabbing her by the throat. Out of nowhere she smiled bringing a knife she somehow got hold of and stabbed his face.

"AHH. YOU BITCH," Blondie screamed just as she began driving the knife into his face over and over.

Dead.

I felt the car come to a complete stop. I don't know how or where I went but my body had me running into the house, my Glock in my hand. Running up the stairs, my voice didn't work as I reached his door. Salem reared back slamming the side table into number two's face, knocking him out cold, just as the third guy rammed something in his hand into her side. Salem's eyes went wide. My hand moved before my mind did, and I shot the fucker in the head right between the eyes.

Looking up our eyes met, and her eyes switched from something dangerous to soft.

"What the actual fuck?" Killian said behind me. "Sal—"

"Killian, take Tobias to the car," I snapped, keeping my gaze on Salem. She continued to hold the side table.

"Aunt Sey, I want to be with you," Tobias began to beg.

"Little one it's okay," Salem whispered. I don't know if he heard her. I barely did. From the corner of my eye I noticed him nodding his head. What the fuck? He listened to her instead of me. I knew they were growing close to each other, but this looked entirely different.

Killian stepped over the two bodies before grabbing Tobias and carried him out. I couldn't look away from Salem. My white shirt she wore was covered in blood, and from the looks of it, brain as well. It was ripped vertically down the middle, and her hair was wet and covered with blood. Looking around her body, she was covered in blood. She looked like Carrie, when they poured pig's blood over her body. I didn't even know what I was feeling at this moment until I saw her begin to sway on her feet. Looking closer I took in the large blood stain on her side.

"You were stabbed," I growled. Stepping closer I tried my best to keep my anger from showing. I was angry about everything at the moment.
Dimitri not answering his phone, Killian taking me around town showing me different properties he wanted to buy, and now Salem. I was angry with her for thinking she could just take down so many

different men without help. Not once did she contact either of us. It was Tobias who did.

Shaking my head, I stepped closer to her. "Let me look."

"I'm okay." Her voice shook, which told me everything I needed to know. She was far from okay.

"Just shut up and let me look," I snapped. Lifting her shirt without waiting for her permission I took in the two stab wounds on her side. Along with bruising that was already turning a dark shade of purple.

"You need to be stitched up."

"I told you I'm fine." She smacked my hand away from her. Taking several steps back she pressed down on her side, hissing the moment she made contact. "Fuck," she whispered. Before I could even blink, she swayed further on her legs before they finally buckled, and she went down.

"Tell me again what the *fuck happened?*" Dimitri growled at us. Killian stood leaning against the doorway. Mila was cuddling Tobias who was passed out on the loveseat, while Dimitri and I stood facing each other in the middle of the waiting area.

"I've gone over this a dozen times, Dimitri."

The moment Salem passed out, we rushed her to the hospital, where they were still operating on her. The blond girl from before showed up cussing at all of us while focusing her attention on Killian, glaring more than I had ever seen a person glare before.

After they took her back, Dimitri and Mila showed up. They had apparently been run off the road and Mila had a gash above her eyebrow. The moment he saw Killian carrying Tobias he had demanded we tell him everything. As if we hadn't planned on telling him.

"Tell. Me. Again." One thing about Dimitri is he hates having to ask for things twice. I just didn't see the reason for having to tell him for what seemed to be the millionth time.

Rolling my eyes, I turned and sat on the chair behind me. "I don't know what happened before we got the call. Tobias called screaming and then the call cut out. We tried calling you guys, but it went straight to voicemail. We were only about ten minutes away, if that. I brought the security cameras up, the ones I placed when we first arrived. From there we saw her take down three men downstairs before we all heard Tobias scream." I couldn't help but glance over at him. I never wanted to hear him scream like that again. Something inside me snapped when I heard it.

"She ran up the stairs and took out one of them before we arrived. When we got into the house and upstairs, she was in the process of the second one. The third stabbed her, and I shot him."

Dimitri looked over at Mila and Tobias as if they would disappear from sight if he looked away long enough. I hated that. Ever since Tobias had been born, it was like a new Dimitri had also been born. He was scared about everything, worried his enemies would find them. This had been the first attack since he'd been here, and it was while none of us had been around.
Just Salem.

A stranger to us all. Someone we can't find any information about. Someone who won't tell us anything about herself. Someone we don't even know. It was like it all fell into place now. I understood why Dimitri wasn't sure about her. I had just been blind to it all. Who the fuck was Salem? Was that even her real name? Sure I found a photo of what appeared to be her family, but how could we be sure she hadn't done something to them?

We were all killers, and she proved that with killing five men in her house just a few hours ago.

The sound of the door opening broke me from my thoughts. Turning around, a small man in scrubs walked in. "Salem Gray family?"

"That's us," Dimitri answered. I knew better than to tell him we weren't exactly her family.

"Is Aziza here?" he asked.

"She went to get something to drink." Killian finally spoke for the first time since we arrived here. "Here she is," he said, just as she walked in.

"Is she okay?" Aziza whispered.

"She's resting right now. We had to repair the damage done to her kidney, along with some bleeding she had. We stitched up the two stab wounds, but she has some bad bruising." The doctor said everything to Aziza, not once looking at any of us.

"When can I see her?" she asked, holding her cup of coffee tightly.

He finally glanced around at us before returning his gaze to Aziza. "You can stay with her tonight. But the rest can wait until visiting hours tomorrow morning."

She nodded her head.

"Let me know if you need anything, Aziza." The doctor smiled before turning towards the door and leaving.

I don't know what was going on between the doctor and Aziza, but glancing over at Killian, he looked like he was ready to tear him apart with his bare hands. "Aziza."

She turned sharply looking around at all of us. I had no idea who this woman was, but by the look on her face, she was ready to tear Killian a new asshole. She was ready to fight any of us if we said a word about Salem. I wanted to hold onto that, but everything about Salem was truly beginning to get under my skin. We had no idea who she was.

"Why can't we find anything on her?" Dimitri turned his full attention to Aziza.

"She doesn't exist, that's why." I was surprised by the fact that she stood her ground. Not many women could. Three it appeared to be.

"Yeah, got that, but we're going to need a little more information," he grunted.

"I'm not going to tell you shit, so don't waste your breath."

"Do not speak to me like that. You know who I am. You know I will not think twice about ending your fucking life right here, right now," Dimitri growled at her, taking a step. I wasn't going to step in unless things got worse, and from the look on Killian's face he was fighting with who he was going to side with.

Aziza laughed, full on laughing. I don't know who was more surprised by that as well, either Dimitri who had stopped stalking towards her like prey, or Killian who stood straight up, arms crossed looking between them both. Even Mila who was two seconds away from falling asleep was now sitting straight up watching Dimitri.

"You think I'm scared of you?" She was still laughing. "That's good, a really good one. But no, buddy, I'm not." Aziza stepped forward now standing directly in front of Dimitri. "She doesn't exist because I made sure no one can find her." She pointed towards

Killian. "Even if you think you have the best hacker, there's always someone better," she said, now pointing towards herself. "Me."

"Wait, what?" Killian stepped towards them.

"Salem no longer exists in this world. No one knows her, and no one can find her. She was never born; I took it all away. And if you ever threaten me again, Dimitri Volkov, I will make sure everything you have in your life disappears." And to top it off she patted his chest. Turning around she headed for the door. "And, Killian, if I ever see you again, I'll stab you. I don't need a *boy* in my life that would ever allow his pussy boss to speak to me that way. I deserve better." With that the door slammed.

Killian punching the wall caused both of us to turn towards him.

"I don't want to hear it. Take Mila and Tobias to Hollow. Zane and I will meet you there." Dimitri then pulled out his phone that I hadn't even realized was ringing.

"How'd you get this number?" He looked at me, his face hardening from whoever was on the other line.

"Excuse me?" After a moment he threw the phone across the room, hitting it, smashing it to pieces.

"Who was that?" I asked.

"Luca." Dimitri stormed towards the door. Following him out, he marched around the fifth floor looking at each door. I had a feeling he was looking for Salem and I wasn't sure what he planned on doing once he found her.

"What did he want?" I asked.

Ignoring me he continued looking around, searching each folder on the doors. I knew better than to try and get him to stop. Once he was on a mission, he stuck his mind to it, no matter what.

I don't know how long we searched, going through the whole fifth and sixth floors until we saw the same doctor the moment we got to the seventh floor.

"You," Dimitri growled and began stalking towards him.

The doctor looked up and rolled his eyes before crossing his arms over his chest.

"What do you want?" he asked not caring that Dimitri was a dangerous man. It appeared everyone in the damn town didn't care. I wouldn't be that surprised if Dimitri ended up shooting him for the disrespect.

"Where is she?"

"Care to elaborate who you're referring to?" Give it to the doctor for not giving a shit.

"Don't give me that, where the fuck is Salem!" he barked, getting loud at the end.

Before he could say anything, the door to our left swung open and Aziza stepped through. "In," she ordered.

Dimitri, not sparing a glance back, walked into the room, with me following behind. I wasn't sure what I expected when I walked in. But seeing Salem lying on the hospital bed sent my heart into a frenzy. My stomach felt like it was in knots. Everything felt uncomfortable.

She laid there with an IV in her arm, an oxygen tube in her nose. The whole side of her left face was bruised, and several bruises sat along her arms. I had yet to see the rest of her body, but I knew it matched.

"What do you want?" Aziza answered after closing the door and stepping to stand next to Salem. A spot where I wanted to stand. I wanted to be the one she was leaning on, holding her hand.

"Who are you?" Dimitri asked. A cool expression.

"I'm not telling you," Salem answered, staring at Dimitri, not once sparing me a glance.

"Tell me why the fuck Luca had his men attack your house and my fucking son!"

"I'm not telling you," Salem's voice hardened.

"The fuck you are." He stepped towards the bed. Everything happened so fast I could barely react. Dimitri approached the foot of the bed, and Aziza punched him in the face. Dimitri went forward to grab her arm. Salem was out of the bed, IVs torn from her arm, and swinging her leg out that knocked Dimitri onto his ass.

"Don't fucking move," Salem ordered. Her knee stuck in his throat, his arms above his head. "I'm not telling you shit, and you don't come into my hospital room asking me shit either. If you don't like what I'm telling you and *have* been telling you ALL, then fucking leave." Her face was inches from Dimitri's. I should have moved, should have removed Salem from what she was doing, but I couldn't find it in me to do so.
Standing up, Salem moved back as Dimitri got to his own feet. "They attacked my son," he growled.

"I protected him," she shot back.

"Barely," Dimitri muttered.

"Excuse me?" Aziza finally stepped around. "Are you kidding me? Salem has done everything to fucking protect all of you!" she screamed. She was hinting at something, but I couldn't tell what.

"It's fine." Salem shrugged, wincing as she did. Looking down I frowned as the side of her gown stuck to her side.

"Salem," I whispered.

"No."

"Your side." I pointed to what I was talking about.

Without caring she lifted her gown up, showing, just like I assumed, bruises covering her legs, along with her stomach. The bandages along her side were coated in blood, along with her stomach where they must have opened her up.

"Get back in bed," Aziza ordered. Bringing her phone out she did something quick before saying, "Tyler will be in here in a second to redo those."

For a moment no one said anything. I couldn't tear my eyes away from Salem. Not even when the door opened behind us.

"They're still here." The doctor who hadn't dealt with Dimitri's bullshit walked in carrying a tray of supplies. "Lay down, Salem."

Doing as the doctor said she laid down, keeping an eye on both of us. "Leave." Her voice was calm. I felt myself flinch from the pure coldness she held. She acted like we were nothing. Not even in the beginning did we treat each other like this.

"Don't contact my family a—"

"Dimitri," I finally spoke. "She can contact me." My words were firm. I didn't care if he ordered me or not.

"No. I won't be talking to any of you." Salem hissed as the doctor began taking her stitches out. "If you can't trust me that I'm protecting you by not telling you anything, then we have nothing." She didn't look anywhere else but at me.

"Salem." I wanted to tell her I did trust her, part of me did. But everything was different. I felt like a fucking teenager, a girl at that. I hated having these emotions, these feelings towards her because everything started to feel like too much. I had told her everything about how I started to work for Dimitri, and even about my damn family.

"I don't want to hear it, Zane, it's fine." Something unfamiliar about her voice made me uneasy. Salem never showed when she was worried, or in fact feeling uneasy. But here, something was so off about it. I had no idea what was going through her head like usual, and suddenly I felt myself getting angry.

"Well, then, I guess we're done here." I was forced out. Even if I didn't mean it.

"I guess we are." Salem nodded. Another part of my heart broke.

Turning on my heel I headed for the door. I couldn't look at her because if I did, I would say something I regretted. I knew the reasons I was throwing in the towel with her, but not knowing her reasoning was like a knife to my chest. This was the reason I didn't get attached to people. I stuck to the four that were my family, and to hell with everyone else.

I don't know why I said it, when it wasn't true. The anger building up inside me was becoming so uncontrollable that I should've walked out the door. Instead I opened my mouth.

"You were nothing but a lousy fuck. This is why I don't fuck virgins."

Chapter 28

Salem

Two months later

Their screams echoed around the house until it went silent. Lee stopped screaming first, then it was Emmy. Mama and Dada screamed some, but Dada mostly just cursed and yelled at the bad men. My lungs burned, and my throat was on fire from screaming so much. I had no more tears in me. Everything hurt.

Mama stopped screaming.

Dada began sobbing.

I couldn't see what they were doing. They had me tied in the front room while they went into the kitchen.

Dada went silent.

I tried to calm my breathing. I knew what they were about to do. They were dead. Mama, Dada, Lee, my sister Emmy. They were all gone. Toby was gone.

My heart ached, and everything inside me was shutting down. Shutting off. I no longer wanted to feel anything.

Footsteps appeared behind me, but I had no energy to fight the rope that held me to the chair. I could only wish they would end me quickly.

I was tired of fighting.

I was so tired.

"Get rid of her." That was Luca's voice, I could tell.

"Leonzo, came and cut this bitch from the chair," Remo ordered.

I tried lifting my head, but everything felt weak. My leg was cut badly. I don't know how I survived that. I couldn't survive much more; I wouldn't make it.

I felt Leonzo cutting the rope around my untouched leg first before reaching around to my useless arms. The moment the rope let go my body fell to the ground. I wanted to yell in pain, but I barely felt it.

"Take the bitch outside," Remo ordered someone near me. I didn't have time to protest, to beg them to stop their attacks. Not before a hand grabbed the back of my hair flipping me onto my back.

Remo was staring at me. Finn and Donato were nowhere to be seen. Giulio and Orlando stood above my sister's dead body. Leonzo stood above my brother's body. I didn't see Luca or Dante either.

Leonzo smirked before grabbing hold of my ankle and began dragging me.

Dragging me through glass. Glass that was now embedded into my back. I couldn't scream or feel or do anything. I just wanted to finally be back with my family.

"SALEM!" a girl screamed. Jolting awake, my heart beat against my ribcage. My skin felt clammy, and the pounding in my head pressed against my eye socket, ready to burst at any moment.

"Salem," someone said next to me. Not wanting to look over, I shook my head instead, climbing to my feet. I rushed into the bathroom and slammed the door shut.

I didn't want to deal with Aziza. Ever since the accident she had become overbearing. Hanging around every minute, always checking on me. Even to the point she had begun to sleep over, stopped her dancing, and tried to take care of me.

I didn't want it.

I didn't want any of this.

It had been two months since he left.

Left me in the hospital, telling me I was nothing but a fuck to him. A lousy one at that. It shouldn't have bothered me as much as it did. Still did.

Everything about us suddenly made sense, on why he "cared" so fast. I was truly just a warm body to him. I was nothing. It hurt almost as much as losing my entire family. It was why I never told them what happened. They would have used it against me, against Aziza. I couldn't let that happen.

Closing my eyes I pushed everything aside and climbed into the shower. Not bothering to fix the temp, it climbed and climbed until I knew my skin was burning. But the heat was much better to deal with than any feelings I didn't want.

Stepping from the shower, I brushed my hair and teeth before returning to my room. Aziza was no longer in sight. Going straight to my closet I pulled on a pair of leggings, a large sweatshirt, and my flat combat boots. Grabbing my keys I headed downstairs.

I had no idea where I planned on going, but with Uncle Walker and Aziza standing over me at every second I barely had time to myself.

"Salem," Uncle Walker called from the kitchen. I stood there with my hand reaching for the door handle before he yelled, "Get in here now."

Rolling my eyes, I fought with myself. I could ignore him, and deal with it later. Or never if I just disappeared. Which was looking better and better each moment they were hovering over me.

"Salem?" Aziza whispered from the doorway into the kitchen. Glancing over my shoulder, I wanted so desperately to ask her to look for him. To tell me where he was. But I couldn't. I was the reason the house got attacked. Why Tobias could've been hurt. I shook my head, ready to bolt again.

"Uncle Walker wants to speak with you," she said, his own personal messenger. "I'm going to head into town for some errands."

Nodding my head, I moved out of her way. Aziza left without sparing me a second glance. Losing the battle, I slowly made my way into the kitchen, where Uncle Walker stood against the farmhouse sink. His arms crossed over his chest, staring at me like he was ready to beat me.

"You need to snap out of this." His voice was rough.

Instead of speaking, I rolled my eyes and went to the fridge. Opening it, I grabbed a water bottle. I wasn't really in the mood for just water. I needed something stronger. But it could be my excuse for why I really came in here.

"Salem!" Walker barked. Turning on my heel I shot him a glare. I didn't need his attitude. I didn't need him. I just wanted to be left alone, for everyone to leave me alone. "I'm talking to you. It's been two fucking months. Grow up," he growled.

Shrugging my shoulders, I turned back for the front door. I wasn't going to wait here for him to lecture me on how I had to get over Zane. How I needed to remember what he told me right after the accident. I didn't care anymore.

"I swear to god, Salem, you walk out that front door, it's the end," Walker snapped, following me out to the living room. "Walk out that door and this little revenge path you're going on will end. I will pack my shit and leave. I will no longer be your uncle and help you."

Stopping in my tracks, I slowly turned back towards him. Uncle Walker had always been there for me, even before my parents were taken from me. He was my best friend, and now he was giving up on me. *But he hasn't been here.* My brain reminded me.

Giving him a smile I inclined my head before turning back for the front door. Stepping out I refused to cry for losing someone else in my life. I rushed to my SUV, getting in. I didn't feel as I drove from the driveway. I wouldn't let someone else hurt me.

I didn't cry when they tried to kill me.

I didn't cry when Zane left.

I wouldn't cry now.

Chapter 29

Aziza

Errands in New York.

I was tired, cranky, and really hungry by the time I pulled up to the house Killian bought. I had left home nine hours ago and now I was pulling into his driveway. I knew they were here. I just had no idea how any of them would feel about me being here.

It's for Salem.

I had to remind myself. She was worth it. She was worth it all.

Before I could talk myself out of it, I climbed out of my car and went to the front door. Knocking a few times, I waited about two seconds before ramming the key into the lock and opening the door myself. Stepping inside I didn't bother looking around. Instead I followed to the back of the house where I assumed the kitchen was.

What I hadn't been expecting was Zane holding a gun to my left the moment I stepped inside the kitchen. Killian sat at the kitchen table with Mila and Tobias. Dimitri was standing behind Mila, his hands on her shoulders. It was almost adorable the way he cared. I just couldn't find it in myself to care for Dimitri.

"What are you doing here?" Zane growled, the gun still raised at my head.

"Zane put the gun down," I answered back, not looking away from Killian. I knew he was trying to find me. He had been since he'd left the hospital. I just couldn't be with him. He broke me. He was also doing whatever Dimitri wanted.

"I won't ask again—"

"Zane put your fucking gun down!" Killian barked. Everyone but me jumped a bit from the force of his words.

Slowly Zane lowered his gun, but not before growling like a damn animal at me. Looking at him over my shoulder, I took in the dark circles under his eyes, and the dark, longer than normal, beard. His clothes were even wrinkled. The other thing was Salem's name tattooed along his hand.

"Aziza, it's good to see you." Mila smiled brightly at me. I wanted to be happy to see her, but I couldn't. They were all controlled by Dimitri. He was a serious problem.

"Wish I could say the same," I remarked back. Ignoring the stares I stepped further into the kitchen and went to the fridge. I needed to eat something quick. I was beginning to already feel faint.

"Watch what you say to my wife," Dimitri barked at me.

"Or what, you'll scowl me to death?" I rolled my eyes, still searching for what I needed. Nothing in the fridge or freezer would help me. I couldn't look at Killian. I couldn't ask him if he still carried his supplies around.

"Aziza." Speak of the devil. Taking a deep breath, I turned. Killian was now standing in front of me, very close. I felt like I couldn't breathe with him standing this close to me. Everything was suddenly coming back. All the feelings I'd shoved away were rushing back in. I hadn't even realized he was speaking to me until he tilted my chin up. Staring up at him, his eyes softened at me.

"Blood sugar?" he asked. It was the simplest question, but it was everything. I didn't trust my words, not this close to him. So instead I nodded my head the best I could while he held my chin. "Here take this." He held something out in his other hand. I just couldn't pull myself together enough to care. I wanted to stay right here in his embrace, he was one of the only two I trusted with my life.

You'll always come second, my head reminded me. I would always come second to Killian. No matter what, Dimitri and his family were first. Killian was a computer soldier for him. I didn't matter, just like Salem didn't matter to Zane.

Remembering why I was here, I snapped out of my head and took a wide step back. Snatching my favorite chocolate bar from his hand I opened it as I walked around him and into the living room. For this conversation everyone was going to need to get comfortable.

Sitting down in the recliner I ate the chocolate while everyone slowly made their way in. Tobias waved at me as he headed towards the stairs, assuming Mila told him to go play while I was here. Dimitri and Mila sat furthest from me. Killian sat right next to me on the loveseat, holding out a water for me. Always thoughtful. I wanted to climb into his lap and remember the good days when he would always have what I needed. Always had this chocolate and had water because I was terrible at remembering to bring any.

"Why are you here?" Dimitri asked, reminding me I was here again for Salem, and not because of Killian and myself. I couldn't stop myself from looking over at Zane. He was standing by the doorway, his arms crossed over his chest, his back to the wall as he watched all exits. He was back to how he used to be before Salem. It made my chest tighten. I wondered if that was how Killian was now. Did he go back to not sleeping? He'd never slept much before.

Shaking my head from the thoughts, I refused to worry about him. "Salem," I said. One word.

One word was all it took for the room to become tense. Dimitri's body looked like he was ready to fight if she was here, Zane looked as though he was in physical pain just hearing her name. *Good.* I wanted him to hurt; he destroyed her.

"What about her?" Zane's voice was low. I wasn't sure I even heard him until Killian glared over his shoulder at him.

"It's been months, wh—"

"Two, to be exact," I interrupted Dimitri. Finishing off my candy bar, I took the water from Killian. I don't know why I wasn't expecting the lid to be just sitting there on top, ready for me to drink. But I couldn't help but glance up at him, to find he was already watching me. Smirking at me. But it wasn't cocky or mean. He was smirking like he actually cared about my opinion about him.

"That's not the point, why ar—"

"I mean, it can be the point," I again interrupted Dimitri. And the look he was giving me told me he surely did not appreciate it. "Here's a question for you…You love Mila, right?"

"Yes." He gave no hesitation, good.

"Then, Zane, I have one for you." I turned my attention towards him. "Do you love Salem?"

All he did was glare at me. I knew he had some type of feelings for Salem, whether it was love or lust. Either way, I knew she had feelings for him. She loved him, even if she never wanted to admit it aloud.

"Zane." My voice was stronger than I felt.

"Don't say my name like that," Zane snapped at me, taking a step forward. Suddenly Killian was on his feet standing in front of me, his hands fisted at his side.

"Take another step towards her, me and you will fucking fight, got it?" Killian never fought, but now he was willing to fight their enforcer for me. Willing to set aside the darkness he had for me. It warmed my heart, and I wanted to once again climb onto his lap and have him take me away from everything.

Instead I tapped the back of his leg with my foot. "It's okay," I whispered.

For a few moments they continued to stare at each other, glaring like their life depended on it. Finally Killian sat back down, keeping his hands in fists on his knees.

"Okay, enough of this. Aziza, I'm glad you're here. Dimitri just has extreme trust issues, and I apologize for him being the way he is. But what are you doing here?" Mila asked.

"What do you guys know about Salem's past?" I asked, looking around at each of them.

"Nothing," Mila answered.

"Well, her whole family was murdered." It was odd saying it out loud. Salem and I never spoke about it, and she never mentioned it. This was all weird. But it had to be done.

"Does this have anything to do with Luca?" Dimitri asked.

"It has everything to do with Luca." Sitting back I tucked my legs underneath me before looking over at Killian. I was getting ready to ask him for a blanket, but before I could open my mouth, he held out the flannel he was wearing. I couldn't stop the smile. He was surprising me, but I just didn't have time for this. I had to worry about Salem.

Taking the flannel from him I covered myself with it, itching to smell it.

"Her parents grew up in New York with Luca. I don't know too much about their lives. But Andrew, her dad, Walker, her uncle, and Luca..." I paused unsure I should mention Jacob or not. Jacob was important but for this part of the story, I decided against it. "They grew up together. Luca had always been crazy, and Andrew knew he was involved in the mafia. Anyway there was this girl, he—"

"Emily Willis," Dimitri suddenly announced. Looking over at him, he was staring directly at Killian. I wanted to ask, but I had a feeling he was looking into Luca. Trying to find anything they could about Salem, but they wouldn't.

"Yes, Emily Willis. She was the daughter of two very powerful people, lawyers, the mafia lawyers. They were arranged to be married, but Luca was batshit crazy. They were supposed to marry but the night before the wedding Emily and Andrew ran. Walker helped, and they went south. They bought a farm and began different lives."

"Luca has a son, Dante. No one knows the mother." Killian looked over at me.

"They got rid of her after he was born. She's not really important."
It was sad, but true. Taking a sip of water, I continued on. "They had
three children, Emmy, Lee, and Salem. By the time Salem was nine,
Luca had found Emily, and he took a team to murder all of them."

"I hate to say this, but it's not uncommon for the mafia to kill
families off," Dimitri started, holding up his hands. "I'm not saying
it's okay, believe me. I would never go after children, but it's
common with a lot of men in our world." I understood what he was
saying, but it still made me angry. They didn't know the worst of it
all.

"I don't know how she survived. When I found her, there was so
much blood." Staring down at my hands, it took me back to that day.
I may have only been ten, but I could remember everything. "We
were supposed to go for our last dance practice, but when I
arrived…" I looked up at Zane, wanting to make sure he understood
everything I was about to say. "She was lying on her stomach. Her
back was completely torn up, and glass was sticking out. God, there
was so much blood, so much. I don't even know how they saved her
leg, it was cut so badly." Taking a deep breath, I tried to calm down
and not let the tears fall. But I couldn't. They began trailing down
my cheeks. "Her throat was slit, s-she fuck." I tried getting my
breathing under control. Thinking back to that time was difficult.
Seeing her there dying while there was nothing I could do.

Swallowing the lump that lodged its way down my throat I
continued on. "She had packed dirt into her throat to try and stop the
blood. She even had her shirt bunched up. But when I t-touched her,
her eyes shot open. She was a-alive."

Everyone was silent.

"H-er brother, he had been stabbed so many times. His face was no
longer recognizable. Emmy, god, she was r-aped, over and over
again. Andrew had been beaten, missing a hand, most of his fingers
and toes. His ear was m-missing. Then it was her mother, E-emily."
I couldn't stop the tears. I couldn't even try. Looking over at Mila,

she was sobbing into Dimitri who now looked pained. I couldn't even face Zane, because I knew if I didn't like his reaction, I would kill him myself.

"Emily was raped, and not just in one place. She was tied down to the kitchen table. Her hands had been nailed down, and her legs were broken so she couldn't move. But worst of all, she was stabbed and left to die. She was left to hear them try and finish Salem off." My voice dropped as I whispered, "She was eight months pregnant."

Mila gasped before her voice broke and she began clutching her own stomach. Her little baby. Dimitri held Mila as she cried her heart out. Killian got up and picked me up, plopping me down onto his lap. I never told him about this part of my life. He knew about my parents. He knew my secrets.

But not Salem's.

"Her parents wanted Salem to name him. She named him Tobes." Again I whispered.

Mila couldn't control herself anymore, as she cried and cried. Dimitri began whispering things into her ear, trying to calm her down. Killian's arms wrapped around me, holding me against his chest like his life depended on it. I still couldn't look at Zane. If this didn't convince Zane over why she hid who she was, then again, I would kill him.

"I'm so sorry," Killian mumbled into my ear. Slowly he began rubbing circles into my thigh. The spot that he always rubbed because it helped with my leg pain. "I'm so fucking sorry."

"I don't believe it," Zane finally spoke.

"Excuse me?" I couldn't stop the bitterness in my voice.

"It's some stupid sob story," Zane scoffed.

"Some sob story? That's why she's gone back to the broken shell since you walked out that door. Since you called her nothing, basically," I snapped. "I don't even understand why you hate her so damn much," I muttered more to myself but loud enough that he must have heard because once again he stepped forward towards me.

"Zane, you better watch yourself." Killian spoke in a calming voice. I wasn't sure if he was moments away from losing his shit or not.

"If you truly cared about her then you wouldn't have said what you did. You would also believe it all. I'm sure you've seen the scars covering her entire body." I shivered at the thought of them. I'd seen them dozens of times. She may hide her body from most people, always wearing turtlenecks so no one saw her scars. But I knew Zane had seen them.

His silence told me everything I needed to know. He cared for her, but because she couldn't tell him the truth, he wanted to treat her like she was nothing. Nothing at all to him. But I wouldn't let him hurt her. Not anymore than he already had.

"She has always been saving us," Mila mumbled into Dimitri's chest.

"Moy tsvetok?"

"I've been keeping a secret from you." Mila couldn't look at Dimitri. "I've known Salem since I was pregnant with Tobias."

"What do you mean?" Dimitri's voice hardened.

Mila swallowed before looking over at me. I didn't know if she needed permission or what. I wasn't involved in this knowledge, but since I'd told them most of Salem's story, might as well tell them everything else as well.

"Four years ago when I was kidnapped, she was there. She was the one who killed them."

Silence.

Silence.

"Wait." Dimitri looked over at us, before his body tensed. "Are you telling me she was the one who tore all those men apart?" He was finally understanding everything. Salem was behind everything.

I nodded my head.

"She was the one who tore Matteo apart, literally. We found his body missing. Luca's men, those murders were brutal. You're telling me, Salem, that girl is the one who murdered all those men?"

Again I nodded my head at Dimitri.

"He was convinced it was some guy..." Dimitri trailed off. Finally coming to the understanding of everything. He looked over at Zane, I don't know why. "Zane?"

"Who is she?" Zane asked.

"Ghost," Mila answered for everyone.

"Bullshit, Ghost isn't real," he snapped.

"Who broke your nose four years ago, Zane?" I was losing all patience with him.

Again there was silence. Zane stared at me like I was a bug underneath him. Dimitri was smirking because he knew, and Mila was trying hard to hide her smile.

"No," Zane finally answered.

"Oh, yeah, big boy. She knocked you out easily. Took a baseball bat to your nose. Broke your poor little nose. Even went through your wallet." I tapped my chin. "What was your full name again? Zane Theodore Rivera. Damn must suck to get taken down by a five-foot-four girl." I cocked my head to the side, waiting for him to say something nasty towards me. Instead Zane watched me for a solid minute before stalking out of the living room. Leaning further into Killian I laid my head against his chest. I didn't know what I expected when I told them the truth. But Zane acting like Salem was still the enemy was not one of them. It shouldn't have bothered me as much, but I felt extremely protective of her. She saved my life in more than one way. I just needed Zane to understand her reasoning behind hiding who she was. Why we were both hiding.

I hadn't realized I'd fallen asleep until I felt the move underneath me. Jerking awake I gasped, feeling like I couldn't catch my breath.

"Shh, it's okay, moya printsessa." I would've known that voice anywhere.

Glancing over my shoulder I noticed the sun was beginning to shine in through the window.
"You fell asleep," he murmured. "They went to bed, and Zane still hasn't come home." He sighed, kissing my temple.

"You're still here," I found myself saying.

"You won't find me anywhere else, little dove." I wish I could believe him, but I couldn't let my heart be opened to him again. Just not yet anyway. Sometimes I felt overdramatic for pushing him away. I wasn't dramatic. I just couldn't let another man control me. And that's all Killian wanted; he wanted the control over me.

"Hey guys, have you seen Tobias?" Mila asked, startling me. Shooting up, Killian grunted as I pressed my ass into his dick.

"I just woke up," I said looking over at Killian over my shoulder.

"He hasn't come down that I've seen."

"Fuck!" Dimitri yelled from somewhere in the house. Killian stood quickly, almost knocking me to the ground. Shooting him my best glare he only smirked at me before turning his full attention back to Dimitri.

"The Cartel has him," he growled out. "They have my fucking son."

Chapter 30

Salem

Everyone makes mistakes in their life.

Mine was not telling them who I was.

I should have told them. That way they could just hate me from the start. Instead I lived in a little fantasy world where I thought Zane could care for me.

My second mistake was leaving Uncle Walker behind without thanking him. I should have stayed and talked to him. Instead I went quiet like I once did before.

Zane had become my happiness, had become something I had no idea had so much power over me. Not until I realized I never wanted to speak again. I wanted to give up. I lost everyone in my life that meant something to me.

Aziza would be okay. She went to see Killian. I knew she did. She would be okay. My uncle would be okay. And Tobias would be okay. Even if I hated Dimitri, he was a great father and could protect him. He didn't need me.

No one did.

Which is how I found myself captured by what I had assumed was Luca's men until the first night. When they came to beat me.

Instead it was Carlos' brother. Carlos, who I killed a long time ago. His brother was apparently very mad that I killed him.

My body was shutting down, I could feel it. Every time I tried to breathe the sharp pain ripped through my body. I don't even know how many ribs were broken. I barely could look anywhere with both my eyes bruised as fuck. Every time I even opened my eyes all I saw was red. The gash along my forehead had bled down my face and gotten into my eyes. I knew I was missing several nails from both my hands and my feet. I wouldn't be surprised if all of them were gone. I barely felt all the cuts that wrapped around my body, mainly my stomach and legs.
I couldn't even remember how many days I've been here. I think four but after the first night I had been beaten so badly, I probably couldn't tell you what my name was.

"Wakey wakey," the bald guard, whose name was Aaron, said barging through the door. He was a big dude; all the fuckers were. At this point they all looked the same, huge men and tattoos with either brown or blond hair.

I still didn't speak. It was what made them mad, they wanted me to scream. Wanted me to beg them to stop. But I refused to give them what they wanted. Instead I kept my head down and closed my eyes.

"Oh, no. I just wanted you awake so you can see our new plaything." Aaron laughed walking in front of me, I think. I could barely open my eyes without the sting of blood coursing through them. "Want to meet him?"

"You know I'm jealous. I love being your plaything," I wanted to say. But I didn't.
It was a smile that lasted only a moment before I saw a small shaggy brown-haired figure being dragged across the floor. Surely my mind was making this up; it couldn't be him. He was supposed to be safe with his family. Surely, he wouldn't be stupid enough. But as soon as his little voice called to me my eyes snapped fully open, ignoring the fiery burning.

"Salem," he sobbed.

"Let him go," I hissed out. My body protested against me sitting up straighter in the chair I was tied to.

"Tie him to the chair in front of her," another guard snapped. I couldn't focus on who was talking or if they were talking anymore. I could only look at Tobias crying, throwing his tiny weight around trying his best to get out of their grasp. His pants were covered in mud, and his white shirt was no longer that white, covered in small amounts of blood and mud.

"Aw, look the lad is pissing himself." A guard laughed. Snapping my gaze down I noticed he was. "You gonna piss more when he starts the real fun?" he taunted, tying Tobias's small body to the chair in front of me. The rope was wrapped around both his legs, his wrists on the arm rest like mine were, and then for extra measure they tied rope around his chest around the chair. His sobs had turned into screaming and high pitched. One of the guards roared and brought his hand back, ready to smack him.

"Touch him and I will kill every single one of you." My voice came out calmer than I thought it would. I watched both guards hovering over Tobias turn to look at me. Even the guard by the door snapped his gaze to me. I kept mine on Tobias. His crying stopped, and he made no sudden movements. "I will make you piss yourself. I will flay every part of your skin from your body," I continued, a smile praying to erupt on my face. "Do not touch a single fucking hair on his body, or I will make everyone wish they were dead. Every. Single. One. Of. You," I warned.

I don't know how long the time passed until the guard by the door laughed, causing the other two to laugh as well. Tobias closed his eyes, dropping his head. I promised I would protect him, no matter what. I may not have been able to protect my own brother, but I refused to let anything happen to him. He didn't deserve this; it was all my fault for bringing it to them.

"I would like to see you try, little *girl,*" Aaron said as he reared back again before his hand connected with the side of Tobias's head. His ear and the right side of his face instantly turned beat red. All I felt was rage, and all I could see was red. I don't remember the last time I was this angry. When my family was killed, I was angry, but I was scared. So scared I didn't do anything, but now I felt the rage rushing around me. I didn't feel the hurt anymore. It was all anger, coursing through, and my heart sped up, adrenaline pumping through my soul. My eyes narrowed at the laughing guards, taunting me, thinking I wouldn't do anything. I refused to let

Tobias be hurt. He didn't deserve this, not even Zane.

My mind worked on autopilot mode. I couldn't think. My body was working without thought of what I was doing. It was as if I watched my body move from the screen above.

I threw myself backwards, the chair breaking on impact, the legs and arm rest still tied to those parts of my body. The guard by the door charged at me, trying to grip my arm. Pulling back I wrapped my legs around his leg before plunging my right arm still tied to the wood armrest into his stomach.

Dead.

"Fuck fuck fuck," someone in the background yelled. I don't know who, but I couldn't stop as I continued stabbing him with the wooden stake. Everything in my mind went blank. I was working like a machine, one that couldn't let the little one down, even if it was the last thing I did.

My mind went somewhere dark, a place I didn't want to be, but I went there so I could save him. "Little one, remember to close those eyes," I remember saying before the darkness in my soul took over.

———————

Zane

Fourteen hours.

Fourteen hours since Tobias went missing.

I had no idea where he was.

After Aziza told us Salem crawled back into the heartless person she was before, it broke me. I hated that I did that to her. I was ready to get in the car and drive all the way back down to her. To beg her to forgive me, that I would do whatever she needed. Be whatever she needed.

Then she told me about her being Ghost, and that she was the one who broke my nose four years ago. I wasn't sure if I was angry or fine with that information. Sure I wasn't happy about my nose being broken, but from her reputation, she hadn't killed me. I was there lying on the ground. She could have easily killed me.

"Uh, boss?" Dean's stern voice startled me. Jolting me from my thoughts I barely had the energy to look up. "Zane!" he snapped,

Dean may be the head of our men, who reported back to me. But that didn't mean I wouldn't lay his ass out right here.

"What!" My own voice jumped out. The tension in the house was becoming unbearable. Until the door was thrown open and I glanced at who thought they could just walk into the house. Why the guards outside had not stopped them was beyond me.

Until I saw who it was.

Salem stumbled across the doorstep, carrying my favorite shaggy-headed person on her back. Her eyes found me the moment she walked in. Dimitri rushed into the living room, Mila hot on his trail. Mila gasped before she ran over, taking Tobias off her back.

"Oh my god, my baby!" she screamed.

I stood there, frozen. Salem was staring at me, her eyes half closed, and then suddenly she turned on her heel and began stumbling out the door.
Dimitri came up behind me, his hand resting on my shoulder. "If you want her, go."

Looking over at him, I could see all the seriousness in his voice and his eyes. He knew Salem meant something to me. I loved her. But I also couldn't understand what was stopping me from taking a step towards her.

"She's hurt, Zane, go to her." Dimitri's voice was stern. Nodding my head I ran out the door, but she was gone. Salem was nowhere to be seen.

Chapter 31

Salem

I felt like my body was shutting down; everything hurt. But the worst was my heart. My heart hurt the worst.

Seeing him was like a punch straight to my chest, and everything was coming back to me. I wanted to forget him, I wanted to get on with my life. I never wanted to see Zane again. Whenever I thought about him it hurt. I was tired of hurting. I was so tired. Tired of wanting revenge for my family and tired of missing and hurting Zane.

I let Zane into my life, and it destroyed me. I wanted to hate him, I wanted to march back to the house he was staying at and take all my anger out on him. But I couldn't.

I loved him.

As much as I wanted to refuse, as much as I realized some part of me must have known that a long time before it was even possible.

"Salem?" someone said from above me. Opening my eyes the best I could, I hadn't even realized I had fallen on the ground. Or that I had my eyes closed at all. "What the fuck are you doing?" Tyler ran towards me.

I didn't speak. I couldn't.

The moment he reached me, he gasped. I must have looked as terrible as I felt. After I'd left the weird building where Carlos's brother was holding me, I didn't think as I drove Tobias to where he remembered staying. I don't even know how I drove there and drove to Tyler's.
I tried my best to stand up, but the moment I put any pressure on my wrist, the pain shot into my arm towards my shoulder. Gritting in pain I fell back down.

"Fuck, fuck, okay stay here." Tyler freaked out, running his hands into his hair, giving me one final look before running towards his house again. I wanted to say, "*I'll be right here, I'm not going nowhere.*" But my voice wouldn't work. Nor did I want to truly say anything. I just wanted to close my eyes. I just needed to rest. Just for a little bit.

"No, no, no, no," I faintly heard someone say, but sleepiness was stronger. And at least there, I couldn't think about him.

BEEP. BEEP. BEEP.

It rang over and over again. The faint sound of the air blowing had my brows furrowed. I felt my body wrapped in a warm cocoon. It was beginning to become too warm. My skin felt sticky, warm, and hurt. My ribs first started to throb, and then everything else hurt. I don't think there was a single part of me that didn't ache and scream in protest.

Without opening my eyes, my one hand reached for the IV in my other hand. I wanted to rip it out; it was too uncomfortable.

"No, don't do that." My hand stopped mid pull. I didn't want to open my eyes and see who it was. I just wanted to get these wires out of my damn hand.

"He's not here." I didn't want to know where he was. I couldn't care, and I didn't want to care.

Peeking out from my eyelashes, I almost laughed at the sight of the big bad Dimitri sitting across from the bed I was lying on. For the first time I truly looked at him. His hair was a bit longer on top than the side, and his blue eyes bored into my own. I wasn't sure why he was here, but whatever it was couldn't necessarily be good.

"Is this going to be a long conversation or one where I need a drink?" I asked, finding more courage than I had. My body hurt, and I wanted to ask where I was. Along with a million other questions but the only one that I found myself truly wanting to know was if Zane was okay.

He chuckled before actually giving me a gentle smile. "I could get us one. That's if you want one." He shrugged, leaning forward, his elbows resting on his knees. I felt unprepared for whatever he planned on doing.

"Let's not take this the wrong way but I wouldn't trust you not to put drugs in it." I tried my best to sit up. Wincing, pain shot from all different spots in my body.

"None taken," he muttered, watching me as I tried to find a comfortable spot. After trying for what seemed like the hundredth time I couldn't, so I laid back blowing raspberries.

"Are you here for something, or did you just plan to stare at me creepily?" I finally snapped after him not saying anything to me.

"What happened when they took him?" he asked. "And you," he added.

"I killed them, got him out, in the end," I stated. I didn't want to think back to that night that I let myself lose control. Every kill I knew what the outcome was. It was me or them. I wasn't going to let them take anything else from me. But Carlos's brother? That was a completely different story. Tobias was there. Because of me.

"Cut the shit, Salem, I want to know. Why does my own fucking son hate me? What the fuck did you do to him?" Dimitri yelled at me.

"First off, you do not yell at *me*. Second off, why don't you ask him? And seriously, Dimitri, I never made Tobias do anything, let alone hate you." Crossing my arms over my chest, I hid the pain that shot from my side. I watched as Dimitri stood from the chair before walking over to me, standing over my bed.

"Salem, if I have to torture you to figure out what happened, I will," he smirked.
Did I actually believe he would torture me? Yes.

No matter what he knew, he didn't care about me. I was nothing but someone who warmed his best friend's bed.

Taking a deep breath, I stopped glaring at him. I had no idea why Dimitri would think Tobias hated him. Out of the times we've talked, he only told me he cared for his father. He didn't want to disappoint him. Even for a four-year-old, it made me sad. I wanted to find Tobias myself, wrap him up, and tell him everything would be okay. But I couldn't.
I was no one.

"Aaron smacked him, that's it," I said. Turning my head towards the window, I didn't know where I was actually going, but I needed a breather from him.

"Don't look away from me," he growled.

"I am not Mila! You have no right to yell at me like I'm your fucking wife or your child!" I wanted to yell more, but my throat began to close up. I don't know what it was, but I could stay quiet around those left of my family. But the moment Dimitri and his bunch showed up I opened my mouth like a fool.

"What happened to you?" he asked me. "The doctor gave me a full report on your injuries, so just fucking tell me yourself. What did they do to you!"

"GOD!" I lost it. I yanked the IV from my hand and swung my legs over the side. I had no idea what I was doing, but I couldn't stay here and take him yelling at me like a child. I ignored the pain as I got to my feet. Walking over to the dresser I pulled out whatever clothes were in there. "You're so fucking impossible, you know?" I yelled. "They tortured me, okay."

I watched as his eyes shifted from anger to something different. I'm not even entirely sure what emotion he was having, but that didn't stop me.

Shoving my legs into the sweatpants, I said, "They think I'm working with you. They think I'm your hired assassin. He's angry I killed his brother. They took and tortured me for four, maybe five days. They cut me, burned me, fucking broke my bones, they fucking did everything you can imagine to me!" I screamed at the top of my lungs. I didn't even think. I whipped the hospital gown off and shoved my arms through a random t-shirt from Tyler's guest room. "I wouldn't tell them anything, I was so ready to give up. I was ready to finally be done until they brought him in." The tears were like a fucking flood gate at this point. "They dragged him into the room, laughed at him. Tobias pissed himself, and they laughed, telling us they were going to rough him up. They were going to make me watch as they tortured your fucking son. I snapped. I don't even remember it. I blacked out. I told Tobias to close his eyes and when I came to, they were all dead. Aaron, his guards, all of them dead." Taking a deep breath, I wiped my cheeks, refusing to let him see me cry anymore. "Then we walked out. He walked for the first two miles, but he was tired. So I carried him. I carried your son until I found a car that I could hot-wire. I carried your son with a fractured foot, broken ribs, and on the verge of dying myself. So if you ask yourself if I care for your son, I do. Ask yourself why he hates you."

"Sal—"

"No, he doesn't hate you. He's hurting, he witnesses more than a four-year-old should ever see. I'm so sorry I was brought into your life. I should have stayed away, I knew I should have. I'm sorry for my part in this. But I will not apologize for killing them. They will all fucking die, Dimitri. So I think it's better if you just get the fuck out and forget me. I won't be seeing Tobias anymore, so fix your relationship with him."

Walking to the bedroom door, I opened it, motioning for him to leave. Dropping his shoulders he walked to me, opening his mouth to say something else. Instead I held my hand up, not wanting to hear anything else he had to say. I already cried in front of this man, opening up more than I ever wanted to.

So I watched as Dimitri walked out of the door, and after I slammed it shut, I broke. My knees hit the tile floor, and I felt the warmth of my tears draining down my face. I cried for Tobias, the one who didn't deserve any of this. I cried for the man I loved walking out of my life. I cried for my family who deserved to live and were taken too early.

I cried for myself.

One month later

I gritted my teeth as I poured a cup of coffee. It should not take this much effort to pour anything. But this time around my body was taking longer to heal.

"You shouldn't be out of bed." Tyler appeared next to me. I wanted to tell him to fuck off, to just leave me alone. But I was in his house, and he also had been nursing me back to health.

After I showed up on his doorstep a little over a month ago, he had been nothing but nice and honestly a sweet person. After he and his husband got my wounds to stop bleeding, they put me under for two days so I would actually rest. When I had woken up it was to find Dimitri staring at me. After the argument we got into I hadn't heard from him or anyone else. I ignored all of Aziza's phone calls. I knew she was with Killian. But besides her I hadn't heard from anyone.

Shrugging my shoulders I gulped down most of my coffee before pouring even more in. I turned facing Tyler, who stood in his scrubs. Glancing at the clock, it read 6 pm. Which meant he was going into work soon, and right now he wanted to check my wounds and make sure they were healing correctly. After two days of telling him he didn't need to check me, I finally gave up, and just let him do doctor things, because even though I had taken care of more accidents than I cared to admit, he was the doctor.

Rolling my eyes, I set my mug down and pulled my shirt off. It was easier than him trying to hold it up while checking. I began tearing off the gauze that was placed on my side when Tyler grunted at me. "Salem Gray!"

Shooting him a glare I ignored his growls at me, tearing off the rest of the tape.

"You're supposed to wash your hands before doing any of that," he muttered but still continued to check on my side that had been the worst. Being burned and then stabbed a few times will do that to you. I still had missing nails, and the gash above my eyebrow still had stitches in it.

"Alright your side looks good, but still apply that burn cream I gave you." He looked over my face. "And your stitches can come out now."

Nodding my head, I pulled my shirt back on before sitting down on the counter. Tyler had most of the supplies already in the kitchen, so it took him no time to pull them out. "The stitches on your stomach can probably come out in a few days. And I know I said you should be resting, but there's someone here for you."

Immediately, my body tensed, and I wasn't even sure who it would be. If it were Aziza she'd march in here. Dimitri would honestly do the same. Zane would have lost his patience waiting out there.

"Please just hear them out?" Tyler smiled, kissing the top of my head before grabbing his keys off the counter and walking out of the back door.

Swallowing, I pushed away from the counter and walked into the living room. No one was waiting there for me, until I saw a tall figure standing on the front porch.

Killian.

Grabbing the throw blanket from the back of the couch I walked out. As soon as the door closed, he turned around and I felt the pity rolling off him. I wanted to scream at him, tell him to leave, and beg him to forget about me. I wanted him to just care for Aziza so that I could disappear.

Instead I stared at him.

"So it's true," was all he said.

What was true, I had no idea. I wanted to ask, but I didn't. I kept my mouth shut.

"I swear you two are the most stubborn assholes I've ever had to deal with." He swung around glaring at me. "If it weren't for Aziza, I'd probably beat the shit out of you," he grumbled to himself.

He could try, I wanted to say but didn't. But why would it be for Aziza...

"Holy shit." I couldn't believe it. "You're him."

"What are you referring to?" he asked, cocking his head to the side.

"The one she's been in love with since, shit, forever, honestly." I couldn't believe it, and also couldn't understand it. Killian and Aziza. Killian was her best friend from New York. The one who left.

It was him.

"She told us about what happened, and then finally yesterday Dimitri told us about Tobias." Killian fisted his hand at his sides, ignoring what I said, but it gave me enough. It was him. "I don't know where Zane is," Dimitri said. He went off to find another Cartel after you left. He's supposed to be back in a few hours. But he told me and Aziza about Tobias last night."

I had no idea what to say to him. Killian and I never really had one-on-one time to talk.

"Dimitri's pride won't let him, but thank you." He turned his full attention to me. "You made Zane into a person. Before he was a walking robot. And thank you most of all for saving them all. You saved Tobias, a few times from what I hear." He smirked. I knew what he was talking about. Mila.

I got her out, and by saving her, I saved him. But I didn't want to be thanked. It wasn't why I did any of this. I didn't save them to be thanked. I did it because I couldn't save my own family.

"Aziza told us everything."

I nodded my head.

"I know we don't know each other much, but Zane does hate himself for leaving you. I won't ask you to forgive him, what he said was inexcusable. But please understand wh—" The sound of his phone ringing cut him off.

"What's up?" he answered, walking away from the porch and down to his car. Turning around myself, I began stalking back towards the front door. Just as my hand turned the doorknob, I heard Killian yell words I couldn't understand.

Turning back around, he ripped his door open before glancing back up at me. I was ready for this conversation to be over.

"He was taken again. Luca took him!" Killian snapped. "Tobias is probably going to die because you couldn't get your head out of your ass and fix whatever is going on between you and Zane," he yelled again.

Dante and Luca were the last ones on my list. The list I had given up on because I thought if I stopped, they wouldn't come after them anymore. But I was wrong, so wrong, and now it was all my fault. Tobias was taken again because of me. The last time Dimitri had no idea who took him, and now he did. They could get him back, Dimitri was smart. He was a killer, he knew what to do. He knew how to get him back. But the aching tightness in my chest just kept getting tighter, threatening to rip my heart apart. It was going to be ripped from my chest leaving me to bleed and die on the floor, alone.

Alone again.

"Fuck," I mumbled to myself. "Killian!" I yelled as he got into his car.

He arched a brow at me.

Fuck, was I really going to walk into a fight again? Was I going to risk everything for him?

Yes.

I ran down the steps and climbed into the passenger side.

"Go to Two Three Two West Road," I ordered.

"What's there?" he angrily asked backing out of the driveway of Tyler's house.

"My weapons."

I was going to finish this. Luca and his son were going to die, even if that meant me going down with them. Tobias and his family would live through this. I was going to guarantee it. I refused to let them die like my family did.

Chapter 32

Zane

That feeling you get in your gut when you know something is going to happen, something wrong. Ever since I walked out the door on Salem in the hospital bed, I had that wrong feeling settling in my gut. Then when I watched her walk out after saving Tobias, everything felt wrong.

I stood there like a fool and watched her limp out of the house. She was hurt, badly from the way she was limping, but I still stood there like a damn fool. I had no idea how she got out of there so fast. After I failed her again, I refused to do it anymore.

Killian and Aziza came home a few hours later, much of Aziza's equipment for tracking with them. Aziza knew where she was and was getting hourly updates but refused to tell me where she was. Until I overheard her telling Dimitri.

Dimitri surprised me when he left for several hours. But when he came back, he looked haunted. For the first time he actually looked upset about something other than Mila being involved.

"*Cartel,*" was all he said before I was running out the door, and tracking them all down. It didn't take long to find the small group of ten men hiding out in some safehouse in New Mexico. They should have been enough to hold the anger I felt, but it didn't do much.

I could barely hold it together when Dimitri actually told me what she told him. That they tortured her for defending us, that she walked miles with Tobias on her back because he was tired and saw too much. I knew she cared, always knew she felt something.

No matter how much I begged Aziza to tell me where she was, she wouldn't tell me. Dimitri wouldn't. No one would. I didn't understand. I still didn't. How did Aziza finally accept Killian after what he put her through? I just didn't understand.

"I'm sick of the states. I can't wait to get back home," Dimitri declared walking into the kitchen. I couldn't agree with him more. My only problem would be convincing Salem to come back with me so I could grovel for the rest of my life.

"Is Aziza coming back with Killian?" Mila asked from behind me. I couldn't help my hand tighten against the glass of water. Just the mention of Aziza sent me into a frenzy. I couldn't understand why she wouldn't tell me where Salem was.

"I don't know." Dimitri shrugged, kissing her temple. I was once again back to being uncomfortable watching their love. I hated it even more now because I lost it.

"How do you not know? We're leaving tomorrow—" Mila was cut off from the sound of Dimitri's phone going off.

Rolling his eyes, he fished his phone out, answering it. His body immediately went tense, and that caused my own body to react. I stood from the chair, looking around at all the entry spots. No one in sight.

"What do you want?" Dimitri spat out. Without having a second chance a dart shot out and landed in my chest. My vision blurred as Mila's body went down, a dart sticking from her own chest. Dimitri's body went down next, his eyes focusing on me. My knees buckled, and I struggled to stand straight up.

"Shoot him again," someone behind me said. A second dart shot into my back before my whole body seized and I fell onto my side.

Everything went black.

Drip. Drip. Drip.

Blood trickled down my chin landing on the gravel road. The gun pressed to my temple, ready to blow my brains out, had Tobias screaming his lungs out, begging for them to spare me. I couldn't even look up.

I had no idea where Dimitri was. Probably dead.

When I woke up, I had no time to prepare as my hands were tied behind my back, my ankles tied together. Mila sat next to me, her body also tied together. Tobias sat in front of us, unable to move from the look of his swollen ankle. But Dimitri was gone.

Even as I tried to look around, I could only see a construction site. Mila had tape over her mouth so she couldn't speak. I could feel her eyes on me as I struggled to breathe. After taking so many beatings you get used to it, but somehow this felt all too different.

"Where is she?" Dante asked us again. I refused to ask who he was referring to. Mila also knew I wouldn't talk. "You can tell us where she is, and I will let the boy down easy. Quick and easy," Dante taunted, holding a knife in front of Mila's face.

"Pl-please just l-let us g-g-go," Tobias screamed. His voice trembled with fear. It was a fear I wanted to take away from him. I just couldn't.

All this was my fault. I shouldn't have gotten involved with Salem. I shouldn't have done so many things. I should have been training harder and been on watch instead of thinking of her.
I was so focused on what was going on inside my head, I didn't realize Dante had his brass knuckles until I felt the pain spread through my face. My breath left my lungs, as I tried holding all my pain together.

"Fuck it, grab the boy," Dante ordered. "I hope you enjoy the show!" He chuckled.

Just as one of his men went to grab onto Tobias who was screaming even more, thrashing around, a loud range of bullets stopped everyone in their tracks. A black Bugatti Chiron Super Sport shootout roared in, tires screeching as two bikes hit the bumper before flying off and whoever was riding the bikes flew off.

A loud explosion went off behind us, sending me and Mila face first into the dirt. Just as a pair of hands began tugging on my ankles, just as I was about ready to fight my way through, I heard, "Calm down."

Killian.

I wanted to ask a million questions, most importantly where had he been. But I didn't have time for that. My hands are let go, and he shoved a knife and gun into them.

He climbed over to Mila and began untying her binds. Tobias was nowhere to be seen, and all I saw was smoking from the explosion along with dirt flying up from the car.

The moment her tape was ripped off she started yelling, "Where is Tobias? Oh my god, Killian, where are they?" she begged over and over again.

"I don't know, sweets; my job is just to get you two out," he whispered. I don't know why the fuck he whispered since this place was going off like it was the fucking Fourth of July.

We all barely climbed to our feet before a large SUV pulled up and Killian was dragging Mila to the back seat. Following because I had no idea what else was going on, we climbed into the back.

Aziza in the front seat driving surprised the fuck out of me, along with the fact that Dimitri was sitting right next to her. The moment the back door closed, Aziza hit the gas and we were off.

"Someone better start fucking explaining to me WHAT THE FUCK IS GOING ON!" Mila screamed, smacking Dimitri on the arm before turning her attention towards us.

Throwing my hands up, I agreed with her that I would also like to know what was going on.

"Aziza, just go a little further and then get out," Dimitri ordered, turning his gaze back to his wife. "Aziza is going to take you to a safehouse she has set up. We're going to meet up with them later," he said as she slowed down just enough for Killian to climb into the front seat and take over for her.

Mila didn't have a chance to speak before Aziza opened the back door and grabbed her. In a blink of an eye, Killian was driving off heading in the same direction we just came from.

"Fine, don't tell your wife what's going on," I muttered. "Are you going to tell me?" I said a little louder from the back seat. "Also, who the fuck was driving that car that took out those men?" I barely got that out before the SUV became target practice for multiple guns.

Chapter 33

Salem

I always knew I was going to die early.

I also knew that when I died I wanted to wear my parents' wedding ring, which sat on a long chain around my neck.

The moment I get a clear view of them, two bikes tried to run me off the dirt road. Shifting the wheel to the right just a fraction caused both bikes to hit my bumper, and both men flew off and landed in an unnatural way. I know I shouldn't but my gaze fell to Zane and Mila, both of who are now lying on their fronts as Killian came out between two large construction trucks.

Shaking my thoughts off, I went back to focusing on the task at hand. Getting Tobias out.

Locking the brakes I slid to a crawling speed. No one can see the car between the smoke from the explosion Dimitri and Aziza set off and from the amount of dirt I picked up. Throwing my door open, I grabbed Tobias around the waist and hauled him onto the passenger seat.

"Shh, little one, it's just me." I smiled before shifting gears again and shooting forward. I didn't pay attention as Killian dragged Mila to the SUV, then I took off.

"Salem, I never thought I would see you again," he cried.

"It's okay, you'll see me anytime you want. But I'm going to need you to pay attention alright?" I asked, shifting gears again, turning right sharply.

"Are we on that secret task?" he asked.

"Remember all those driving lessons we've practiced?"

"Secret two or four?" he asked.

"Definitely four."

"Alright, let's do it!" He smiled over at me. Taking the ear plugs, he climbed over into my lap, and his hands went to the wheel, tightening them.

I reached to my side and grabbed both Glocks, just in time as the SUV came in behind us. Letting a breath go that I didn't realize I was holding, I said a silent, "Let's go." It was time to end this once and for all.

I shot out the windows at all the men coming towards us. All we had to do was reach the end of this road, and then they could take Tobias and run.

"Salem, do you love Zane?" Tobias yelled out of nowhere.

"With everything," I whispered. I knew he couldn't hear me, but he always asked personal questions that he knew I'd answer because he couldn't hear me. It was how we started training.

"If Uncle Zane doesn't get his shit together, I might make you my wife first." He giggled.

That is what made it all worth it.

Looking out the windshield, I barely had time. A dozen men stood there. I yelled at Tobias to get in the back and buckle up before my hand flew to the wheel. I slowed down, yanking the wheel to the left hard. The right bumper flew into the wall, Tobias let out a little yelp. Causing my eyes to wander to him. I knew I shouldn't have done that because when I turned back around the car jolted over something on the ground, causing the car to flip.

"Tobias…" I mumbled the moment the car stopped rolling. I could feel the gash above my eye reopen, along with every other wound that had been stitched up and was now bleeding. My body suddenly felt very weak. But I couldn't stop, not just yet.

"SALEM!" Tobias screamed from the back.

Trying my best to climb out of the window, it wasn't until I felt two sets of hands grab hold of each arm that I realized how truly fucked I was.

"Well well well, what do we have here?" A deep Italian accent invaded my head. I couldn't look up to face him. If I did, it would cause too much rage. I would become too angry. I always knew I

304

would face Luca and Dante, but I was never prepared for the feelings it would cause. My chest felt on fire with hurt. My body ached from my emotions.

"What do we have here?" His voice.

The voice that haunted all my nightmares, haunted everything inside me. Everything in me burned with rage. I felt my skin ignite. I was ready to drive any sharp object into his body.

"Dante." His father nodded at him. The blow to my cheek should've done something to me but instead I felt numb. As I looked up, for the first time I faced Luca since that night.

"Get rid of her."

"Get rid of her."

"Get rid of her."

Blow after blow to my face should've been enough to again make me react to something, but I felt nothing. I was numb.

Numb to feelings.

"Stopppp." A little voice broke me away from my rage. Looking over, Tobias filled my sight.

How did I forget he was here?

I was so filled with my own rage, my own revenge, that I forgot Tobias was here. I couldn't die, not with him right here.

"Ple-please, get up," he begged.

Just like I begged. I begged them to let us go, to let me go. I promised them I wouldn't tell anyone. I promised I would disappear, and they would never see me again. I lived in fear. I *had* lived in fear.

But no more. I had to make it through this. If not for me, then for Tobias. He had to get back to his family.

Even if it was the last thing I did.

Looking up at Luca, I fought against the rage that wanted to cloud my judgment. That wanted to suck me down and make me do more than kill everyone here. He looked the same, dirty blond hair, a little grayer, and deep brown eyes. The same evil look in them.

He had no idea who I was.

"Why have you been killing my men?" he demanded.

I wondered how long I could keep my mouth shut before they began hitting me. But I didn't have to wait long before Dante grabbed me by my hair and dragged me to my feet.

"I can do this all night if we must, but I prefer to do something else with my evening." Luca dragged on. I fought to look around, but from what little sight I had he barely had any men around. Dante held me by my hair, and two men stood by Tobias, keeping watch, while two men stood behind Luca.

I had killed most of his other men, and the rest he had must have been killed from when we had the explosion. I wanted to smile at the fact that his whole empire was going under. I wanted to laugh in his face and ruin everything for him.

Dante punching me in the rib jerked me back to the present. Luca was glaring down at me while Dante gave me three more solid punches.

"Abbastanza!" *Enough.*

Swallowing down bile that I definitely was seconds away from throwing up everywhere, I looked back up at Luca.

"Who are you!" he roared. His temper was getting to him. Again I wanted to laugh in his face.

"Don't remember me?" I asked back.

"Why the fuck should we, you stupid bitch." Dante pulled on my hair again. My skull screamed in protest.

"Avrei dovuto controllare il polso." *Should've checked the pulse.* Throwing my elbow back into Dante, he loosened his hold on my hair, giving me time to sweep my leg, knocking him to the ground. I grabbed hold of the knife from his belt in time to turn and throw it towards one of the men holding Tobias.

The second one didn't think twice before charging at me. Swinging a punch towards me, I blocked it, throwing my own into his face. He roared, giving me time to grab him around his neck and twist. Twisting took more strength than I cared to admit.

Two down.

Four more to go.

Turning to face Luca, his eyes were wide as he really gave me a good look.

"You're alive," he whispered. I couldn't hear him, but reading his lips gave it away.

"Your worthless son couldn't even finish the job," I snarked back.

Dante got to his feet, in a fighting position.

"But how? How could you be alive?" Again he was whispering, a little louder this time. But it was ironic he was surprised to see me alive. They had made sure everyone else was good and dead, but not me?

"You took everything from me," I spat out.

Dante moved in closer, edging to try and take me down. I itched for this fight. Glancing over at Tobias he was now peeking around a barrel. He would be safe for me to finish this.

"I'm going to end your life, your son, and everything you ever built. Just like how you gutted my family and tried to do the same to me," I smirked. Luca backed away, his men flanking him as Dante moved at me.

He swung his fist, but I blocked him just like I did before. I swung my leg knocking him back again, but this time he grabbed hold of my leather belt across my back, taking me down with him.

A sharp pain shot through my stomach. But I didn't have time to focus on the pain. Instead I head butted him. Getting to my feet left me open as a shot rang out.

"Fuck." The words left my mouth. The pain in my shoulder left my right arm useless.

I was tackled, my head bouncing off the ground. Everything went blurry, even as I felt someone straddle me. Hands wrapped around my throat, pressing down. I no longer had oxygen as I was being choked.

My lungs struggled, my arms struggled, everything was struggling. Until I felt the weight being pushed off me.

"Salem, come on, plea-please." That little voice called to me again. Blinking my eyes open, Tobias's face filled my sight. "Come on, please, you gotta get up."

I tried my best to sit up, but everything screamed at me.

"G-gu-gun," I stuttered out. Tobias left quickly before shoving something in my left hand. Thankfully he didn't try my right, as it was completely useless.

"Little boy got away from her!" Dante spat out somewhere to my left.

Looking over, he pulled a knife from his side, blood pouring from it. Luca was nowhere in sight; it was only us three. Pointing the gun at Dante, I whispered, "Close those eyes, little one."

I didn't have to wait. I knew he had done what I asked. "Say my name," I growled at Dante.

He shook his head. Refusing.

Shooting his leg, he barked out in pain, falling face first onto the ground.

"Pl-please, I'm so s-sorry," he begged, peaking at me from the ground. "I-I-I was yo-young, I just did w-what my fa-father told me t-to do," he continued explaining. As though I cared what he actually said.

"My name."

"S-Salem Gray."

A bullet in his head, and he dropped to the ground.

My head fell back down onto the ground. I knew Tobias was speaking, but I couldn't hear the words. I could barely see his face. Exhaustion was threatening to take over. The darkness was begging to drag me down.

"No!" Tobias screamed. Other voices screamed, but the only one I heard was his.

Zane

Fear.

That's all I felt.

I didn't let the SUV come to a complete stop before I yanked the
door open, and I was running to them lying on the ground.

"NO!" Tobias screamed at her. My knees hit the ground the moment
I was beside her and I couldn't believe my eyes. She was covered in
crimson, blood pouring from her everywhere. I had no idea how to
stop it.

"Oh, fuck!" someone behind me said. I couldn't be sure who it was.
My hands wrapped around my shirt, tearing it from me as I pressed
it to her side.

"Salem…" My voice broke.

Her eyes found mine, tears welling in them. I couldn't handle her
crying anymore.

"I'm so sorry." I leaned into her. "CALL THE AMBULANCE!" I
found myself screaming.

"Zane…" she whispered. "I'm sorry I never told you."

Shaking my head, I didn't want to hear her apologize for being
afraid. Nothing seemed to matter anymore. All I wanted was her. I
needed her.

"Listen, plea-please," she begged. "It was you; it has always been you. From the moment I broke your nose almost five years ago. It was you, you saved me from myself, and I'm sorry I never told you. I love you." She coughed, blood spewing from her mouth. "I lost myself when they were murdered, but you, you gave it back to me." More blood spewed from her mouth. I could hear the sounds behind me, but the only thing I truly heard was her. "It's okay, you'll make it through this. I'm okay... I don't even feel it..." Her voice slowed.

Everything faded before my eyes. Her eyes closed, as her breathing stopped.

"NO, NO, NO, FUCK. SALEM!" I screamed, my hands pounding at her chest, unsure of what I was doing. Not even as I felt two pairs of hands grab and drag me away from her.

One month later

"Hey."

My body tensed and my legs almost fell from the bed they rested on. Looking up from my lap, I stretched my sore muscles over my head, groaning as my shoulder popped and everything felt like I was hit by a train.

"Any news?" Mila asked, closing the door behind her. Shaking my head, I focused back on the window. I didn't want company. "Here, Killian made some turkey wraps and there are some other things in there for you," she said handing me a large box and a cup of steaming coffee.

"Thank you," I murmured while taking a large drink of coffee.

"You should go home and shower," Mila whispered. They always tried to get me to leave and either shower or just get out of the room. I just couldn't.

I couldn't leave. I left once before, and now I refused to let her out of my sight. I had security surrounding her entire room, along with the fact that she was on her own floor. That way I could work out and still keep an eye on her.

It had been one month since my world imploded in front of my eyes, where everything went to hell. I couldn't do anything. We were too late. I was too late. There was so much blood, so much.

I hadn't even realized I was staring at my hands, my entire body shaking.

"Zane?" Mila whispered. Looking over at her, tears welled in her eyes. I couldn't take it if she cried again. "I'm so sorry."

I couldn't tell her it was okay because it wasn't. None of it was okay. I was broken. And the only one who would and could truly fix me was in a coma, unsure when or if she would wake up.

Chapter 34

Salem

Two months since the accident

Darkness was holding onto me with no chance of letting me go in sight. The only thing I felt was soreness, and someone's hands holding my own. But these hands were much bigger than my own, but they felt nice. They felt like home.

"Salem… Come on, Kitten, you gotta wake up." His voice was soothing all the pain I felt. I could feel his lips pressed against my ear as he spoke. His breath was hot against my skin, but this felt natural. "I'm kind of losing my mind here, beautiful. It's been so long since I've seen those bright blue eyes. I kind of need them right now." Something warm and wet landed on my neck. Was he crying?

Wake up? What could he be talking about? I tried opening my eyes, but they wouldn't. I tried moving my hand but again nothing. *Why couldn't I move?*

"I have those feelings for you, the words you spoke to me. But I'm not saying it to you while you're asleep here. So wake up, you hear me? I need you to wake up," he begged over and over again.

I wanted to fight the darkness that felt so heavy, taking me over again. I wanted to hear his words. I needed them. I've missed so much, but even with my eyes closed, everything felt like too much. I felt too heavy.

Until everything faded.

He never leaves.

I know he barely talks, even when others come into the room. But I always felt the side of the bed dip, along with his hand always holding my own. My heart ached and cried for him. I needed to tell him I was here. That I'm right here with him. But nothing I did worked. I felt them poking at my skin, changing my IVs, even the softness of someone braiding my hair, and brushing it out.

But nothing I did would allow me to wake up.

"You know this is the first time I think he's actually left the building since you've been here. He made everyone clear this floor out, it's kind of creepy to be honest." He let out a low chuckle. "I can't wait for you to see the big guy. If you thought he was huge before… man. He's changed you know." His voice whispered closer to me, "It's my fault you know, he never wanted to leave you. I got into his head, and it's all my fault. I don't trust well, and when I knew something was up with you, I voiced all my concerns to them."

I begged my body to open my eyes, to look at Dimitri and tell him I forgave him, that I was just too stubborn to let them in. That it wasn't all his fault.

"He's drowning, Salem, you really need to wake up, please. He's losing himself, and I'm afraid you're the only one who can save him." Something warm touched my forehead, as though he was giving me a kiss. "Your family needs you."

I'm sure I was about to open my eyes, I was ready. I was done fighting, I needed to wake up.

"WHY THE FUCK IS SHE NOT WAKING!" he yelled. The walls could fall down from the pure anger in him. Zane's fury was suffocating everything. It was making me angry as well. Why couldn't I wake up?

"Mr. Rivera, please listen to us. I've explained to you many times, along with countless other doctors. Every doctor we've brought in here has said the same thing over and over."

Zane growled like an animal, and I so desperately wanted to pull him to me. To calm him down, to tell him again I'm right here.

"Do something to wake her up. She's breathing on her own! She's basically healed, why won't she wake THE FUCK UP!"

"Zane," Mila's sweet voice called out.

"Mr. Rivera, her scans are clear, but the damage that has been done to her over the years, along with the fact that Miss Gr—"

"Mrs. Rivera. She's mine, her last name is Rivera. Not fucking Gray," Zane barked out.

"The brain is special, no one's brain is the same. She is healed for the most part, but her brain needs time to heal."

"YOU SAID HER BRAIN IS HEALED!" Something crashed, along with loud footsteps barging into the room. "Get the fuck out!" Zane screamed.

I heard the sound of the door opening and closing, and for several minutes I thought I was left alone. I was ready for the darkness to take me once again until I heard his boots pad across the floor. His large hand covered my own again, and his hot breath covering my ears.

Home.

"I'm losing it, Kitten. I'm utterly losing it. I need you to come home. I want you to be my wife. You want kids, I'll give them to you. You want to see the world, let me take you. Anything, just fuck… come back, Kitten." His tears were hot against my neck again.

Home.

Beep. Beep. Beep.

The same heart monitor was annoying me. The bright sunlight shined into my room, blinding me. My eyes followed the light from the blinds to a long arrangement of flowers, with a teddy bear laying in the chair in the corner.

My eyes.

They were open.

I almost laughed until I felt the pain in my stomach. My hands traveled up until they reached the top of my blanket, pulling it down with too much energy. I yanked my gown up to find more scars, fresh ones. But overall healed, stitches to be removed. Fixing my gown, I covered myself.

The hospital room was large, covered in an uneasy white that I hated. I've always hated hospitals. My bed sits in the middle, with four chairs surrounding my bed. The one to my left is well worn, like the person who'd sat there hadn't moved.

The sound of the door opening and Zane walking in made my heart flutter. My breath caught in my throat as I stared at him. He was different, bigger somehow. His muscles had always strained against his shirts, but now his muscles had muscles on them. He hadn't realized I was awake, his eyes staying focused on the ground, as he tightened his grip on the cup. His eyes had dark purple bags under them, and I wanted to scream that I was awake. But I didn't.

I didn't want to close my eyes, but I felt very tired. I was scared if I closed my eyes they wouldn't open again. I barely kept them open as he walked to the chair and sat down, grabbing my hand and closing his eyes. I couldn't fight it anymore, and I let myself sleep.

———————

When I woke up sometime later, he was still holding my hand. But there was something else in the room as well. My eyes blinked a few times trying to get used to the lighting. This time the sun was beginning to set.

"Oh my god." A gasp left someone on my right. Looking over, Mila sat there. "You're awake," she whispered. Tears streamed down her face the moment our eyes connected. Looking her over, Mila looked the same, but her stomach was now much larger.

I tried telling her to shush, I didn't want to wake him up just yet. Thankfully she understood, and standing up she squeezed my other hand. Not saying anything she walked out the door. Turning my head, I looked over at Zane, whose head was still fallen back, in a very uncomfortable position.

His beard was longer and fuller. His hair was even a little longer. It made me want to drag my fingers through it. But the weight of trying to pick my hand up was exhausting. So instead I settled on just staring at him, enjoying the freedom to admire him.

I must have stared at him longer than I thought. The next thing I knew the sun was setting and his phone was going off. Zane jerked awake, his hand immediately going to his phone before answering.

"Da." I would never get tired of him speaking Russian. "Net, net novostey. Mila byla zdes', no ushla." *No, there's nothing new. Mila was here, but she left.*

Whoever was on the other line spoke for a long moment before Zane hung up and pocketed his phone. His eyes closed, before tightening his hand in mine. He still had no idea I was awake.

Squeezing his hand back, I felt his whole body tense, unsure if it was just moving in my sleep or if I was awake. His head shot up, his eyes burning into my own, just as they widened. He dropped my hand, rushing closer to my side, clasping my face in his hands.

"Fuck…" His lips pressed against my own in a punishing way. Pressing his forehead against mine, he said, "Please tell me this is real." Pulling away, tears filled his eyes. For the first time I actually witnessed this man cry. It broke my heart.

"Is this the part where you grovel?" I deadpanned, trying to hide my laughter that I want to let go so desperately.

"I will grovel for the rest of my life. I'm going to buy you everything you ever wanted. A new farm, animals, weapons, those weird bellbottoms you wear, or even those sexy black boots."

He continued kissing my cheek before resuming talking. "You want anything in the world, it's yours. We can go anywhere. You want to kick my ass once you're healed enough, please do it."

I could fall into him, that was if my body didn't ache and wanted to fall apart. Instead I began crying, crying so hard my body shook, and surprising me the most was Zane holding me. He held me as I cried because he was okay with me never having children. He was okay with me.

"I want a new car. Mine was trashed. New boots would be nice. I'm sure the ones I was wearing are destroyed. Also a farm would be nice. I think you'd look super-hot in some cowboy boots and a hat," I muttered into his chest.

He laughed, pressing a kiss to the top of my head. "Anything, Kitten."

"Tobias, be careful please." Mila's voice was soft but strong.

"Mama, I just want to be close to her." God, I missed that voice. I missed him so desperately, his smile, his laugh. Everything about the little man made me miss him.

I felt his hands trying to ease his way on my other side. I could still feel Zane pressed against my other side. It warmed my heart that they were both here with me.

"Dada, I thought you said Aunt Sey was awake," Tobias tried to whisper but failed. But I didn't mind at all. I wanted him to yell, and laugh, and whatever else he wanted to do.

"She is, right now she's just resting her eyes with Uncle Zane."
Dimitri surprised me with how soft he spoke. This was the first time
I had ever heard him speak nicely and calm.

"I want her to wake up," Tobias declared. If I hadn't been awake
before, I would be now. I could feel Zane beginning to stir next to
me, his arm that was wrapped around my waist tightening.

"Tobias, you need to be quiet, they're resting," Dimitri said
somewhere closer.

"Yeah, be quiet, Tobias," Zane muttered into my neck, his hot
breath clinging to my skin. "We're resting."

The door opened and closed before I heard, "Well, I see she has a lot
of visitors today. I'm Dr. Beckett. I heard she woke up last night."

After Zane and I talked a little, he fell asleep curled up next to me.
The doctors had come in trying to get me up and moving but I asked
to just be left until the morning. It was surprising they allowed it,
but I guess they did since it was only a few hours. I felt Zane
moving up, so my head was lying on his chest, his thumb rubbing
circles into my hip.

"Well, I'm glad everyone is here. Has she woken up again?" Dr.
Beckett asked.

Deciding it was time to stop fake sleeping, I opened my eyes and
was met with three sets already focused on me.

"Well good morning!" Dr. Beckett was a little too chipper for me.

"Salem!" Tobias squealed next to me, his arms wrapping around my
sore waist. I tried to hide the groan, but it still hurt, nonetheless.

"Tobias, be careful!" Mila jumped from her seat rushing over to
remove his arms from me.

Shaking my head, I smiled at her. "It's okay."

"Well, since you're awake I would love to go over your chart," Dr. Beckett announced, waiting for everyone to get comfortable.

"Alright, so when you were brought in, you were dead." Dr. Beckett's words should have surprised me, but they didn't. I remembered Dante beating me and Luca shooting me. I remembered it all. "You had internal bleeding that we stopped, multiple wounds that had been reopened, along with three new stab wounds, and a gunshot wound." I wish she could've stopped there, but I knew that wasn't the end. "You had four broken ribs on your right side, and three on your left. You had a collapsed lung that we had to repair, and your throat was terribly damaged. We'll need to run tests on, well, basically everything to see where we need to do work." Dr. Beckett's sad eyes burned into me. I knew this was going to happen. I'd gone through this more times than I'd ever wanted to do.

"How long has it been?" I asked. My voice was raspier than it had been before, and I wasn't sure how I felt about it. The silence should've told me, but I still needed to know.

"Three months." Zane pressed his lips to the top of my head.

I sucked in a breath not expecting that answer. I had been in a coma a few times before, but usually only for a few days.

"Alright, I'm going to grab some nurses and we're going to start running some tests."

For the next few weeks, I had tests done repeatedly. Relearning to walk was a bitch. I had to relearn how to do a lot of physical things.

Thankfully, after three weeks I was moved to a physical therapy center. Zane stayed with me the whole time. Mila brought Tobias almost every day. Dimitri always stayed by the door when they visited. Aziza and Killian showed up the first few weeks.

"Alright, Salem, let's get you up and moving. Let's see if we can get you moved back home soon."

Nodding my agreement for that, I carefully swung my legs off the side of the bed. Zane stood but kept close to my side, and Dimitri walked over next to him. Michael reached his hands out ready to catch me if I fell.

When I first arrived here, and Michael became my doctor, Zane wanted to kill him. Even after I told him that Tyler and Michael were happily married Zane still hated the idea of Michael helping me, especially in the shower.

"I think your boy toy is seconds away from murdering me, so I'm going to let him help you stand." Michael rolled his eyes.
Zane gave me a knowing smile as he held my left hand and Dimitri held onto my right. Planting my feet on the ground, it took everything to stand on my weak legs. They were both holding me up.

Walking was rough. My legs were extremely weak. Even after a few weeks of practicing, it was still rough. I was able to walk down the hall and halfway back before my knee started to give out. Trying to take another step, my knee finally had enough and buckled. Dimitri's hand tightened, holding me close.

"Thank you," I murmured.

"You think you can make it back to your room?" Zane asked.

I wasn't honestly sure, but I refused to be weak, especially in front of them. Nodding my head, I took another step. The moment my foot hit the tile, my knee gave out and my body began to fall. Zane swept an arm under my knees and back, picking me up bridal style.

"They have wheelchairs, Zane." Our faces were so close I could feel his breath on my cheek.

"I prefer to carry you."

Deciding not to give him an argument, remembering all the times he begged me to wake up, I wrapped my arms around his neck and kissed his cheek. "I need to shower," I whispered.

"Let's get you a shower then, Kitten."

Dimitri opened the door to my room letting us inside. Michael stood off to the side talking to Tyler.

"She wants a shower," Zane announced, not bothering to wait for anyone to speak.

He stepped into the huge bathroom, closing and locking the door behind us. Setting me down on the small counter, I watched as he flicked the water on before quickly undressing himself. His broad chest always amazed me, but what was different was that fresh tattoo. An outline of my side profile over his chest. Underneath was my name in what I knew was my mother's writing. My eyes filled with tears. I couldn't believe it.

His hands reached behind me to untie my gown, his eyes never leaving my own. "I never thought you'd wake up." His voice was so low, barely a whisper. "I never prayed before, but those months I did every day. I prayed for you to come back to me. I promised I'd never disappoint you again." I wasn't sure if he was speaking to me or himself. He couldn't look at me as he untied my gown. He had just undone the first one, before he moved to the second. "I lost myself, you know. I barely remember these past two months. But I also remember it all. I don't even feel like this is real…" His voice trailed off as he untied the last knot. The gown fell to the floor, and immediately I felt self-conscious. I wanted to cover myself from his unreadable gaze. My hands automatically went to cover my middle, where the scars were the worst.

"Net ne." *No, don't.* His Russian did things to my body. I had no idea I would have this reaction, and it made me realize this was the first time I'd ever heard him speak Russian. "Don't hide yourself fro—"

"Mne nravitsya kogda ty govorish' po Russian." *I like when you speak Russian.* Though my accent sounded so odd, a southern girl speaking Russian was an odd mix.

"Ty takoy krasivyy kotenok, samyy krasivyy, kotorogo ya videl. Shramy i vs." *You're such a beautiful kitten, the most beautiful I've seen. Scars and all.*

My whole body shivered at his words, and he could see it because he shook his head. "When you're feeling better, Kitten." He tried to smile, but it didn't reach his eyes. Instead of speaking he picked me up from the counter and carried me into the shower. Holding me in one arm he grabbed a cloth and somehow managed to pour body wash onto it. Setting me down on the side seat he began washing my shoulders and back.

"Tell me about your family," he mumbled as he kneeled down and began washing my legs.

"Mom and Dad met when they were really young, like I think seven, Dad was ten. They were best friends. I think Dad always loved her from the beginning." I had to stare at the shower wall because if I looked at him, I was afraid I'd break down and cry. "They used to dance in the kitchen. Sometimes there would be no music, and sometimes Mom would sing." I laughed remembering all the times she would sing for him. Zane grabbed my foot and began washing it. It shouldn't have been sexual but something inside me was wrong. Very wrong. Because I was beginning to get very wet from him just washing me and I knew he wouldn't do anything about it.

"Lee was the best brother and he was good at everything. He used to have such a potty mouth. Mom would always threaten him if he taught me any more curse words. He wanted me to be named Megatron and he would always call me a pain in the ass. I would always follow him around when he was doing chores outside because I loved being there and it was like a game to see how long it would take him to get annoyed with me. I don't think he ever really got mad at me. He pretended but I think he loved it."

Zane moved to my other foot, washing it with the same amount of care.

"Mom used to sing 'Mississippi Girl' all the time with me. It made Dad laugh. Emmy was much older than me, so she didn't like to hang out with me much. She was into makeup and always wore dresses. She was a lot like Mila in a way, shy, but when needed she was outspoken. She always did my makeup when I asked. It was what we did to bond, I guess."

Zane listened as I talked about my family, from taking care of the farm, to dancing with Aziza. I talked about when we got Pumpkin and how Dad showed me how to properly take care of a horse. We discussed vacations we took around the country, how no matter where we went Lee and I always got into trouble. I even told him about my aunt and uncle, and how Michael was the one who taught me to defend myself.

"Tip your head back, Kitten," he muttered. Doing as he asked, I closed my eyes as he poured shampoo and began working his fingers into my hair. Even if he was the one who helped me every day to shower, it always felt like the first time. This felt like magic; this felt like heaven.

"This is a good way to start that groveling," I started to whisper but ended up moaning with the way he massaged into my skull.

"Yeah, and you keep moaning like that and that groveling I'll be doing will be with my tongue inside your pussy," he grunted. This grunt was different, though. He wouldn't do anything that pushed my buttons.

"That works for me," I mumbled as he started to rinse my soap from my hair.

"You need to heal, beautiful."

I didn't speak as he conditioned my hair and rinsed it out. I sat there as he quickly washed himself and toweled off. Once he was done, he helped me dry off before drying my hair with the towel, setting me down on the counter once more.

"You want that oil in your hair before I brush it?" he asked. It warmed my heart that he even asked, I didn't know why I wanted to cry because it was a simple question. But, fuck my emotions were all over the place.

"Uh, oil on the ends."

Doing just that he poured some oil on his hands before running his hands through the middle section down to the ends. Brushing my hair out, he began braiding it. Once he was done, he took a wide step back. His eyes wide, his nose flared as he stared down at me. I couldn't stop the overwhelming need to drag his face down to my pussy. Which he must have understood because the moment our eyes connected, he said, "I need to taste you. It's been months. Fuck it's been so fucking long." He wasted no time as he kneeled in front of me, his mouth at perfect height for my pussy, and fuck I was wet. The ache was becoming too much. I needed his mouth on me.

"Are you going to make me beg?" I raised a brow at him.

"No, Kitten, I want to do the begging." His thrilled smile told me all. "Can I lick your pussy?" he actually begged.

His large fingers spread my lips apart, and he stared at me. "Please, Kitten, I need a taste of you." My body felt like it was on fire. I wanted him to keep begging, but I also wanted his mouth on me. Giving him a quick nod, he wasted no time before he dragged his tongue from my ass to clit. I shouldn't have moaned as loud as I did. There were people outside. But I didn't care. The only thing that mattered was his mouth.

"Fuck I've missed your pussy," he mumbled. "I want to stay here between your legs." Another long drag. "Fuck, Salem please let me have more."

I acted as though I was thinking about it, when I really wanted nothing more than to make him stick his tongue inside me as I fucked his face. He stared up at me, his hands holding me open for him.

"Three," I stated.

"Three?"

"I want three orgasms," I said my fingers running through his hair. "Right now I want you to make me cum three times, and you won't touch yourself after." I grinned.

"Deal." He wasted no time before he did just that. His tongue worked into my hole, fucking me with his mouth as he held me open. It had been so long that I nearly came from just that, and the moment one of his fingers entered and curled inside hitting that perfect spot, I came apart.

"Fuck, fuck, fuck," I chanted over and over again. He refused to let up and began sucking on my clit. Adding a second finger.

In and out.

In. Out.

Twist.

"Zane, please…" I didn't even know what I was begging for. But whatever it was, he somehow knew. Letting go of my clit, he spit on my pussy for diving back in. Flicking my clit over and over again, his fingers pumped into me.

I covered my mouth, trying my best to be quiet as I came for the second time. If this was how I went out, I think I would be okay with it.

"Zane… please, it's enough," I panted out. Zane moved his mouth away from me, gazing up at me with hungry eyes.

"You said three," was all he said before once again going back to eating me. This man was eating me like it was his mission. "Hold yourself open for me, and Salem…" he smirked. "Do. Not. Let. Go."

I had no idea what he had planned. I did as he asked. Reaching down I held myself open, two fingers still curled inside me. He reached his second hand up. "Suck," he said, giving me his pointer finger. Doing again as he asked, I sucked on his finger, sucking it like it was his cock. Which I wanted so desperately.

Removing his finger from my mouth I didn't know what he planned on doing until I felt it at my back entrance.

"Whoa there, big guy." The words flew from my mouth. He rubbed against my asshole, still fucking me with his finger and tongue. It was all too much. I had no idea how I was going to come again. Everything was becoming too much, but at the same time it was not enough.

The moment we locked eyes, his finger pressed against my asshole. My body tensed, but he latched onto my clit again making me relax. He worked his finger into my asshole, before he added a third finger and once again curled them. Hitting that spot that I was beginning to lose control.

Which is what he wanted.

"Zane…" I moaned out. Our eyes locked onto each other, and my fingers were itching to move and hold his face to me. Which is exactly what I did. I didn't care about the pain in my body. I latched my fingers into his hair and held his face to my pussy. I didn't even care if he could breathe or not. I just needed this.

The pressure built, and my mouth fell open as no sound could make its way out. My vision blurred, and I threw my head back as a gush poured from me, pouring way more than should have been possible. Even as I removed my hands from his head, he didn't remove himself. Instead he kept a finger lodged into my ass, fucking me there, while his other hand held me open.

I was surely going to pass out.

"God damn, Salem." He drank from me. "I want another," he declared. But I couldn't. "It's okay, I'll give you a few hours," he smirked.

Removing his hands from my body, he stayed in the kneeling position staring down at my pussy. I could feel self-conscious but I didn't. I closed my eyes and leaned back. I could hear Zane moving around but I couldn't force myself to open my eyes. I felt so tired.

The feeling of something warm on my thigh made me flinch. "It's just me, Kitten." Zane's soft words let me relax as he cleaned my thigh.

"I'm tired."

"I know, come on let me get this gown on you." He tried pushing my arms through the sleeve.

"I want your shirt," I stated.

He didn't respond. Instead he moved around again before he helped put his shirt on me. "Come on, wrap your arms around me."

Doing as he said, he picked me up, and I felt at home. In his arms, I felt safe and for the first time I fell asleep feeling as though everything would be okay.

Epilogue

Zane_

Five months later

When Salem woke up, I nearly lost it. I had just got done doing a workout and was so tired that I nearly fell asleep trying to do push-ups. I thought caffeine would help, but when I got done with my second cup, I knew I just needed a little nap. The moment I walked in the room and saw her still lying there, I wanted to yell and break everything in the room.

Instead I sat next to her bed and fell asleep the moment my ass hit the seat. I knew Mila showed up and sometimes she left, but when Dimitri called, I tightened my hand just on reflex. She tightened her hand back. At first, I thought it was just her body reacting, reflexes. But our eyes connected, and it was as though all my prayers had been answered.

After that, Salem struggled to walk. The damage to her left leg made her walk with a limp. The first week was the roughest. She had CAT scans and MRIs, along with tons of physical therapy. By the second week she was angry and screaming at me. At first, I wanted to fight back with her, and make her hurt back. Until one night she broke down and told me more about her parents' death.

Finally, a month after she woke up, we were able to take her home. Back to North Carolina, where she practically scared the doctor half to death, threatening that if she didn't get to go back home to her things, and where she was comfortable, she was leaving with or without their permission.

A blow to my face nearly knocked me on my back. "Fuck," I cursed. I could feel blood trailing down my chin. Thankfully, she hadn't broken my nose.

"You're too distracted!" Salem growled at me.

It was true, I was very distracted. For the past two hours we had been training. I could see sweat dripping down her body, and the fact that after only twenty minutes of us starting, she'd ditched her shirt. So now she stood in spandex shorts that frankly let her ass hang out and a sports bra that didn't hide the fact her nipples were hard.

She stood across from me, a few feet away, breathing hard. Her body was beginning to form bruises along her legs and arms.

"You're pushing yourself pretty hard," I grunted, planting my feet in position.

"One more round." She laughed, smirking at me.

"One more," I said, stalking towards her.

I watched as her eyes began to narrow at me, her glare becoming more and more intoxicating. I could tell she was beginning to struggle, favoring her right side more than her left.

"Ready?" I asked. I had to end this quickly, or she was going to keep fighting until she dropped.

"Yup, ten seconds and I'll have your ass on the ground." Slowly she brought her hand up, telling me to push forward. Taunting me. Laughing to myself I wondered what her end game was. She barely could hold herself, yet she wanted me to pounce first. Granted, most would probably go after her first. All my enemies would. They wouldn't allow her to strike first.

I held her smirk and charged forward. I could wrap my arms around her waist and tackle her. Just as I reached her, my arms begin to wrap around her, and everything slowed down. She grabbed hold of my left arm, knocking it off her body. Holding me by my wrist stretched out she spun around and elbowed me in the back of the neck. My body launched forward, but before I could go any further my left knee was kicked out. *What the fuck?* The burning sensation of my scalp had me gritting my teeth together. She wrapped her hand around the top of my head, gripping my hair so tight and pulled me backwards onto my back. As soon as my back connected with the floor mat, the air left my lungs, and then she punched my face. Fucking shit.

I don't even know when I closed my eyes, but when I finally opened them, I watched Salem walking off the mat, her pony tail swinging back and forth. My eyes never left her as she walked to the bench where our waters sat. She chugged hers before picking mine up with a towel.

"Are you still distracted?" she asked, walking back towards me. I had no idea what to even say to her. I have no idea what just happened, or how it happened. I couldn't even catch my breath.

"No," I said, my voice coming out like a whisper.

Slowly sitting up she sat down across from me, shoving the water into my hand before nodding at me. Bringing the water bottle to my mouth I welcomed the cooling sensation.

"You okay?" she asked.

"I'm good, just haven't had my ass kicked in a while," I said, chuckling to myself. Which was a lie. Salem always seemed to be able to kick my ass.

"It's about marshmallow time." Salem smirked at me when I narrowed my eyes at her calling me a marshmallow. Since the hospital she'd begun calling me that, and though I claimed to hate it, I secretly loved it.

"I'm confused. Maybe because I just got the wind taken out of me," I said, taking another swig of my water. "But I don't even know what I'm trying to ask—"

"There's a lot you don't know about me, Zane," she mumbled, cutting me off. "I've been training secretly," she whispered. Probably hoping I wouldn't hear, but I did. That is why she was tired more than normal.

"Okay," I tell her.

"Can you kiss me now?" she asked.

Before I could even nod or do it myself, she jumped into my waiting lap, her arms resting around my broad shoulders. Crashing her lips to mine she tasted like mint and sweat, and I craved her taste. Opening her mouth and allowing my tongue to dip in, I licked her teeth, and sucked on her tongue, bringing it into my own mouth, claiming her mouth as mine. She straddled my waist and began to grind against my growing cock. Fuck she was incredible. I craved her. She was like my lifeline, and I had to have her. I swallowed her moans, my cock becoming painful inside my pants as she just continued rubbing herself against me, her hands flying into my hair. Yanking my head back she broke our kiss just to latch onto my neck biting down hard.

"Fuck," I moaned.

"I need you," was all she said before I had ripped her shorts off her body and pulled my shorts down.

"Have me," I barely had the chance to get out before she impaled herself on my cock.
"FUCK," she screamed.

Still, I forced my body to relax before I did one pump. I hadn't even done that as a teenager, but with Salem it didn't matter how many times we went at it, how many times I tasted her. It would never be enough.

"If you don't start moving, I will fuck myself in front of you, and you will NOT be able to touch me," Salem growled at me. Smacking her ass, knowing it would leave a handprint, I began moving my hips, working myself back and forth. Her moans grew louder and louder as I watched my cock move in and out of her cunt. It was such a pretty sight. I couldn't look away, her pussy was dripping wet.

"Fuck," she moaned again. Her moans were like music to my ears. I lived for them. I wanted them all. "Fas—" Wrapping my hand around her throat I cut her off with another smack to her ass.

"Spread your legs further," I groaned out.

"I nee-I need to…" she started to stutter. Reaching forward I began rubbing her clit, earning another loud moan mixed with a scream. "Pl-please."

"Come for me, Kitten." Pinching her clit she came with a loud scream of my name, and hearing my name on her lips, I didn't give her time, flipping us over. I pounded into her not caring that she needed to catch her breath. Wrapping a hand around her throat, her eyes went wide, smirking at me. Clutching her pussy on me, I stilled, fighting against myself. I didn't want to cum just yet. I wanted more from her.

"Fuck you, Salem, clutching around me like that is going to cause me to lose my mind. "Open your mouth."

She opened her mouth, allowing me to spit in her mouth. I watched as she swirled her tongue around and swallowed.

"Fuck," I gritted out.

"Please." She begged me. Rubbing her clit, I pressed further on her throat. She could still breathe. Thrusting harder into her, her eyes began to close. "Open your fucking eyes."
Immediately, she did.

"Hold your pussy open," I growled. Moving back, I let go of her throat and moved her legs open more, holding her thighs until her knees touched the mat. I fucked her like a madman. I couldn't get enough of her.

"Fuck, fuck, fuckkkk," Salem screamed. As she had her second orgasm, her pussy clenched around me, and I couldn't hold back anymore. My own release poured out of me, soaking her.

Falling forward, I laid on her.

"I think I just died." Salem giggled, wrapping her arms around my neck, holding me close.

"If you die, then I'll follow you," I mumbled into her neck. "No matter where you go, I'm following you."

"You better." Salem kissed the side of my neck, before latching on and biting me.

"Wanna make chocolate chip or sugar cookies?" Salem asked Tobias. I sat at the island watching them take out random shit from the cabinets.

"I dunno know." Tobias giggled.

"I'm thinking about both." Salem smiled, pulling out way too many bags of chocolate. But if there was anything I learned about Salem, she loved her chocolate. She literally had a drawer upstairs filled with different kinds of it.

"Yeah, me too," Tobias declared.

Since Salem came home from the hospital, Tobias had been following her around. Dimitri tried to get him to stop, but it was like they needed each other. Salem was actually smiling and laughing with him. They watched all the Disney movies together and worked on puzzles that Salem had. Fuck they made meals together every day, even baked like this was some actual bakery. It was honestly cute.

"ZANE!" Dimitri yelled from the front of the house.

"DA!" I yelled back.

The moment he stepped into the kitchen, he glanced at Tobias before saying, "U nas yest problemy." He only spoke Russian around his son when something was seriously wrong.

Both Salem and I tensed. Salem was better at hiding it, as she continued measuring out the sugar and flour. Thankfully, she spoke way too many languages and she understood exactly what he was saying.

"Killian i Aziza bol'she net. Oni ischezli." *Killian and Aziza are gone. They disappeared.*

Salem slowly turned around, never breaking eye contact with him. I could feel the anger radiating off her. There was going to be no stopping her. There was no way she was going to just let him handle this. I could see that look in her eyes.

"Rasskazhi mne vse." *Tell me everything.*

Fuck.

Acknowledgments

First and for most I would like to thank you the readers. Thank you for letting me tell you the first half of Salem's story. This girl has been stuck inside my head for the last year, and no matter what she was staying. Her story demanded to be told.

Lazzie, my best friend for the past nine years. Thank you for helping me navigate through, not only life, but when I called over and over again talking about Salem. Telling you her story, coming to you with new ideas.

Jordan, we may have just recently became friends in the past two years. But you have always been there when I needed to vent. You helped me figure out how to even start this process. Without you I would still be pulling my hair out trying to figure this out. You're welcome for your first smutt book.

Lastly **my husband**. Thank you for listening while I talked about all the different books I read. Listening to me while I talked about monster dicks. You're a real one for that. You stuck by my side when I told you I wanted to publish a book, you never doubted me. Always said we'd make it happen. So thank you for believing in me, even when I didn't.

Lastly thank you to the people who thought I wouldn't make anything of myself. That I wouldn't be someone. Fuck you.

Printed in Great Britain
by Amazon

20341098R00193